ENDLESS ENCHANTMENT

"I'm sorry," Charity finally said.

He looked confused. "For what?"

"For the way I treated you," she declared without hesitation. "I was so stupid back then. I put popularity before friendship."

Keelen shrugged. "We were young. We're supposed to make mistakes," he said reassuringly, trying to put her mind at ease.

Her eyes darkened with emotion. "I know, but there's no excuse for the way I behaved."

Drawing her eyes to his, he saw the old Charity he knew. The Charity he had fallen in love with. He clasped her hands in his. "It's all in the past," he said, cutting short any further argument.

She tipped her head back and gazed in his eyes. Beautiful eyes. Why hadn't she realized years ago how wonderful he was? After a prolonged silence, she blinked rapidly and smiled as she said, "Thank you."

A nervous chuckle came from her throat. Even in the darkness she could see the sparkle in his eyes. Her curiosity swelled up inside her about the boy who was now a man.

Keelen almost shook from the growing heat spreading through his loins. He took her hands in his and inhaled. Her rose scent was driving him mad. His eyes slid from hers and fastened on to her lips—the most sensuous lips he'd ever seen. After all these years he had never forgotten how her lips molded with his or the desire that had spiraled within him.

She had been the first woman he had ever kissed and although the kiss had only lasted a matter of seconds, it had always carried a special place in his heart.

Now the time had come again.

BOOK YOUR PLACE ON OUR WEBSITE AND MAKE THE ARABESQUE ROMANCE CONNECTION!

We've created a customized website just for our very special Arabesque readers, where you can get the inside scoop on everything that's going on with Arabesque romance novels.

When you come online, you'll have the exciting opportunity to:

- View covers of upcoming books

- Learn about our future publishing schedule (listed by publication month and author)

- Find out when your favorite authors will be visiting a city near you

- Search for and order backlist books

- Check out author bios and background information

- Send e-mail to your favorite authors

- Join us in weekly chats with authors, readers and other guests

- Get writing guidelines

- AND MUCH MORE!

Visit our website at
http://www.arabesquebooks.com

ENDLESS ENCHANTMENT

ANGIE DANIELS

BET Publications, LLC
http://www.bet.com
http://www.arabesquebooks.com

*This book is dedicated to the memory of a woman
who was just like a sister to me:*

*Teresa (Reese) Hill
December 28, 1963–February 9, 2001*

*We never truly realize how much someone meant
to us until they are no longer there.*

ACKNOWLEDGMENTS

To my family, especially my loving daughter, Ashlie Renae, for making me a cup of peppermint tea when I needed it most.

To my critics Beverly Palmer and Sherry Branch—your opinions mean the world to me.

To my mother, Kathleen Anderson. If there was no you there wouldn't be me. Thank you for always being there. I love you!

To Cindy Porter for her flair with names.

To my Aunt Cynthia for making my first cruise memorable enough to write about.

To Elizabeth Simon for line editing my submission packet.

Special thanks to Adam Z. and Becky C. at the Missouri Kidney Program for saving me from weeks of retyping when my system crashed.

I would like to thank all of my families—the Moores, Andersons, Hills, and Daniels—for all of their love and support. Yes, ladies, Terrance Moore really is my brother!

Prologue

She had been standing at the corner less than ten minutes when yellow school bus number twenty-nine turned onto her street. A wave of uneasiness swept through her. Taking several deep breaths, she reminded herself, *don't let them get to you!* But how could she not? They'd been getting to her for almost four years with their teasing and malicious jokes. Even as seniors nothing had changed. It never would. Not until she could find the strength to do something about it.

The bus squeaked to a halt, causing her heart to hammer rapidly against her chest. Then, sooner than she hoped, the driver pulled the lever and the door slid open. Shielding her eyes from the rays of the sun, she noticed someone new was seated behind the wheel. The school district never could keep a driver for long. No one ever seemed to come back. *I wish I could do the same.*

Reluctantly, the girl climbed the steps, forcing a smile for the ebony man just as she reached the top. She tried to ignore the flutters in her stomach as she pivoted on her heels to face her peers. However, her spark of courage quickly fizzled as she found more than two dozen pairs of eyes boring into her.

They know. They have to. Why else would they be watching me?

With that single question she knew someone had made

it their business to spread the painful gossip. Now her heart was pounding so hard she was sure the others could hear it.

There were no seats available at the front of the bus, which left her with no choice but to move toward the back, passing everyone before she could reach an unoccupied seat. Inwardly she groaned, *when would it all end?*

After taking a stabilizing breath, she shuffled down the aisle, trying not to look at anyone, but found her eyes being pulled in every direction. As she passed them she heard whispers and giggles echoing around the vehicle. She neared the Cutie Pies, an elite group of senior girls who'd made her high school life a living hell, and a lump the size of a golf ball rose to her throat. Arika and Olivia to the right. Kimora and Charity to her left. Swallowing, the teenager hoped just this once they'd spare her feelings. She was uncertain how much more she could endure in one week. Before she could make it past them, Arika stuck out a slender arm and blocked her safe passage.

She flinched, causing Arika's magenta glossed lips to quirk with amusement. "Girl, relax," she said, her voice spreading silence throughout the bus. As ringleader, she was fully aware that she had everyone's undivided attention. Leaning back against the bench, she gazed up at the girl's nervous expression with icy contempt. "I'm just curious. Why are you wearing that stupid-looking cap?"

The girl had enough sense not to reply. Instead, she shrugged as a revealing flush tinted her cheeks, allowing Arika to guess her reason.

She tried to ignore the gulping coughs as the others tried with little effort to conceal their laughter. Her stomach churned. Swallowing despair, she strained for control.

While the girl was looking down at her tennis shoes, Kimora rose and swiftly yanked the cap from her head.

The girl's trembling hand sprang to finger the tendrils that spilled around her face. Out of habit she reached for the ponytail that used to hang to the middle of her back, only to be painfully reminded that it was no longer there.

When a single tear escaped from the corner of the girl's eye, Arika's jaw twitched with satisfaction. "I kind of like your new look." Her words were saturated with ridicule. Edging closer, she taunted, "It kinda reminds me of my older brother."

Snickers were heard until finally one of them—she was unsure which one—burst into a hearty laugh. Arika set off additional laughter by releasing an animated high-pitched sigh. Then she settled back against the seat and finally lowered her arm.

With renewed humiliation the girl stumbled to the back of the bus, sinking low onto an empty seat where her cap landed beside her.

Resting her forehead against the cool leather in front of her, she allowed the tears to flow freely. Deep sobs racked her body, but she pressed her lips tightly together to contain them. *What have I ever done to be treated this way?* Reaching up, she touched the hair at the nape of her neck where her mother had tried to repair the damage. Someone had taken away her prize possession: a ponytail that had taken forever to grow.

Only yesterday someone had switched off all the lights in the girls' locker room while someone else knocked her to the ground, swiftly cutting her hair. By the time the power was restored, no trace of the ponytail was found. When questioned by the gym coach, no one seemed to have known what had happened. *Jealousy.* That's all it was. Pure and simple jealousy.

Lifting her head, she lowered the silly blue cap safely onto her head again, then roughly wiped the tears away from her eyes. Crying was useless. It only made matters

worse. They would never feel remorseful. Nor would anyone ever confess. They didn't have to. She already knew
the ones responsible: Arika, Olivia, Kimora, and Charity.
The Cutie Pies. Folding her arms across her chest, she
rocked back and forth as anger brewed inside her. *I'm
going to get even with them, even if it takes a decade,* she
vowed.

Graduation was closely approaching and the torment
would soon be over.

But she would never forget.

One

Ten years later

Charity Rose shook her head. "I don't think it's a good idea."

"Why not?" Tia Rose asked. "I think a cruise is a wonderful plan."

Charity had just put a batch of her famous chocolate chip cookies into the oven and set the timer. Now, resting her hip against the dishwasher, she picked up the letter again and gazed at it before mumbling, "A cruise is a fabulous idea, sis. A ten-year class reunion isn't."

"But this isn't just another reunion held in a stuffy ole' high school gymnasium." Tia swung around in the chair as she spoke, her voice bubbling with enthusiasm. "Yours is going to be aboard a cruise ship. How romantic!"

Charity raised a blue mug to her lips and took a sip of her favorite orange spice tea. Charity knew her sister could be overly dramatic at times. Tia believed love could happen anywhere, and felt she proved her point when she met her fiancé on a Colorado ski trip. To her, love was like a game show—it was either behind door number one, number two or number three. Charity groaned at that, thinking not everyone is lucky enough to get it right the first time.

Her face thoughtful, Charity glanced again at the invitation she'd received in the mail only the day before.

She had to admit the concept was intriguing. Rockbridge Senior High was hosting her ten-year class reunion aboard an Enchanted Cruise Line ship. She'd always wanted to take a cruise. Her ex-husband had even promised to take her on one for their ten-year anniversary.

Well . . . that day never came, did it?

Charity looked up from the letter with her brows slanted in dismay. She had just remembered. "Tia, you forgot one thing . . . Donovan will also be there."

Tia responded with a grunt and looked at her sister with contempt-filled eyes. "All the more reason to attend. Show him how far you've come without him." She raised her own mug to her lips and took a large gulp of tea.

Gazing down at her sister's chubby, cinnamon face, Charity shook her head and said, "I don't think so." She couldn't imagine spending five days on the same ship with her ex-husband.

High school sweethearts, the couple had married immediately after graduation with dreams of being together forever. She had loved Donovan as much as she thought any woman should love her man. Charity closed her eyes against the heart-wrenching memories. *What a fool I was to believe in him.* Divorcing him had been the smartest move she'd ever made. With an awkward wave of her hand she tried to brush aside the past; the rustle of paper quickly reminded her of the issue at hand.

Lowering her mug to the Formica countertop, she mumbled in a low, raspy voice, "Besides . . . what do *I* have to show for the last ten years?"

"Do I have to break it down for you?" Tia asked, eyes wide with disbelief at her sister's lack of confidence. "You've got a *lot* to be proud of." She ticked off on each finger as she spoke. "Let's see . . . you're finally attending college. You've started your own bakery. Not to mention you're doing a fabulous job raising my niece alone. I'd call that a huge accomplishment in itself."

Charity's frown deepened. "It's not *that* great," she protested, meeting her sister's direct gaze. "Donovan's supporting us."

Tia rolled her hazel eyes with growing annoyance. "As he should. You supported his sorry behind for eight years. The least he can do is provide for you and Taylor."

"There you go again," Charity mumbled before the timer went off a few minutes later, and she got up to remove the finished chocolate chip cookies and put the next batch in. She was glad for the interruption; facing the stove, her sister couldn't see the scowl that framed her eyes, or see her draw in her bottom lip in thought. Charity knew that Tia thought she still had a soft spot for Donovan.

What her sister didn't realize was that Charity regretted having put her life on hold for the selfish bastard. In fact, she wished she'd come to her senses a lot sooner. Putting aside her own plans for college, Charity had supported Donovan while he attended medical school. She'd planned to enroll in college during his last year, but by the time her husband had started his residency program in Springfield, Taylor had come along. And then . . .

Tia pursed her lips with extreme agitation. "Humph! I think you were too lenient with him. I would have asked for a lot more." When Charity's lips twisted in a half smile, Tia hastily added in her own defense, "Well, plastic surgeons *do* make a lot of money."

Charity didn't think it was any of Tia's business, and therefore had never disclosed the full amount of her divorce settlement. In actuality, when she found Donovan in the arms of another woman, leniency was the furthest thing from her mind. With the help of a lawyer, the courts had generously granted her alimony, child support, college funds for both her and their daughter, the two-year-old

BMW she was still driving and the four-bedroom house she had sold shortly after the divorce. She'd since returned to her hometown of Columbia, Missouri, a small college town located an equal distance between Kansas City and St. Louis, and she was now living in her parents' home since they'd retired to Mobile, Alabama, a year before.

After placing the hot cookies on a plate to cool, Charity returned to her chair, crossed her ankles and said, "Taylor and I are doing just fine."

Tia leaned forward, rested her elbow on the table, and gave Charity a loving smile. "I know you are, girl. Still, I was worried about you there for a while. I didn't think you'd ever stop letting Donovan walk all over you."

Charity rolled her eyes and sighed, uninterested in another discussion about Donovan's adulterous behavior. Reaching for her tea again, she finished the lukewarm drink in one gulp, then shrugged. "Well . . . all that's in the past."

Eager to change the subject, she reached for the teakettle on top of the old gas stove, poured hot water into her mug, then moved across the shiny taupe linoleum to refill Tia's.

"Thanks, Sis." After dipping a fresh tea bag into her mug, Tia rose to her full five-foot-five-inch height. "Here's to your ten-year class reunion." She held up the piping hot liquid in a salute. "Let the world know Charity Rose has arrived!"

Charity moved back toward the stove to turn off the burner and couldn't resist a slight grin. "Don't say anything when you burn yourself."

"Honey, hush." With a dismissive wave, Tia lowered herself back into the chair. "Don't worry about me. If I burn myself Jonathan will be more than happy to kiss my wounds." A smile tipped the corner of her mouth at the mention of her fiancé. Leaning forward again, she added, "It's time for you to live a little. Maybe even find your soul mate."

Mug in hand, Charity moved to the table and seated herself across from Tia. While liberally sweetening her drink, her eyes moved upward and found her older sister watching her.

Two months before, Tia had showed up for dinner minus her shoulder-length hair. Now she was sporting short honey-brown dreads that looked fabulous surrounding her round face. Tia had always been the daring one in the family. Five years ago she had opened the city's only African-American bookstore. No one believed she would survive in a small college town, but Tia proved them all wrong by tripling her sales over the last three years.

While Tia was a risk taker, Charity had always done what others expected of her. Never a leader, she had been so caught up in making others happy that along the way she had lost an important piece of herself—her self-confidence. For once she was doing something *she* wanted to do and was finally starting to feel in control of her own life. Maybe Tia was right. Maybe it was time for her to stand up and take a bow.

After taking a hearty sip, Charity's eyes traveled to the brochure lying on the table beside her. Food, sunshine, relaxation. She really could use a vacation. But was the ship large enough to keep her away from the two people she wanted least to encounter?

Between clenched teeth, she murmured, "Arika really outdid herself." But then Arika Anderson had always striven for perfection. As a newscaster for Channel 8 News, she was a familiar face in homes across the city. Former class president and head of the reunion committee, the nutmeg beauty was once again in charge. As a teenager she had been the most popular girl in their class, which meant if she allowed you to be her friend you were one of the fortunate ones. If not, she made your life hell. It wasn't until recently that Charity realized that even a friend could stab you in the back.

Tia shifted in her seat. Noting the change in Charity's expression, she tried to probe her sister's thoughts by asking, "Have you seen her since you got back home?"

Charity shook her head, trying to mask her inner frustration with a deceptive calmness. "No. Not yet."

Slapping a palm across the table, Tia exclaimed, "See! There's another reason for you to go. You can catch up with an old friend!"

Charity made a rude snorting sound before murmuring. "I wouldn't call us friends."

Tia looked confused. "But . . . I thought you and—"

"It's a long story," Charity interrupted before it went any further. "I'd rather not get into it." With an irritated sigh she rose from her chair and moved toward the oven to check the progress of her cookies, grateful for the diversion. Several months ago, she had shared with Tia the pain of finding her husband with another woman. However, she hadn't mentioned that the woman was Arika.

Tapping her fingertips lightly against the table, Tia noted her sister's flushed face and the agitated rise and fall of her breasts. Something was bothering Charity, but she wouldn't push for details. Tia knew whatever was on her sister's mind would eventually be shared, or she'd find a way to work it out of her. What she did know was that something had finally happened between her sister and Arika. "Actually, I never liked her," was all she said, but she still remembered the day Charity came racing home to share her excitement at becoming a Cutie Pie. She knew Charity had been longing for acceptance, and Tia had been happy for her little sister. That is, until she had a chance to meet the group.

Dropping her gaze, Charity spoke in a low, troubled voice. "Yeah, well . . . it takes some of us longer than others to realize what was always staring them right smack in the face."

Tia would say or do anything to convince Charity to take a vacation. She deserved it. "Don't let Arika spoil your fun. Go anyway." Raising her mug, she blew on the hot liquid before bringing it in contact with her lips. "And don't worry about Taylor. She can hang with her aunt Tia."

At those words Charity met her sister's gaze, her lips pursed with false annoyance. "So you can spoil her." As if on cue, she crossed the room to look out the window at her daughter playing in the backyard with Karen, the little girl next door. Looking over her shoulder she remarked softly, "I'm still trying to undo the damage you did during finals week."

Tia waved her hand dismissively. "No harm done. What are aunties for?"

Charity turned her head slightly to roll her eyes and chose to ignore the question. Having no children of her own, Tia catered to her niece's every desire. Taylor had her only aunt wrapped around her finger and she knew it.

Watching her five-year-old play with a new Barbie Tia had bought, Charity's heart was warmed by her daughter's adorable grin. Taylor was the best thing that had ever happened to her.

Tia's cell phone rang. While she answered the call, Charity stared through the window, her expression solemn. Outside, the air was warm for spring. Tulips were already in full bloom. She loved the house where she'd grown up as a child. Theirs was a modest neighborhood with traditional two-story homes and large oak trees in the yards. Long before the development of several new subdivisions, Chapel Hill had been one of the most prominent neighborhoods in the city.

Charity had never wanted for anything as a child. The Roses had both been in their forties when their daughters were born. After being unsuccessful for years the couple believed they were unable to have children. However, when their assumption proved to be false, their mother, Deirdre, ended a career as principal of Oakland Junior High to be a full-time mom. Her evenings were consumed with chauffeuring the girls from one fine arts class to the next. Charity had always wanted the same for her own children, and had expected to sacrifice a career when the time came to start a family. The plan had been that she would work to support Donovan while he attended medical school, and once he started his practice, she would become a full-time mother. It was supposed to have been an investment in their future. Instead, everything had gone downhill as soon as Donovan had been offered a position with Mount Carmel Hospital.

Bringing a hand up to cup her chin, Charity took a moment to reflect on how much her life had changed in a decade. If it had been due to different circumstances, she would have been glad to be back in her old home. She sighed. Charity never imagined that at twenty-eight she would be right back where she started. Even though it had been her choice to return to Columbia, being home again made her feel like such a failure.

She glanced down at her watch and saw that it was almost three-fifteen. Moving away from the window, she reached for a mitt, opened the oven door and removed the cookies.

The moment the aroma reached Tia's nose, her radar went off. "Ooh! I've got to go," she said into the receiver. She snapped the phone shut and set it down on the table. Rising from her chair, she moved swiftly to the stove where she removed a spatula from Charity's hand and scooped a hot chewy cookie off the sheet. "Mmm!" She took a bite and handed the spatula back to her sister before returning to her seat. "You know I like them hot. Hurry and bring them to the table."

Shaking her head, Charity reached for a saucer in an overhead cabinet. Tia was something else. Even though she was bossy, she couldn't have chosen a better sister. What Charity needed in her life was plenty of unconditional love, and between her sister and Taylor, Charity was granted more than her fair share. While the rest of the cookies cooled, she placed six on a saucer and carried them back to her seat.

Tia reached for another and took a bite. "You know I live for your cookies. Mmm! No wonder I can't keep these on hand." Last year she had added a coffee shop to the back of her bookstore. When Charity returned home three months ago Tia had come up with the idea to also sell fresh-baked cookies. They were an instant hit.

Baking cookies cleared Charity's mind, gave her balance. During her divorce she had needed that balance more than she had ever needed anything before in her life.

Charity settled back against the chair, her eyes clear and observant. "That's a new recipe. What do you think?"

Tia chewed slowly. "I love it! What did you do, add chocolate mints?"

Charity nodded.

"An excellent combination." She took another bite and raised her brow. "How could you possibly think you've nothing to be proud of?" Her question received a shrug. "You bake kick-ass cookies. You've got a list of orders for baked goods scheduled for the next six months and the orders are still coming in."

Charity beamed with pride. Business had been good. Since she began baking cookies for Heritage Bookstore, some of Tia's business sense had rubbed off on her. She distributed flyers and placed a weekly ad in the local newspaper, and before she knew it word got around. The orders were coming in nonstop. "Speaking of which, I don't know how much longer I'm going to be able to conduct business from home. This oven isn't big enough." She glanced around the white accented kitchen. Although it was spacious, with plenty of cabinet and counter space, the stainless-steel stove was not large enough to hold the volume of orders she'd been receiving lately. "I'm considering leasing a shop downtown."

Tia wagged a finger in front of Charity's face. "See what I'm talking about!" She rose and carried her mug to the sink. Reaching into a cabinet overhead, she removed a tall glass. "Girl, please. You need to send in your deposit and get on that boat."

"It's a ship," Charity corrected.

"Whatever," Tia mumbled. She reached into the refrigerator and poured herself a glass of milk. "I don't care if it's a canoe, you need to be there." She offered Charity a glass, but she declined with a shake of her head.

Tia was never going to let up until she agreed. "Okay, okay." Feeling cornered, Charity said, "I'll give the reunion some thought."

After taking a swallow of milk, Tia plopped back down in her chair. Reaching for another cookie, she took a bite. "I can't understand what there is to think about. If money is an issue, I can foot you some."

Charity groaned. Now she knew why her sister was once captain of the debate team. "No, money is not an issue." She pressed her lips firmly together. "I'm just not sure if I want to see my former classmates again. They would probably prefer not to see me, either."

Lounging back in the chair, Tia decided to break her rule and press the issue. "Why?"

Charity couldn't come up with a plausible explanation. "There are reasons." Lots of reasons, but she wasn't about to go there.

Tia shrugged. "Then forget them. Soak up the sun and enjoy the Bahamas."

Charity read the concern in her eyes. Smiling softly she said, "Maybe."

Tia leaned across the table, eyes sparkling with mischief as she met her sister's gaze. "You might even see Keelen again," she sang.

Charity's smile faltered as the name stirred old memories. How could she have forgotten Keelen Brooks?

In grammar school, he had lived right next door. They once had been best friends and had spent hours climbing trees and riding bikes. During seventh grade Keelen's father's job moved his family away, but they had returned to Columbia during his junior year. Keelen had always been overweight. But Charity didn't mind; that is, until Arika and the others zoomed in on their tight-knit friendship.

There was a selective group of "misfits" the group had made fun of on a daily basis. Suddenly Keelen had been added to that list. Although Charity never participated in any of the name calling, she had never bothered to say anything in his defense. Instead, she had stood by and watched, which in her opinion made her just as guilty. Not that he needed defending. Keelen had never taken the taunting personally and chose to ignore them. Because he gave no response they eventually lost interest. Torn between acceptance and her relationship with Keelen, Charity had allowed the group to make the difficult decision for her.

It had been so long since she'd seen him. Charity wondered if he still hated her.

Her mouth dropped at the rush of memories. "Oh, no," she groaned. "Another reason for me not to attend."

Tia waved a hand at her foolishness. "You're nuts. That was kid stuff. He'll be glad to see you. The *real* you."

Charity couldn't help wondering who "the real" her was. She allowed her eyes to fall to her waist. After giving birth to Taylor she had lost the slender figure she'd held onto for almost twenty-three years. Now with her increasing interest in baking, she'd never lost the extra weight. Her size six had somehow escalated to a ten. Doubt continued to creep into her thoughts as she remembered Donovan telling her on numerous occasions that he found her new body repulsive.

Tia knew what Charity was thinking. Quickly stuffing another cookie in her mouth, she reached for her sister's wrist and practically yanked her out of the chair.

Startled, Charity asked, "Where are we going?"

"Come with me and you'll see."

Charity allowed herself to be pulled down the long narrow hallway into the guest bathroom. Once inside, Tia shut the door. "Now look."

Charity turned and found both of them standing in front of a gold-trimmed mirror mounted to the back of the bathroom door.

Tia pointed to her reflection. "There is nothing wrong with the way you look. What isn't there to like?"

Charity patted her auburn hairstyle in a blunt cut that fell below her ear. She had an even complexion that complemented stunning chestnut eyes. At five-eight, with a medium build, her abdomen was firm and her body toned even after childbirth. Yes, she could still turn the head of a man.

Tia wrapped an arm around her sister's waist. "Now tell me . . . what's wrong with you?"

Charity frowned at her sister's reflected image.

Releasing her, Tia turned and faced her. "Girl, please! Don't believe anything Donovan told you. You're far from fat." Wearing a cheesy smile, she moved her hands to rest on her own ample hips. "Now, *this* is what we call fat."

Charity smiled down at her sister. A size sixteen, Tia was heavy, but quite adorable with large eyes that sparkled like the pair of diamond earrings dangling from her lobes.

Tia raised one hand to rest across her chest and the other high in the air, palm forward. "As God is my witness, you're going on that cruise even if I have to hog-tie you and carry you on board myself."

Charity laughed, knowing her sister meant every word.

Two

Charity removed a second suitcase from the conveyor belt. Lifting the heavy bag, she quickly dropped it on the floor before her feet. She took a deep breath, wondering why she had packed so much for a five-day cruise. It was an easy question to answer.

Tia.

Over the weekend, her sister had dragged her to an all-day shopping spree at the Columbia Mall. Judging by her enthusiasm, anyone would have thought Tia was the one going on a trip. Patronizing almost the entire mall, they left with their arms loaded with everything from swimsuits to a satin evening gown. Against Charity's wishes, Tia had even insisted on buying her a little somethin' somethin' at Victoria's Secret, "just in case." The only sensible purchase she had made was the matching luggage on wheels.

Swinging a tote bag across her shoulder, she rolled the suitcases away from the baggage claim area, hauling them toward a woman in a blue jacket holding up a sign bearing the word "Enchanted." Charity joined the crowd that had already begun to gather around her. As she quickly scanned the bunch, she realized that none of the faces were familiar. *Maybe my plane was one of the first to arrive.* Chewing on the inside of her lip, she watched the others conversing among their friends. A wave of loneliness stabbed at her. She wished she had invited Tia along. Her neighbors had generously offered to keep Taylor while she was away, but Tia wasn't having it. She had the remainder of the week off with plans to take her niece to Six Flags, among other things.

The guide finally signaled for the group to follow her through an automatic door, where two chartered buses were waiting outside.

"We'll begin boarding momentarily," she said in a perky voice. With a warm salute, she went back inside the terminal to direct other passengers.

The group formed a single line. With several dozen people ahead of her, Charity dropped the bag from her shoulder and sighed. Looking down at her wristwatch, she noticed it was a few minutes past twelve. Already the heat of the afternoon Orlando sun had caused trickles of perspiration to travel down the valley between her breasts. She was glad that she had dressed coolly in a pink racer-back tank dress with her feet comfortable in white canvas mules.

"Charity Rose!"

Charity turned toward the direction of the voice and found a woman moving quickly in her direction, waving a hand vigorously in the air. Charity raised her sunglasses from her small, perched nose and rested them on her head. Hmmm, the woman looked familiar, but she couldn't remember who she was.

Moving in closer, she gave Charity a weird look. "Girl, don't act like you don't know who I am."

Taking a closer look and comparing it with the zesty voice, she finally recognized the petite lady. "Beverly Thomas?"

The woman dropped a large straw bag and planted a dainty hand to her girlish waist. "The one and only." Her face broke into a wide smile as she pulled Charity into a tight embrace as if they'd been lifelong friends. "Girl, how have you been?"

"I've been fine," Charity answered as she moved away and looked her over. "I almost didn't recognize you. You've changed!" Gasping in amazement, she noticed that Beverly was no longer wearing the extra twenty-five pounds she'd carried throughout high school. In their place were small tapered hips and slender legs. Shoulder-length pinched braids framed a mocha face and a long delicate neck. Who would ever have guessed her face had once been covered with a severe case of acne?

Beverly clicked her tongue, pretending to be insulted before her face melted into a gentle smile. "I hope that's a compliment. I'd know you anywhere. You still look wonderful."

"Thanks," Charity said, relieved Beverly was happy to see her. They'd known each other since junior high, and during high school they had shared several classes and often found themselves working together on numerous projects. However, outside of class time they'd had little contact. It wasn't because Beverly hadn't tried. Charity had been the reason why their relationship had never blossomed into anything further. Had she really behaved that badly? She suddenly felt guilty and wondered if she'd have the same feeling every time she ran into someone she'd shunned during high school.

Beverly removed a handkerchief from the pocket of her white shorts and mopped her forehead. "I lost track of you after high school. Didn't you marry Donovan Gross?"

Swallowing her regrets, Charity wrinkled her nose. She had spoken with Donovan the week before, long enough for him to make plans to pick Taylor up the following week so the two could fly to Chicago and spend a couple of days with his parents. He had informed her that he also was attending the class reunion. Charity didn't even bother to share with him that she would be on board as well. She rocked back on her heels with silent laughter. *Won't he be surprised.* "We're divorced now. What about you?"

Beverly tossed up several fingers. "Twice divorced. No kids, but I do have a schnauzer."

Charity chuckled, then stooped down and took a seat on top of her luggage. Beverly followed her lead.

"I have a daughter, Taylor." Reaching into her purse, she removed several pictures from a black billfold and handed them to Beverly.

"She's beautiful," Beverly commented after going through the entire stack and handing them back.

Charity tossed the stack back into the bottom of her purse and stretched her legs leisurely in front of her.

Beverly took a deep, cleansing breath and stared up at the bright Florida sky. "The weather is going to be beautiful. I'm living in Minneapolis now and the weather there is either mild or too cold. This is going to be a nice change."

Her companion's excitement was contagious and Charity felt herself finally relaxing as she anticipated the days to come. "I'm back in Columbia, and you know how the weather is there. I'm looking forward to the fabulous tropical weather I've heard so much about."

Eyes sparkling, Beverly grinned. "I almost didn't make it. I'm so glad Keelen persuaded me to come."

"Keelen?" Charity croaked the word in a hoarse rasp, then remembered the two were first cousins. How could she have forgotten? The first time she had met Beverly was at a barbecue the Brooks had held in their backyard one Fourth of July weekend. "Is . . . is Keelen coming too?"

"Heck, yeah." Beverly rose from her luggage when she noticed that people were beginning to board the bus. Shielding her eyes, she scanned the area for him. "He stopped by the men's room after he retrieved his luggage. I guess he's around here somewhere."

Charity felt a mixture of excitement and fear at seeing

her old friend again. Would he still be angry? However, she didn't have much time to ponder. The driver moved to retrieve their luggage and loaded the bags in the cargo space underneath the bus.

Beverly swung an arm around Charity's shoulder and squeezed. "This trip is going to be fabulous! I'm so glad you're here."

Charity met her gaze and found her words to be sincere. "Me, too." She swung an arm across Beverly's shoulders and smiled with genuine pleasure.

They boarded the bus. As they moved down the aisle, Charity recognized few familiar faces from high school. However, Beverly knew almost everyone and stopped to speak, even asking several times, "Do you remember Charity Rose, the cheerleader?" Charity noticed sagging smiles and weak waves, realizing that outside the Cutie Pies, she hadn't made many friends. She felt some of her excitement fade, but quickly reminded herself that the next several days would be an opportunity to show people just how much she had changed. Tossing her tote bag in the compartment overhead, she sat on the seat next to Beverly.

Turning in her seat, Beverly's hazel eyes were filled with mischief. "I want to hear all about Columbia."

Charity smiled broadly. "I can't tell you much. I just returned, myself."

Beverly sighed dramatically. "I left the same year we graduated. When Tony Wayne returned from basic training, we ran off and eloped."

Charity's eyes grew wide. "You married Tony Wayne?" Surprise was obvious in her voice. She remembered the lanky olive-skinned teenager. Outside of tutoring her in algebra, Tony had always been quiet and kept to himself. She would never have guessed he was even interested in anything other than books.

"Yeah." Beverly grinned. "We were on the student

council together. When Tony mentioned he was ready to get out of Columbia, he began to look really good to me. I'd always wanted to get out of that dead-end town. We lived overseas in Panama for almost two years. Fabulous experience! I could spend hours telling you stories. I was so wrapped up in my life as a soldier's wife that it took me two years before I realized a woman was not what Tony needed in his life." Her left brow rose. "If you get my drift."

Charity's mouth gaped open. "I knew something was strange about that boy."

The two giggled like teenagers. While passengers continued to board the bus, Charity brought Beverly up to date on the changes that had occurred to their hometown over the last decade. They were engrossed in a discussion about a Barnes & Noble moving into the area when someone caught Beverly's attention.

"Oh, look! Here comes my cousin." She rose in her seat, frantically waving her hand. "*Yoouu whooo*, Keelen! We're over here."

Peeking down the aisle, Charity's smile slipped into an *O*. She blinked to make certain she was seeing clearly. There he was, moving toward them with long, powerful strides. He was wearing khaki shorts and a blue polo shirt unbuttoned at the nape of his neck, showing off rich pecan skin sprinkled with sandy-brown hair. Her mouth went suddenly dry. *This handsome critter couldn't possibly be four-eyed Keelen,* she thought. However, seeing the lopsided boyish grin she had grown accustomed to, Charity knew it couldn't be anyone but him. She stared up at gray eyes complemented with heavy dark eyebrows that were once hidden behind thick glasses. Gone was the Jheri curl. In its place was hair cut so close it lay in waves across his head. Keelen had grown significantly and stood about six feet tall. What had once been a soft build was now chiseled into a work of art. Age had done him well. He was gorgeous.

Charity suddenly remembered to breathe.

Stopping in front of their seat, he greeted her with a warm smile. "How have you been?"

She jerked slightly at the sound of Keelen's voice, deep and sultry. Focusing on him, she was forced to lick parched lips before speaking. "I've been fine."

"Good." He gave her an award-winning smile, showing off perfectly aligned white teeth.

She tried to tell herself to remain calm, but his scent was sending her heart into a tailspin. *Snap out of it.* "I see your braces paid off," was all she could think to say.

He chuckled lightly at her keen observation. "Thank you." Pausing, he allowed his eyes to travel the length of her before returning to her face. "You look great."

"Thanks," she spoke softly. A blush crept up her shoulders all the way to her cheeks. Despite her best effort to appear unfazed, she felt a flutter at the pit of her stomach. Charity's eyes were glued to him while his heated gaze warmed her body. She wasn't sure how long they stood there staring at one another as if no one else in the world existed. Suddenly Beverly cleared her throat.

"Cuz, take a seat," she said with a twinkle in her eye. "I think the driver is ready to go."

His gaze briefly met his cousin's before swinging back to Charity. "I'll see you later," he said.

All she could do was nod. It wasn't until later that she found it strange he hadn't appeared surprised to see her. It was almost as if he'd been expecting her.

Keelen was happy to see that Charity had made it. His secretary had assured him she had paid her fees, but he didn't want to get his hopes up until he saw her for himself.

A lot of preparation had gone into planning the reunion, and he wanted everything to go smoothly.

As CEO of Enchanted Cruise Line, Keelen knew it was important everything went according to schedule. Currently they had three cruise ships, with a plan to add an additional two by the end of the year. He was working with a prestigious marketing firm, and a team would be aboard during the cruise, taking pictures for an upcoming brochure. He was also scheduled to meet with three potential investors when the ship docked in the Bahamas. Otherwise, the trip was going to be his first attempt at a vacation in a long time.

Making himself comfortable, Keelen reclined in his seat and allowed his eyes to leisurely observe Charity. Arms folded beneath ample breasts, she was engrossed in conversation. Even though he was two rows back to their right, Keelen could still see the silky hairs on her arm. She was still as enchanting as ever. Full ruby lips. Chestnut eyes surrounded by thick long lashes. Gone was the long ponytail. In its place was a short sleek look. A white headband secured her hair away from her face, exposing smooth cinnamon skin. Her short cotton dress revealed long shapely legs, visibly attractive to the male eye. Although she was seated, he could tell Charity had added about ten to fifteen pounds to the rail-thin frame she'd had in high school. He saw that the extra weight added power to the total package.

Keelen remembered when they first met. He was sitting on the porch when Charity had walked over and introduced herself by telling him she didn't like boys and that he'd better stay clear of her and her yard. He had responded by tossing a mud ball in her face. She retaliated with a mud ball of her own. By the time both of their parents came out of the house, the two were covered from head to toe. That was the start of a very long friendship.

When his father's job transferred them to San Diego, they

were pen pals for years. They did not see each other again until his family returned to Columbia their junior year. The two families met for dinner one evening. Keelen took one look at the teenage beauty and instantly fell in love. Instead of the feisty, strong-willed friend he had once known, here was an insecure teenage girl desperate for acceptance. They buddied around for a while, but all she ever talked about was being a Cutie Pie and what it meant to be popular. He tried to steer her to other interests, which included him, but being in love with her proved to be useless. He wasn't an athlete or popular, and therefore he had been in a league of his own.

When Charity was finally initiated into the group, their friendship became practically nonexistent. The other girls made certain to ban their relationship by finding humor in his appearance. Charity never participated in the taunting, but he could see how uncomfortable the situation made her feel. Keelen had always known why she had never come to his aid. She was afraid of being on the other side. Eventually the group realized their jokes didn't faze him and left him alone, but by then he had become so involved in after-school activities that he no longer bothered to pursue their friendship.

Keelen had even tried to hate Charity, but never could. Now, after seeing her again, he realized that his feelings for her hadn't changed. The strength of the reaction surprised him. It had been ten years since he'd last seen her, but he found himself still reacting to her the same way he had in high school. Even now, her beauty intrigued him. Strange and erotic thoughts were racing through his mind. Blood flowed hot through his veins. Keelen tried to convince himself that because she was beautiful it was only normal to react this way.

Leaning back in his seat, he rested a hand under his chin. He'd thought he was over her and had hoped to display a cool, nonchalant demeanor when in her company. He had even anticipated the goofy look on her face when she learned he was the CEO. However, the longer he watched her dress creep up her sexy brown thighs when she shifted in the seat, the harder the idea of a nonchalant attitude became. Suddenly, Keelen found himself looking forward to some relaxation, soaking up the sun, and renewing an old friendship.

"Oh, my God! We're roommates!" Beverly exclaimed as the two compared their room assignments. "I couldn't have planned it better myself." Bubbling with mutual excitement, they moved down the narrow hallway in search of cabin 4B.

Charity was relieved. She hadn't given it much thought, but she would have dreaded it if she had ended up sharing a room with someone she didn't know. Or even worse, Arika. Part of the reunion's concept was the random pairing of students, allowing peers a chance to reacquaint themselves with students they had lost contact with over the years. Charity could almost guarantee Arika made sure she was rooming with either Kimora or Olivia.

Beverly slid the key card in the slot on the door, and they slipped into the room. After a quick observation, she added with a chuckle, "Well, if we aren't close, we will be after this."

Although their quarters were no bigger than a walk-in closet, they both found it quite charming. The walls were decorated with almond print wallpaper and trimmed in white, with contrasting beige carpet. A sliding closet was to the right, just as you entered the room, and next to it was a desk with four small drawers. There were two tastefully decorated single beds covered with an elegant taupe spread. One was positioned against the left wall beneath a color television mounted high near the ceiling and the other was directly below a small porthole window. The shades were drawn, allowing sunlight to pour into the room.

Charity opened what she thought was a closet and gasped. Inside was the smallest bathroom she'd ever seen. The size of a coatroom, it contained a toilet, sink with counter and a narrow shower stall. "My goodness! I can use the toilet and brush my teeth at the same time," she joked. Beverly agreed.

Although they laughed, neither could complain. The bathroom was quite nice. It was decorated in the same color scheme as the rest of the cabin, with an abundance of beige towels hanging above the toilet. A mirror above the vanity took up an entire wall. There was even an assortment of soaps, lotions and shampoos, just in case they had forgotten to bring their own.

Beverly flopped down onto the twin bed next to the window wearing a wide smile. "Ok, homey, what're we doing first?"

Charity looked down at her enthusiastic roommate, feeling the same anticipation bubbling up inside of her. "First, I'm taking a shower. Then let's go and have some of those piña coladas I've been hearing about."

An hour later, Charity was showered and feeling comfortable in a pair of white shorts and a lime-green halter-top. Moving across Beverly's bed, she gazed out the window. They were still docked at the pier. Below, she could see workers loading supplies onto the ship. Above, the sky was a magnificent blue, without a cloud in sight.

While waiting for Beverly to get ready, Charity sat across the bed and took the opportunity to go over the itinerary for the evening. She found a planner on top of the desk labeled DAY ONE, which listed all the ship's activities for the day, including the hours of operation for the casino and the numerous lounges on board. Currently, a buffet was being served on the top deck. Other than a meet-and-greet at five, there wasn't anything scheduled for their class until after dinner. Charity stifled an overwhelming feeling of nervousness that assailed her at the thought of seeing everyone again. She was thankful Beverly would be there with her.

The phone on the wall rang. She was able to reach it from the bed. "Hello?"

"Bev?" asked a sensual deep voice.

"No. It's Charity."

"Hi. This is Keelen."

A smile parted her lips. "I'd know your voice anywhere. Beverly and I are roommates."

"I see." He had already known the two were sharing the room. He'd arranged it that way. "Are you planning to come on deck before dinner?"

"As soon as Beverly gets out the shower we're going to find ourselves some frozen drinks."

A throaty chuckle came through the wire. "Good. I'll see you both on Deck Eleven."

Charity hung up the phone, feeling the best she'd felt in a long time. She reached over for her purse, and before she knew it she was pulling out her compact. She wanted to look her best. Applying translucent powder to her face, she was surprised to find her hand shaking with anticipation. What had gotten into her? It was only her old friend Keelen. However, he *was* a drastic contrast to the boy she remembered. She swallowed hard just thinking about how he had matured, like fine wine. Keelen had certainly gotten better with age. Yet she barely knew him now. They had lived worlds apart for too long. Keelen was not the same person, at least not on the outside, but neither was she. Her change had occurred on the inside. Now she hoped for a chance to make amends and renew what they once had had. She had translated his expression earlier as one that appeared pleased to see her again. She hoped that her interpretation was correct.

She stared thoughtfully into the small mirror while she tried to tell herself that all she was interested in was being friends again. However, as she envisioned Keelen's handsome face, she felt her pulse race. Since she and Donovan had split a year prior, she had not found herself attracted to anyone in particular. Keelen was the first man in years who'd made her feel a flutter at the pit of her stomach.

Excitement rose inside her. She was looking forward to seeing him again.

Three

"This is the life," Beverly said with a sigh. Taking another sip of the fruity concoction, she sagged back against the padded chair. "Four days of being waited on hand and foot, I could get used to this."

"So could I," Charity chimed in. Making themselves right at home, the two were already on their second round of piña coladas. Legs stretched out, she drank in the surroundings. She wasn't sure when she had ever seen a sky as beautifully blue as the one above her. Perched high above the ocean, they were reclining in a pair of lounge chairs in a shaded area on the promenade deck.

Directly across from where she was sitting was a large swimming pool already filled to capacity with guests eager to launch their vacation. The deck was alive with the talk and laughter of hundreds of people. People were celebrating with drinks in their hands. Large tables were off to the right covered with an assortment of fruits and cold cuts. A small band to her far left played Latin jazz. The powerful hypnotic music drifted around the deck and blended with the soft roar of the ocean.

Charity marveled at the beauty of it all. The ship was like nothing she could ever have dreamed about. It was like being a guest at a luxurious hotel. Upon boarding, she found herself entranced by the red plush carpet covering the floor of the lobby. A skylight illuminated the room;

glass encased the elevators; chandeliers hung from the ceiling, and rich mahogany trimmed the walls.

Resting the frosty glass beside her, Charity felt her eyelids growing increasingly heavy. She inhaled a lazy breath and allowed them to drift closed. She found herself falling under a tranquil spell.

"You two look right at home."

Eyes fluttering open, Charity found Keelen standing over her with a warm smile on his face. Her senses exploded as she took in denim shorts that barely had enough room to accommodate his massive thighs, while his biceps stretched the cotton of his T-shirt to its capacity. With narrow hips and broad shoulders, she knew such a body could only be obtained by spending hours at the gym.

During their senior year he'd had less than a dozen strands of peach fuzz covering his upper lip. Now he was sporting a sexy mustache. It would be so easy to get lost in his looks. He certainly was a fine specimen of a man. Thank goodness she was already sitting down, because she suddenly felt off balance.

"Kee, have a seat. You're blocking the view!" Beverly complained.

"My bad," he chuckled.

Charity smiled as Keelen dropped down in the chair to her right. In only a matter of seconds the tantalizing smell of his cologne—maybe it was soap—wafted to her nose. *Girl, get a grip!* Charity took a deep calming breath then lowered the sunglasses from the top of her head to her eyes, concealing her strong attraction to him.

A Jamaican waiter in white shorts and a colorful rayon shirt strolled by, balancing a tray of tall frozen drinks garnished with pineapples. Keelen signaled to him and selected a Bahama Mama. Beverly bought another piña colada. Charity graciously declined, as she was still working on her drink.

"How do you like the ship?" Keelen asked after the waiter had departed.

"It's fabulous," Charity breathed.

"Yes it is," he agreed. "I've probably taken over a dozen cruises, but I still feel the same level of excitement every time."

"Well, this is my first, and I can already say it definitely won't be my last."

"Good." He was pleased to hear that she was enjoying his ship. "Are you planning to sign up for any excursions? If so, you'd better hurry, they fill up quite fast."

They were scheduled to port in Nassau at ten o'clock the next morning before traveling to Freeport. There was an entire schedule of activities available, from dolphin feeding to snorkeling. Charity didn't plan to do anything as daring as parasailing, but she had considered taking a tour of the historical city. "Mainly, I'm looking forward to spending a few peaceful hours aboard this ship," she commented, stretching an arm above her head. "I could probably spend the entire trip sleeping in my cabin."

Keelen leaned closer, whispering in a low seductive tone for her ears only, "Not if I can help it."

The combination of his words and warm breath against her cheek caused her to shiver. She took a larger sip of her drink than she intended, resulting in a brain freeze. Sitting up suddenly, she spilled the drink on her white shorts. "Damn!" She removed her glasses to take a closer look at the damage.

"I see some things haven't changed." Beverly chuckled. "You're still as clumsy as ever."

Charity's gaze fell as she tried to conceal her embarrassment. She had always been a klutz. While trying to mop away the liquid with a small napkin, she murmured, "I know, I know. What can I say?" She gave a joyless laugh then slid out of the chair. "Will you excuse me?"

Keelen sprang to his feet and peered at her flushed face with concern. His eyes scanned her face while his mouth quirked with amusement. "You need some help?"

Charity smiled. He was still as considerate as ever. "No, I'll be right back."

Keelen stared after the departing figure, watching the enticing sway of her voluptuous hips. He enjoyed the way her shorts hugged the slimness of her waist. In fact, he liked what he saw so much he had to quickly sit back down to conceal the sudden bulge in his shorts.

However, Beverly was a keen observer. She hadn't missed her cousin's observation and couldn't resist the upward curl of her lips. Now she knew that what she had long ago suspected was true. Keelen had feelings for Charity. "She looks good, doesn't she?"

"Yes, she does," he agreed, his eyes glued. That was an understatement.

Charity leaned against the weight of the bar while she waited for the bartender to return with the cup of seltzer water she had requested. Dropping her eyes, she sighed and looked down again at the stain that had begun to set. She would probably have to return to her cabin and change.

Stretching her neck, she glanced over to where she had been sitting and observed Keelen and Bev bent close together, sharing a conversation. He suddenly broke out in an irresistible smile. Her heart leaped. He was the best-looking thing she'd seen in a long time. Catching herself, she frowned. She enjoyed looking at him a little too much. The last thing she needed was mixed emotions. She did not need the complications of a man after taking a year to get her life back. Her divorce had given her freedom and a future she clutched tightly and selfishly to her heart. She wasn't sure that she was ready to give up either for anybody.

The bartender returned. Charity dipped the corner of a napkin in the glass and rubbed it lightly against her shorts. Completely engrossed in what she was doing, it took her several seconds to realize someone was tapping her on the shoulder. Swinging around, she found two women she hadn't spoken to in months.

"Olivia, Kimora!" she gasped. After they exchanged air kisses, she looked from one to the other. The two had already changed into their swimsuits. "How are you?"

"I'm doing great," Olivia answered, relief apparent in her brown eyes.

"So am I," Kimora chimed in. Standing in front of her, she clasped Charity's wrist. "The big question is, how are you doing?"

Eyes traveling from one to the other, Charity did not miss the identical look of curiosity etched on both their faces. She wished they were genuinely concerned and not just being nosey. Looking from Kimora's green eyes to Olivia's chocolate face, she frowned at the rush of memories. She had hardly spoken to either of them since the day she found her husband with Arika. The two had contacted her on three-way calling, voices dripping with curiosity, wanting all the juicy details, while pretending ignorance about what had happened between the two. Charity knew Arika well enough to know she had already shared her version of the embarrassing details. Over the months they rarely kept in touch except for an occasional greeting card, until the contact had finally stopped all together.

Forcing a smile, she answered. "Taylor and I are doing fine."

"Good," Kimora said, although she looked unconvinced.

Charity took a moment to study her small oval face. She read remorse in her eyes.

"I'm so sorry about Donovan," Kimora blurted out, sympathy evident in her voice.

"Me too. If I'd known, I would have . . ." Olivia allowed her voice to trail off, her eyes pleading for understanding.

Charity's face stiffened slightly, but it did not stop her eyes from brimming with suspicion. Even though they were both wearing a mask of innocence, she saw the guilt. She had always wondered if either of them had known all along that her husband had been having an affair with Arika. She'd known Kimora long enough to know that even if she had known about the affair she would never have said anything, preferring not to take sides. Olivia was a different story altogether. She and Arika, the originators of the Cutie Pies, were close. They had often shared secrets that they preferred not to share with her or Kimora. Arika would gladly have flaunted her latest conquest in Olivia's face. She, in turn, would have instigated both sides.

"Donovan and I are old news now," Charity murmured, ignoring the pang of loss. In light of the awkward situation, she tried to force cheer into her voice.

Not one to let anything go quickly, Olivia dropped a hand to her waist, then huffed, "I think it's a shame that Arika would stab—"

Charity cut in eager to change the subject. "Well, it's all in the past."

Kimora gave Olivia a warning stare that said, *don't even go there*. Turning back to Charity, she let out her breath, looking at her with genuine concern. "Don't pay Olivia any attention. We haven't heard from you in so long I was beginning to wonder if we were still friends." Her expression relaxed. "I've missed you."

Charity studied her face. Kimora Kincaid was high yellow with shiny ebony curls that framed a face of delicate beauty. A product of a biracial marriage, she had inherited her African-American father's full lips and wide nose. She was petite like her Asian mother, with small breasts and large eyes that were green with a hint of gold.

"I've missed you both." Charity gave them a weak smile and wondered how much truth was really in her response. In actuality, she hadn't thought much about either of them during the past several months. Her life was different now. Donovan, as well as the Cutie Pies, were part of her past. Shaking her head, she continued. "I needed time to myself to sort out things without any outside interference. I'm better now."

"Outside interference," Olivia mocked, sounding outraged by her statement. "Friends are supposed to share things with each other."

Sensing Charity's discomfort, Kimora nudged Olivia in the ribs. "Shut up," she mouthed. Olivia made a show of being offended and took a swallow from the glass she held. Kimora draped an arm around Charity's shoulders. "Good. Now we can catch up."

Charity grinned. Although quiet, Kimora was a no-nonsense type of girl. What you saw was what you were going to get. She spit out men as fast as she could chew them. The petite beauty was in the process of ending her second marriage. Tolerance and patience were qualities of which she wanted no part. As a result, her relationships were many and short-lived.

Olivia moved to Charity's other side and hooked her arm. "Girl, I've got months of gossip to share with you."

"Sure . . . maybe later." Charity gave her a weak smile, certain the gossip was centered around Arika or Donovan. She wasn't interested in hearing about either one. Looking down, she noticed Olivia was still sporting the engagement ring she had received three years ago from her fiancé Timothy Wallis, a running back for the Kansas City Chiefs. The ring had been given to her as a tactic to shut her up.

Years ago, Olivia had suspected Tim of messing around. After getting pregnant on purpose, she threatened him with child support, of "taking him to the cleaners," as she had put it. She wanted a piece of the pie, so when the NFL picked him, Olivia made sure she wasn't left behind.

Charity could tell Olivia Broadus hadn't changed a bit. Loud and obnoxious, at one time she had been respected by half their class and hated by the other. She was a strong believer in an eye for an eye. Charity remembered the window of Deon Thomas's Mustang, through which she had thrown a brick only hours after he'd broken a date with her. Then there was the math teacher whose career Olivia had almost ended by accusing him of trying to sleep with her—until her father had beaten the truth out of her.

They were quiet as they all tried to think of something else to say. Growing increasingly uneasy, Charity shifted from one foot to the other. "Well . . . I better get back before someone takes my seat."

Kimora looked toward the direction of her finger. Squinting, she asked, "Who is that man?"

"That's Keelen."

After glancing at each other, the two asked in awed unison. "Kooky Keelen?"

Charity nodded.

"Oh, my!" Wanting a closer look, Olivia licked her lips, then sauntered over to where he was sitting. She waved her hand frantically as she sashayed toward him, long cornrows swinging. "Keelen! Keelen Brooks, is that you?" Kimora moved quickly to Olivia's side. Shaking her head, Charity trailed behind them.

So many years had passed since Keelen had heard that soft whiny voice that reminded him of nails on a chalkboard. It could belong to no one but Olivia. He turned in the direction of the sound. Sure enough, there she was.

Following close behind her, as always, were Kimora and Charity. He chuckled. The only one missing was Arika. He rose to greet them.

Being the marketing major that he was, he flashed both of them a charming smile. "Hello, ladies."

"It's so good to see you, Keelen." Olivia's voice rang with false sincerity, as if they were long-lost friends. Resting a slender hand against his solid chest, Olivia rose on tiptoe to plant a kiss on his cheek, then possessively clutched his arm. The lustful gaze she gave him made Keelen feel uncomfortable.

Olivia's other hand was curled around a tall glass that contained dark liquor stronger than anything he could handle. Still a beautiful woman, she was wearing a white swimsuit that revealed skin as smooth as melted chocolate. But her large sable eyes, once clear, were now bloodshot, and a heavy concealer failed to camouflage the dark circles beneath them. Rumor had it that she was a recovering alcoholic. Normally, he didn't listen to gossip, but the tall glass in her hand and the stale scent of her breath were clear indicators that her rehabilitation had been short-lived.

Kimora stepped in, running an appreciative gaze over him from head to toe. "My, my," she mumbled, amazed at the dramatic transformation from fat to *fine*. She wiggled her hips. "The proof is in the pudding. Milk definitely does do a body good."

Still smiling, his gaze roamed over her smooth creamy face as he searched for a sign that she had changed over the years. He failed to find one. "It's ironic you would say that, especially since the two of you used to throw your milk cartons at me."

"Oh, my!" Kimora laughed. "How could I have forgotten?" She moved forward and slid her arm through his. Looking up at his gorgeous face, she flirtatiously batted her eyes. A pretty pout marred her face. "I hope you can forgive me. We were so childish back then."

"She's right," Olivia chimed in.

They both continued to squeeze his arms, and he looked from one to the other, his face twisting into a butter cream smile. "No apologies are needed." He turned to the star-struck Kimora and winked, watching her eyeing him hungrily like she wanted to sop him up with a biscuit.

Observing the entire incident, Beverly nudged Charity, who had returned to her seat. As Olivia and Kimora chatted away, competing for Keelen's attention, Bev found their theatrics were even worse than they had been during high school.

As the small talk between the three continued, Beverly waited to be included. After several more minutes she realized that was not going to happen. She hated being ignored. The two acted as if she wasn't even sitting there. Dying to get in the game, she cleared her throat and interrupted. "Hello, Kimora, Olivia."

"Hi . . ." Olivia's voice trailed off. Raising a perfectly arched eyebrow, she studied the familiar face for several seconds before her vision rested on Kimora for help.

Unable to identify her either, Kimora dropped a delicate hand to her bosom. "Forgive me. Do we know you?"

Beverly observed them a moment, then with pursed lips she replied, "It's me. Big Bertha Beverly."

Olivia threw her head back and laughed. "Oh, my God! You've changed."

Kimora gasped, "Yes, she has." Giggling alongside her friend, she blurted, "I must admit you're now quite adorable."

"Thanks," Beverly mumbled. Looking sidelong at Charity, she quirked a brow and added, "I think."

Keelen knew there was no love lost between his cousin and the two women, and decided it was a good time to speak up. "Would any of you care for another drink?"

Never one to pass up a delicious offer, Olivia lifted the glass of brandy to her lips and finished it in one gulp. "I would love another—"

"No," Kimora stated firmly before returning her attention to the group. "We're going to take a stroll. Would any of you care to join us?"

All three declined.

She flashed them a final smile. "Then we'll see you all later." Letting go of Keelen's arm, she pulled Olivia along with her. "See you later, Charity," she tossed over her shoulder.

They were barely out of earshot when Beverly hissed, "Talk about fake."

Keelen appeared amused. "Cuz, don't let them spoil your trip."

"Humph!" She crossed her arms belligerently across her chest. "I can't believe they had the balls to pretend they were your friends."

"Not much has changed," Charity admitted sadly.

Turning in her seat, Bev's brow rose. "Oh, some things have changed all right. Didn't you see the size of Olivia's boobs? Talk about plastic surgery."

Charity chuckled then Beverly broke down. The two of them were laughing so hard they had tears in their eyes.

Dropping back in his chair, a smile twitched at Keelen's lips. "I hadn't noticed." This set all three of them off. Actually, how could he have missed them when Olivia made certain to rub the pair against him every chance she got?

When the laughter faded down, Beverly asked, "You guys still close?"

Quickly sobering, Charity dropped her eyes and stared off into the blue ocean surrounding them. "Not as close as we once were."

Resting her head comfortably against the chair, Beverly snorted. "I don't know how you hung around them."

Charity shrugged. "Back then popularity was important to me."

"They were a bad influence on you. I remember when you used to act just like that."

"I did not!" she lied, eyes wide.

Beverly rolled her neck in time with her voice while she sang, "Yes, you did." Tilting her head, she added, "Ask Keelen."

Chewing on the inside of her mouth, she looked toward Keelen for help. "Did I, Keelen?"

He pressed his lips together before he admitted with a sympathetic shrug, "I'm afraid so."

She pressed her lips together regretfully and pulled her legs up, cupping them with her arms. "I'm so ashamed."

"Girlfriend, don't even trip. I've never held it against you," Bev said, hoping to put her at ease.

"Thanks, Bev," she smirked.

"Well, I'm going to find myself another Bahama Mama." Bev said, rising from the chair. "I'll be back," she sang as she swayed away to the beat of a reggae tune.

Suddenly feeling uncomfortable, Charity leaned back in her chair.

Keelen placed a hand on her knee, "Bev's right. Cheer up."

Charity gave him a weak smile.

Cupping her chin, he forced her to look at him. The concern reflecting in his gaze warmed her. "Hey! No gloomy faces. Look around you. We are on a luxury cruise ship with everything at our disposal. Now close your eyes and take a deep cleansing breath."

Charity obeyed, enjoying the cool wetness of the air in her nostrils.

"Much better."

When she opened her eyes, she found Keelen staring

down at her. "Thanks." She returned her childhood friend's warm smile.

He lowered his hand and leaned back in his chair, turning slightly so that he was facing her. "I hear you're back in Columbia."

She inhaled leisurely. "I'm living in my parents' old house."

"Wow! They still have that place?"

She nodded. "I'm afraid so. They've retired to Alabama. Dad decided he wanted to be near his roots."

His dark eyes widened. "How are they?"

"Living it up," she commented enviously. "Last week they spent five days in Vegas. Now they are on their way to Colorado Springs."

His brow rose. "Don't tell me they're taking up skiing?"

Her luscious lips curled into a broad smile. "You got it. Now that Dad's retired, he wants a chance to do anything and everything before it's too late."

Keelen shook his head. "They always were something else."

While both his parents worked outside the home, he felt the Roses were a traditional middle-class family. As a matter of fact, Mrs. Rose had been a real *Leave It to Beaver* mom: carpools, PTA meetings, and homemade cookies.

Charity kicked off her sandals and Keelen noticed how perfect her feet were. Her dainty toes were painted plum to match her manicured fingers.

"Where are you living now?" she asked.

"Delaware."

"Delaware?" she scrunched up her nose. "What's in Delaware?"

"Me."

"Ooh, well, excu-u-use me," she sang with laughter.

"I also have a condo in Miami."

Her eyes narrowed with amusement. "You might be

interested to know that your childhood home is now the residence of a he/she/it and lover."

Keelen watched her face light up as she chuckled. Seeing that look on her face reminded him of the time when they were ten and she had baked a batch of oatmeal cookies. Instead of adding a cup of flour, she had used baking soda.

"Do you ever come home?"

He nodded. "Sure, Mom and Dad are still in Columbia. I come home quite often."

"I didn't know that." The thought of seeing him in a familiar setting excited her. "I'm surprised I haven't run into them. How are they doing?"

"Good. Dad had a stroke two years ago and had to give up his lawn service. He's around the house, driving Mom crazy," he paused to release a hearty chuckle. "Kay just had twins and Tristian is still in the air force."

The Brooks were once her extended family. When her mother still resided in Columbia, she kept Charity abreast of everything happening in the small city. Charity had already heard that Kay had tried fertility drugs for years hoping to get pregnant and was now pleased to hear that it had finally happened. She would have to remember to give her mother a call when she got home and share the good news. Little Tristian, whom she once had considered as her own little brother, had grown into a fine man, and after college had become a commissioned officer.

Those were the good old days. She and Keelen practically lived at each other's house or in his backyard where they spent weekends sleeping in a tent his father had bought.

"Bev tells me you've started your own bakery," he said breaking her reverie.

Charity nodded and told him about Tia's bookstore and how her business emerged. "I'm hoping to move downtown this fall. Temporarily, I'm working out of my kitchen."

"You can do it. I've always had faith in your ability," he said emphatically. He knew how important fulfilling dreams meant to her.

Charity looked into the face as dear to her as any brother, if she'd had one. But what she was feeling could not be classified as sisterly love. "Thanks," was her only answer.

She couldn't resist another sidelong glance at him. "What are you doing these days?" she asked.

"Investments," he answered without missing a beat.

"What happened to your dream of becoming a construction worker?" she teased.

He gave her a sheepish grin. "That dream died after one summer of labor in the hot sun."

Her eyes danced as her mind drifted back. His parents had a sandbox put in their backyard just for his Tonka trucks and she suddenly remembered a toolshed he and his father had built together. Keelen dreamed of someday building a mansion for his family.

There was a poignant silence before he asked, "Are you living alone?"

"No." She hesitated only a moment, pleased he was fishing for information. "My five-year-old daughter lives with me."

He looked down at her finger and noticed she wasn't wearing a ring. He couldn't resist asking, wondering what had happened between her and Donovan. "No husband?"

She shook her head, looking down at her drink. "No." Didn't everyone know that she had married Donovan?

Keelen had suspected she was divorced when the two registered separately. He could barely suppress the urge to cheer at his good fortune. "Me, either."

"You don't have a husband either?" she teased.

He scratched his head sheepishly. "I meant . . . I don't have a wife. Never have."

A gentle smile teased her lips. "How come?"

"How come what?" He flashed a slow sensual smile.

"How come you never married?"

"I never met the right woman," he answered, winking at her.

Keelen reached out for her soft brown hand and laced her fingers with his, then met her gaze with an intense stare that spread warmth through her. She could not escape the penetration of his smoky eyes that looked as if he were trying to see inside her.

"You've turned out to be quite a lady."

She lowered her lashes with a blush. "Thank you."

"I'm glad you're here," his voice caressed. He then flashed a familiar smile, only this time it did something strange to her insides.

She swallowed visibly. "So am I."

They grinned stupidly at each other, and Charity realized the years put between them hadn't killed their friendship after all.

Keelen was sitting so close she could see the curl of his long dark brown lashes and the curved line of his bottom lip. So clearly defined, so damn desirable, she had to fight the urge to trace it with her fingertips.

Just then a horn blew and the captain announced their departure.

"Come on, guys!" Beverly shouted from over near the railing.

A broad smile lit Keelen's face as he responded, "I guess we'd better go."

Charity eased her hand from his firm grip and pushed herself out of the chair. When she rose she found him standing with his hand out. Charity placed her hand in his again and felt a surge of energy radiating from his fingers. Together they walked over to the railing to join Beverly, who had removed the camera that was dangling around her neck and had begun snapping pictures.

As the ship slowly pulled away from the dock, the horn blew and the passengers on deck waved.

While Charity joined in the farewell, Keelen took advantage of the opportunity to observe her. Her shorts gave him a full view of a firm round behind and long, sexy legs.

"Do you work out?"

She was so involved in the beautiful scenery his voice startled her. "Did I hear you right?" She asked while glancing over her shoulder.

He chuckled softly. "I asked if you work out?"

This time she swung around to face him and rested her elbows against the rail. Tilting her head, she stared up at him. "Yes, I do." A slight frown now marred her forehead. "It's probably all the recreation I get aside from chasing my five-year-old."

Beverly turned to them. "Come on, you two, stand over near the life preserver so I can take your picture." They followed her lead and moved in close together. Keelen placed a palm to her bare back. A tremor rippled from her throat down to the warm spot between her thighs. She was anxious for Bev to finish so she could move away from his contact. Her attraction to him was scaring her.

As soon as they were done, she put a little distance between them. Turning around, Charity leaned against the guardrail and gazed out at the sun reflecting on the ocean. She was anxious to get wrapped up in the tranquility of the cruise. Capturing the spicy scent of his body, Charity was well aware that Keelen was standing less than a foot away. She didn't have to turn around to know his gaze rested on her. She felt as if he were undressing her, his eyes stroking her flesh as his hands would. Gripping the rail tightly, she tried to maintain her composure. She had seen the interest shining brightly in his eyes. Man, she was so out of practice when it came to the opposite sex! Donovan had been her first and only lover. Now she found herself wondering what it would be like to have Keelen hold her tight, showering her with kisses and making love to her. Staring down into the ocean, she quickly reminded herself that she had not come on board with the hope of meeting anyone. She wasn't interested in a vacation fling. Although romantic, cruises were intended to reel in individuals, to make them become a part of the tranquility surrounding them, but she would not allow herself to be caught up in the moment.

"You look ready to jump overboard," Keelen commented.

Shaking away her thoughts, she glanced over her shoulder long enough to say, "No. I was just enjoying the beautiful scenery."

"I know how you feel. My first cruise was a mind-boggling experience. I've traveled the entire Caribbean and even been to Alaska."

"Wow," she answered, not bothering to turn around this time. "That's some place I am dying to see."

He leaned in and nuzzled her neck. "Play your cards right and I'll make that dream come true," he whispered with that same dangerous softness.

She felt heat rush down to the most intimate part of her body. Keelen was flirting with her. It was too much for her to absorb. Suddenly feeling uncomfortable with where the conversation was heading, she looked toward the direction Beverly had taken and saw two women waving at her. Her lips curled into a smile.

She moved away from him. "Will you excuse me?" Looking over her shoulder again as she walked away, she added, "It's time to meet and greet. I see someone I haven't seen in years." Turning away, she was happy for the distraction. She needed time to think.

* * *

After spending an hour sharing photographs and catching up on the last decade, Charity returned to her cabin long enough to change into a pair of clean shorts and grab her life jacket for a mandatory evacuation drill. With a beach towel draped across her shoulder she headed back toward the elevators and pressed the up button.

"Isn't this a nice surprise?"

Charity turned toward the familiar baritone voice that once sent chills swimming through her veins. It had been three months since they had last seen each other, but Donovan still looked as handsome as ever. Standing at six-two with broad linebacker shoulders, he'd once been an all-American football player before a serious knee injury had ended a promising career during his junior year of college. His Navajo heritage had gifted him with fine wavy hair and a broad nose. Dark walnut eyes identical to their daughter's bore down at Charity, full of interest and obvious lust as they leisurely traveled from her face down to linger at her breasts.

"I didn't know you were planning to attend."

She speared him with a fierce glare. "That's because I didn't tell you," she retorted with a defiant lift of her chin. Her lips had thinned with barely concealed sarcasm.

Shaking his head at her indifference, Don couldn't help chuckling. It was unlike her to be so frank, but he guessed he brought out the worst in her.

His tongue slowly circled full lips complemented by a neatly tapered goatee. "You look beautiful as ever." In fact, he couldn't remember her ever looking as radiant. He stared at her as if he were seeing her with new eyes. After only a couple of hours, the sun had already kissed her skin. Having always worn her hair long, the short new style curling softly around her heart-shaped face gave her an air of sophistication. She was wearing a halter-top that revealed her midriff. Even after the birth of their daughter her ab-

domen was flat and her waist shapely. How had he ever
thought her to be fat? He raised his eyes back to her ample
cleavage. Only a thin piece of material was hiding what he
once believed to be her strongest asset.

Feeling a growing discomfort at his lustful stares, Charity folded her arms over her chest. "I don't need your
compliments, Don."

He smirked with amusement. She only referred to him
by his nickname when she was angry. "Are we ever going
to get along?"

She stiffened. "That depends on how far away we stay
from each other." She turned on her heels to depart. Before
she could board the elevator, Donovan's large fingers caught
her upper arm.

He smirked. "Don't be like that."

The lines of her jaw tightened. "Don't be like what?" she
countered while she watched with dismay as the elevator
doors closed. "I find my husband on top of his desk with one
of my friends and now he expects us to be friends." She met
his unwavering gaze. "The most I can do is be civil when our
daughter is around, otherwise I don't have anything to say to
you."

Donovan released her, and being the clown he could be,
slapped a hand over his heart and staggered backward. "I
don't know how much more rejection I can take." When
his stunt did nothing to soften her expression he looked
down at her with the same pathetic expression he'd used
for years to manipulate her. "How many times do I have to
apologize before you forgive me?"

"What does it matter?"

The slight narrowing of her eyes revealed a coldness he'd
never seen before. Growing exasperated at the level of
resentment in her words, he answered softly. "It matters."

"Look, Don . . ." she paused, bitterness filling her
mouth. "I didn't come on this cruise to argue with you."

"Good." He smiled. "Then let's try to get along."

She hesitated, considering his statement before managing to nod in agreement. Nevertheless, she continued to eye him suspiciously. Hearing the sound of the elevator arriving again, she turned away and stepped in, joining the other three passengers.

Donovan stared at the door long after she left. Although it was a big surprise to him to find her on board, he was glad. How could he have ever allowed himself to lose her? Charity and Taylor meant everything to him, yet somehow he had let himself fall into a trap and had given into his lust for her friend.

Arika had been after him for years, and when she popped into his office one evening, he finally decided to give her what she wanted. Now he realized what a mistake he had made.

Things couldn't possibly be over between them. Sure, he was guilty and as a result had allowed Charity her space and even humored her by signing the divorce papers. He'd always made sure Charity was dependent on him. He believed that without his money and influence she would eventually fold like a house of cards.

His smile deepened into mischievous determination. The cruise was the perfect opportunity to weave his special magic and get his family back.

Four

She closed her locker and hurried toward her English class located on the other side of the building. Turning at the end of the hall, her determined steps slowed when she found Arika and Olivia coming her way. Quickly, she dropped her head and stared down at the red binder, hoping the two would just keep on going. As usual, they halted before her.

"What were you talking to Bobby about?" Olivia spat out in a rush of words.

Looking up with a start, the girl stuttered, "W-what?"

"Don't play dumb!" Olivia moved in closer with both hands balled at her waist. "I want to know what you were talking to my man about," she demanded.

Swallowing, she had known it was only a matter of minutes before word would get back to Olivia that she had been seen sharing a bench in study hall with Bobby Barnett. She should have moved to another spot. However, ignoring Bobby was virtually impossible.

She had thought she would have a heart attack when he took a seat next to her, greeting her by name. And when Bobby asked her if she could explain how to work a three-step algebra problem, she had almost fallen onto the floor.

"N-nothing," the girl mumbled in a strained voice. "He asked me a question."

"What kind of question?" Olivia asked suspiciously.

The girl clutched her books tightly to her chest until

the whites of her knuckles were showing. "Homework."
She shrugged trying to blow it off as if it were no big deal,
but with Olivia everything was a big deal.

Pointing an index finger inches away from the girl's
nose, Olivia sneered, "Look-a-here! Stay away from my
man."

"But I wasn't do—"

Olivia raised a hand palm-forward, refusing any type of
explanation. "Everybody knows you have a crush on
Bobby." She gave a cynical laugh. "What would he want
with you?" She fluffed her hair then returned a hand to her
narrow waist. "You don't have a chance in hell of taking
him from me!"

The girl stiffened at the sharpness of her tongue. It was
no secret that she had had a crush on Bobby since kinder-
garten. But even she knew she could never measure up to
someone as beautiful as Olivia.

She whispered in her own defense, "I don't want your
man."

"That's cause he don't want you!" Olivia's voice had
raised several octaves.

Looking around, the girl noticed that several people had
stopped to listen. Feeling heat rise to her collar, she
wished Olivia would just hurry up. She was growing increasingly fidgety under their attention. Nothing seemed
to mean more to them than embarrassing her on a daily
basis. The Cutie Pies had made a hobby of her pain and
she should be used to it. But some things she just couldn't
get used to.

"Don't make me have to tell you this again. Bobby is
mine."

The girl nodded, wishing she could run and hide.

"Now, now, Olivia," Arika cooed. "Don't be so harsh."
She turned toward the girl and sized her up with one stare.
"You're dismissed." She shooed her away like a fly. There

was no mistaking the glint in her eyes as anything but malicious humor.

The girl stepped forward and did not see the foot that Arika stuck out in front of her. She stumbled onto the floor.

"My, aren't we clumsy," Arika giggled. Olivia laughed along with her as the two sauntered down the hall.

After taking another hot refreshing shower, Charity exited the bathroom to find Beverly standing outside the door.

"Which one do you think?" she asked.

Bev held up the two dresses she was considering. One was a long coral knit with spaghetti straps. The other was short, black and spandex.

Charity looked at them both decisively before pointing to the one on the right. "I like the black one."

Smiling, Beverly's eyes twinkled in agreement. "Then the black one it is." She tossed the other on the bed and padded into the bathroom to shower and change.

Lowering herself onto the bed, Charity toweled off then sprayed her moist skin with her favorite Pear Glacé body spray from Victoria's Secret. She had chosen a simple white rayon dress, midthigh length with a racer back.

Charity opted not to wear panty hose. Instead she smoothed the scented lotion over her legs then reached in her suitcase to remove a pair of white two-inch canvas mules. She was just sliding her feet inside when she heard a musical knock at the door.

As soon as she opened it, her brow shot up in surprise. Standing before her dressed in a short blue halter-dress was a woman who hadn't aged a bit in ten years.

"Tasha Lewis?"

"Charity Rose!"

"Go Rockbridge! Go Rockbridge! Go! Go!" The former cheerleaders shouted in unison.

"Oh, it's so good to see you again." The two found themselves embraced in a warm hug. "Come on in!" Charity moved aside and Tasha entered just as Bev came out of the bathroom.

"Hey, girl." Leaning forward, she landed a loud smack to Tasha's cheek. "I thought maybe you had missed your plane. I checked at the desk before we set sail and they said you hadn't checked in yet."

"You know I wouldn't miss this trip for anything in the world." Tasha lowered herself onto Bev's bed. "They had me registered under the wrong name."

"That explains it." Bev twirled around, her eyes bright with delight. "All right, what do you think?"

Tasha answered without hesitation. "You look like a hoochie in that dress."

Bev lowered a hand to her hip. "Don't hate cause you can't get your wide behind in one," she snorted. "Look at what you're wearing. Your boobs are about to spill over the top."

"That's the plan," she retorted. Tasha took a deep breath, presenting her ample bosom enticingly. "If you haven't noticed there are a lot of fine fellas on this ship."

"You ain't lying," Beverly cooed in agreement. Brow lifted, she added, "Did you see the head chef, Pedro, at dinner tonight?"

"Did I?" she exclaimed, amber eyes twinkling. "Girl, he was *fine!*" They gave each other a high five while Charity sat on the bed chuckling.

With dark curls framing her caramel face and high cheekbones, Tasha turned to Charity. "Girlfriend, you are going to have to excuse us. Bev has been my home girl since we ran into each other in St. Louis four years ago. We've been inseparable ever since."

Standing in front of the mirror applying her lipstick, Bev snorted rudely at the unforgettable memory. "I was trying to have a long-distance relationship with this fool I met over the Internet. The brotha was fine but damn he was a disappointment in bed!"

Charity gaped. "What possessed you to meet someone on the Web?"

Beverly sucked her teeth. "Some of us have to take what we can get."

"I know that feeling," Charity chimed in. Her bed had been empty for over a year.

"Charity's divorced," Beverly said by way of explanation.

Tasha twirled around. "Girl, what happened to you and Donovan? I thought the two of you were the perfect couple."

Before Charity could open her mouth to respond, Beverly intervened with a friendly warning. "Girl, don't tell her anything you don't want broadcasted on the six o'clock news."

Tasha rolled her eyes and mumbled, "Whatever," before looking to Charity again for answers.

Taking her roommate's advice, she shrugged. "We grew apart."

Tasha leaned back against the pillows, disappointed but undaunted. "Join the club," she replied. "Breakups are the story of my life. I can't keep a man long enough to make room for his clothes in my closet."

Beverly stopped applying her mascara long enough to laugh. "That's cause you're too picky," she commented with wicked affection.

"Who's picky?" Tasha replied defensively. "All I ask is that he have a job and spend some of his money on me."

While blotting her lips with a tissue, Bev added, "In this day and age, that's asking too much."

"I know that's right," Charity mumbled.

"Amen to that," Tasha chimed in.

Standing sideways in front of the mirror, Beverly heaved a sigh of frustration. "I ate too much at dinner. I hope I can suck my stomach in tonight."

Tasha shook her head in agreement. "Girlfriend, that food was sinful! I think I tried everything they put in front of me."

"So did I," Bev frowned as she studied her reflected image disapprovingly. "And that's the problem."

Charity shrugged. "Who could resist? Everything was sooo good." The evening's theme, Little Italy, prompted a menu consisting of everything from veal to cannelloni. The cruise line employed several top-ranking chefs from around the world who created superb international dishes.

"A cruise is not the time to be trying to diet. We paid too much to go hungry. Besides, you look fine," Charity said, admiring Beverly's girlish waistline.

"Thanks, Charity." Rolling her eyes at her best friend, she added, "Tasha doesn't know how to make a sista feel good."

Lips pursed, Beverly retorted, "The only thing I'm trying to make feel good tonight is a man. Speaking of men, where's Keelen?"

Charity dropped her gaze. Hearing his name spoken stirred a flurry of emotion within her chest she hoped neither of them had noticed.

Beverly shrugged. "Probably still in his stateroom."

Eyes wide, Charity's head snapped up. "He has a stateroom?"

Bev nodded. "Nothing but the best for my cousin."

Tasha sucked her teeth then mumbled, "Some of us ain't able."

Charity nibbled on her lip. Keelen had told her he was in investments. *It must be a lucrative venture if he can afford the luxury of a stateroom.*

As soon as Beverly moved to find her shoes, Charity replaced her in front of the mirror. She took extra care in applying her makeup while telling herself it was not at all for Keelen.

Thirty minutes later the group exited off the elevator. Charity paused to suck in her stomach.

"Relax. You look fabulous," Beverly whispered near her ear.

"Thanks," Charity answered although her nerves fluttered with anticipation. It was important for her to make a good impression. Tonight she was going to reacquaint herself with peers she hadn't spoken to in years and introduce herself to the ones she never cared to meet.

Moving through the foyer, she could hear music coming from the ballroom straight in front of her. Outside the door was an easel holding a sign that read ROCKBRIDGE CLASS RE-UNION. Next to it was a table where two former classmates were seated.

"Welcome, ladies." They were greeted by identical smiles.

Charity looked down at the twins dressed in outfits representing their old school colors—green and gold. Since her return to Columbia, Charity had run into the two on several occasions.

"Diane, Danielle, how are you?" she greeted them warmly.

"Ready to get my party on tonight," Danielle replied after she acknowledged the other two.

"Same here," Diane agreed as she handed all three their name tags. "Almost everyone is here. Go on in and have a good time."

Tasha waved. "See you later."

The three women looped their arms together. Name tags in place, they were ready. "Come on." Taking a deep breath, Beverly stepped forward. "Let's do this."

Tasha's smile was bursting with excitement. "You don't have to tell me twice."

The recorded sounds of "Purple Rain" greeted them at the door. Charity was amazed at the decorations. Dozens

of electrical candles lined the walls. Green and gold stars
dotted the ceiling. There was a banner overhead welcoming the class. Someone was walking around dressed as the
school mascot—a six-foot bruin wearing a football jersey.
Life-size posters of all their former teachers and staff were
strategically positioned around the marble dance floor,
from their principal Dale Carter to the cafeteria supervisor
they had all known as Jewel. Pages of their senior year-
book had been blown up and decorated the walls.

As Charity's gaze swept over the assortment of guests
she realized she had somehow separated from both Beverly and Tasha.

She moved across the plush red carpet over to the bar
and ordered a virgin daiquiri. While the bartender prepared
her drink, she nibbled on her lower lip nervously and hoped
she'd find someone that she recognized. To her amazement
she saw numerous familiar faces. She recognized a partially bald man who used to be in her homeroom, a woman
who looked like she was pregnant with twins who had been
a cheerleader. Her gaze shifted to the former homecoming
queen and king as they sashayed across the dance floor.
They were still a striking couple. She even spied Beverly's
ex-husband who was there with his life partner. Then she
found several cheerleaders. She was worried that she
wouldn't remember all of their names; thank goodness they
were each wearing name tags. Greg who had been voted
most likely to succeed was now mayor of Detroit. Hanna
who spent all four years skipping classes was now a pedi-
atrician. Some had lost their hair, others had gained weight.
Several geeks had matured handsomely. It was amazing
how much had changed in ten years.

The band had not yet arrived; in the meantime tunes
flashing back to the eighties and nineties were played
from a sound system. Charity talked to several more
classmates as she went through the motions of weaving

through the crowd shaking hands, exchanging hugs and polite greetings. Charity was pulled into several embraces by former classmates who she wasn't sure knew who she was. There had been 125 students in their graduating class and it appeared at least half of them were present, including several spouses. She experienced very little of the animosity she had expected. Instead, everyone was wrapped up in the excitement of it all. Instantly she felt more at ease.

"This is it, girl," Beverly appeared suddenly out of nowhere and moved up beside her. "We're about to catch up on ten years of gossip!"

"You're crazy!" she commented with a flash of laughter in her eyes.

"I wouldn't have it any other way." Beverly pointed to the group standing near the door. "You see Marla Robinson over there?"

Charity's eyes darted to a slender honey-colored woman sporting shoulder-length dreadlocks.

"Well . . ." Beverly whispered. "I heard she just got out of drug rehab." She then tilted her head to the right. "And Rochelle over there, she won the lottery two years ago and is already broke."

Charity hid her amusement. "How do you know all this?"

"I've got my ways," Beverly sang. Looping their arms together, she maneuvered them through the crowd. "Watch this." She ushered Charity over to a stout lady sitting at a table in the corner. "Hello, Linda," Beverly crooned sweetly.

"Hi, Bev," she responded with a wide snaggle-toothed grin.

Charity dragged Beverly away. "You were wrong for that!" she gasped trying her best not to laugh, but was failing miserably.

Beverly huffed, "Correction, she was wrong for that grill of hers."

They strolled through the crowd together, Beverly mingling with everyone they encountered.

Rounding the room again they saw Tasha moving their way. She mouthed for them to look toward their left. Beverly squinted trying to get a good look at the person in question. "That couldn't possibly be Mary Helen!" she gasped.

"Where?" Charity asked, her eyes darting back and forth across the room.

"Over there, standing next to Brandy," she whispered.

She took in the former student council president. Once a slender brunette, she was now pleasingly plump.

Tasha tsked. "Oh, my! Girlfriend, look at those hips."

Beverly nudged her in the rib. "Look at that butt." They brought hands to their lips trying to stifle their laughs.

Charity shook her head, suppressing a fit of her own. "You both are being bad."

"Excuse me, but we're acting like *you* used to act," Tasha said without malice.

"She's right," Beverly agreed before draping a friendly arm across Charity's shoulders. "But enough of that. Let's catch that *fine* waiter with the drinks."

Conversations and laughter drifted around the room. Servers carrying trays with a wide selection of appetizers such as finger sandwiches and stuffed mushroom caps strolled the area.

Drinks in hand, they were just starting to circle the room a third time when Charity found Keelen standing off to the right talking to two former soccer players whose names she couldn't remember. She stopped in her tracks as desire coursed through her at the sight of him. Studying him freely, she watched his luscious lips as he spoke and the attractive narrowing of his eyes when he responded. Standing there in a navy blue suit, Keelen was so handsome he stole her breath away. She raised the drink to her lips and took a sip, her eyes never wavering.

Without warning, Keelen turned in time to catch her watching him. She wanted to look away, but couldn't. Instead she found herself drawn to the heat in his gaze. With a smile twitching at his lips he raised his glass in a silent salute. Feeling self-conscious, she smiled in acknowledgment then dropped her eyelids and moved to stand next to the other two.

With her arms folded across her chest, Tasha gave an audible sniff. "Girlfriends, look who's coming this way."

Beverly glanced over her shoulder and mumbled, "Oh, brother. Here comes Dolly Parton."

Dropping her head, Tasha coughed to disguise a laugh.

Charity followed the direction of their eyes to find Olivia and Kimora sashaying their way.

Kimora was wearing a yellow handkerchief tube top and a long low-rise matching skirt that left her tight abdomen exposed for all lookers.

Olivia was wearing her signature four-inch black heels to complement a short rayon shirt-dress made of one hundred percent spandex.

"Hey, girl." Olivia blew a kiss in the air. "You look gorgeous."

Charity smiled. "Thanks. So do both of you."

Kimora looked over at the other two women. "Hello, Tasha." She greeted her with mock surprise. "I haven't seen you in years. Where have you been hiding?"

Even though Tasha was smiling, the flare of her nostrils gave indication of her irritation. "I still work in the unit upstairs from you," mumbled the registered nurse.

Kimora's brow raised a fraction as if to say *oh*.

Olivia cast a glance at Beverly. "Good seeing you again, Beatrice."

"It's Beverly," she sputtered, shooting her an icy look. Before she could retort, Tasha clapped a hand over Beverly's mouth and pulled her to the end of the buffet line, cracking up with laughter.

"Did I say something wrong?" Olivia asked with a sly smile.

Charity rolled her eyes heavenward. Olivia was back to her old tricks.

She looked around the room in search of Keelen. He had disappeared in the crowd.

Kimora's mouth thinned with displeasure. "Why are you hanging out with them?"

Folding her arms defensively, Charity answered. "Beverly's my roommate."

"We looked for you at dinner," Olivia added after a long swig of her drink.

Charity shrugged. "My dinner hour is at six."

"We didn't come down until seven." Kimora huffed. "Are you avoiding us?" It was a statement, not a question.

She blew a strand of hair from out of her face. Where did all this insecurity come from? "Why would I do that?"

Giving an impatient shrug, Kimora answered, "I don't know. I just feel like you are." Her face became pouty. "I thought we'd gotten past the animosity and could spend some time hanging out."

Biting her lip, Charity shifted uncomfortably on her feet. "We've got plenty of time for that."

"If you are avoiding us because of Arika, don't worry. I know how to handle her."

She shook her head. "I'm not worried about Arika." Neither of them looked convinced, but it was pointless to argue.

"Have you seen her?" Olivia asked.

Irritation marred her beautiful features. "No, not yet, but I'm sure I will."

"Now that the room is crowded I'm sure she'll show up soon." Kimora paused to roll her eyes for added emphasis. "You know Arika has to make an entrance."

"I think the four of us should sit down and talk," Olivia said.

"What?" Charity gaped. She couldn't possibly have heard her right.

"She's right, Charity," Kimora agreed. "You shouldn't let a man tear apart our friendship. Men are a dime a dozen, but friends are forever."

The display of loyalty was making her sick. Charity opened her mouth to object but Kimora cut her off.

"Olivia, look!" Kimora had averted her attention to their right.

"Where?"

She was pointing frantically. "Over there. There's Bobby Barnett!"

"Oh, my God, where?" Her eyes were bulging out of her head.

"Over there!" She repeated with an exasperated sigh.

Turning toward the direction of her finger, they found a tall slender man at the buffet table. Olivia squealed with delight. Placing her empty glass on a nearby table, she patted her hair to make sure there wasn't a braid out of place. "I know that backside anywhere. How do I look?" she asked, gesturing to her slinky gray dress. Her breasts strained against it, the buttons threatening to give away at any moment.

Charity nodded and told her what she wanted to hear. "You look great."

A satisfied smile softened Olivia's mouth. "Cool." She latched on to Kimora's arm. "I'm suddenly hungry again. Let's go."

Charity let out a heavy breath as soon as the two had left and took a seat at a nearby table covered with a gold cloth. Those two were already getting on her nerves. How had she ever hung out with them? She wasn't going to let them get to her and she sure wasn't trying to reconcile her relationship with Arika. With all that said and done, the trip was turning out better than she had hoped. She was really enjoying herself.

Gazing out the window at the moonlit sky, she watched the lights from the ship reflecting off the ocean. It was a beautiful sight; nothing but ocean for miles. She couldn't wait to spend time on the beach with the sand between her toes.

Chin resting in the palm of her hand, she allowed her eyes to travel around the room. The band had finally arrived and was setting up in the far corner. Several porters were clearing the displays and tables away from the center to be used as a dance floor.

Looking to her right she found Keelen again. Even from the other side of the room she felt a shiver of desire. She sucked her lower lip between her teeth as their eyes met and held. She knew it was rude to stare but it was hard to ignore his compelling eyes, his sensuous mouth, and his tall sexy body. He didn't have to say a thing, however, her heart fluttered with awareness. Raising her hand, she waved, and he returned the gesture then turned his attention to the pair in front of him.

Tasha and Beverly flopped down at the table interrupting her thoughts. A waiter arrived shortly after.

"Would you ladies care for something else to drink?"

They all smiled up at the tall blond. "Hans, we'll take three Island Punches," Bev responded, reading the waiter's name tag.

Eager to please, he handed each of them a tall drink from the tray.

Charity sipped. "Mmm, these are so addictive." The other two agreed.

The lights dimmed except for the candles mounted on the walls circling the room. A bright strobe light beamed down on the dance floor as the sounds of Janet Jackson filled the room.

"Heeeyy! That's the jam," Tasha shrieked.

"This place is on and poppin'," Bev said as the two rocked in their chairs to the beat of the music. "As soon as I get done with this drink, I'll be ready to get my party on."

"Does that mean you finally learned how?" Charity joked, staring at her from across the table.

While sucking her teeth Beverly murmured, "Girl, I'm good enough to be on 'Soul Train.'"

Tasha gave her a quick glance then snorted. "I wouldn't say all that."

Charity burst out laughing when Beverly rolled her eyes.

While sipping their drinks the three moved in their seats and sung along.

"Uh, oh!" Beverly motioned with her head. "Here comes Tweedledee and Tweedledum."

Tasha smothered a groan. The Forest twins moved their way wearing matching outdated black suits and Afros.

"Hello, ladies," Jerome greeted, flashing a dimpled smile.

"Hi, Jerome, Gerald," Tasha said sweetly.

"Would any of you ladies care to dance?" Gerald asked, glancing from one face to the next. Jerome also looked uncomfortable but determined to dance with one of them.

The band changed to a rap song that Charity had never heard before.

"That's what I'm talking about!" Beverly rose from her seat. "Come on, Jerome." She grabbed his arm and led him out on the dance floor. Tasha considered Gerald for a moment then shrugged and reached for his hand.

Leaning back in her chair, Charity watched the two and cracked up laughing as the twins began doing the Cabbage Patch.

Out of the corner of her eye, she saw Keelen coming her way, moving with the grace of a lion. A light-headed sensation took over. His suit fit him to perfection. The dark material spread tauntingly across his broad shoulders and molded to his powerful thighs. There had always been something about a good-looking man that made her feel all queasy inside, but with Keelen there was something extra. It wasn't just his good looks but his personality, the way he dressed, his confident walk, just everything about him. He had an air of self-confidence to which people gravitated. Flooding with emotion, she couldn't seem to look away. Shifting in her seat, she flashed a warm smile as he approached.

"Looks like you're enjoying yourself," he commented, returning the smile.

His deep voice radiated through her. Nervously, she moistened her lips. "Isn't that what I came here for?"

"Yes, it is," he replied with a wide grin. Their eyes locked and Charity thought she was going to fall through the floor before he extended a hand and asked, "Care to dance?"

She smiled up at him, lips quivering, eyes crinkled with delight. "I'd love to." Heart thumping, she placed the half-empty glass on the table, took his hand, and allowed him to lead her onto the floor. While they danced, she watched the way he moved. Keelen had found rhythm along the way.

The music changed to a Baby Face slow song. Excitement coiled through Charity as she anticipated being in his arms. He pulled her close, wrapping both arms around her waist. Charity felt as though she had been waiting all evening for this moment.

"You smell wonderful." He spoke softly, his breath warm and moist.

"So do you." Her voice was almost a whisper. She noticed the catch in her voice and took a deep breath trying to steady it by reminding herself that this was only Keelen.

Pulling back slightly, he looked into her eyes. "And you

look fabulous," he continued. His breath warmed her temple and then her cheek.

Admiration was obvious in the depths of his eyes, causing her to blush furiously. "Thank you," was all she could manage.

Curving her arm around his neck, she rested her head on his shoulder, and felt firm muscles shift with every move. He held her with a possessiveness that thrilled her, the heat searing her skin through the fabric of her dress. Her breasts tightened. She could stay like this, in his arms, with his body pressed against her, forever. They were made for each other. Tingling from the contact, her pulse quickened with the beat of the music. She closed her eyes and tried to still the runaway beat of her heart. She was certain Keelen could feel it beating rapidly against his chest. His body moved in a rhythm against hers that stirred all kinds of wants and needs. His breath fanned her forehead and she felt him grow hard against her abdomen. She looked up at him and saw desire burning in the depths of his eyes. Her heart was hammering in her throat as the song drew to an end.

Keelen felt a tap on his shoulder. It was Olivia, pressing her big breasts against his back.

Batting her thick lashes, she flashed a sultry smile. "Can I have this dance?"

He traded glances from Olivia to Charity before saying, "Well, uh . . . sure."

Still clutching his arm, Charity cleared her throat. "What happened to Bobby?"

Rolling her eyes, Olivia blurted, "Girl, he wouldn't give me the time of day. I think he's gay."

Or maybe he just isn't interested, Charity thought.

Another slow song came on and Olivia reached for Keelen's hand.

"I'll see you later," Keelen promised in a rush as she pulled him away.

As Charity was making her way back to her table, Donovan caught her arm. He swung her around restraining her snugly against his body, gazing down at her with faint amusement. "Dance with me."

Noticing his devilish smile, she struggled in his embrace, pushing both palms against his chest. "I'd rather not," she declined with a frown.

"I insist," he growled against her ear in an uncompromising tone as he swung her into the circle of his arms again. "You used to enjoy dancing with me."

Feeling a shiver of annoyance, she eased back to meet his gaze. "That's in the past, Don," she muttered.

His lips thinned noticeably. "You're right. It is." He gave her a long penetrating stare and then as if an afterthought he added, "You look beautiful tonight, but then you have always been beautiful."

His compliment pleased her and she grinned despite her best effort. Resting her hand on his shoulder, she didn't leave the floor but she did put some distance between them and agreed to one dance.

It was easy to ignore her ex-husband as she found herself looking past his shoulder at Keelen and Olivia dancing in the middle of the floor. One of Olivia's hands rested on his shoulder, the other seductively caressed his back. As she spoke, she brushed her lips against his cheek. Charity felt an unexpected wave of jealous. She had no right to be jealous. They were after all just friends. But she was totally green with envy. Every time Olivia batted her eyes at Keelen, Charity wished the buttons on Olivia's dress would pop. She couldn't tear her thoughts away from Keelen and how good it felt being in his arms flush against his rock-hard chest. Her body sizzled with wonder. She also knew that Olivia was thinking the same.

As she danced with several other persistent classmates, her gaze strayed often to Keelen who was being passed from one single female to the next. She studied his strong profile, his smooth sideburns and the tilt of his nose.

Before Gerald could drag her onto the dance floor, Beverly and Tasha came to her rescue. She looked around and her heart sank. Keelen had disappeared.

Helping themselves to another drink, the women sauntered around the room. They moved toward a large piano where Charity spotted Arika leaning against the keys. She was surrounded once again by admirers. She was a tall, striking woman and with three-inch red heels her legs appeared even longer and shapelier than they were. She was wearing a lipstick-red knit dress with a halter neckline and a fringed scarf tied in back.

It was too late to ignore her. Arika approached them slowly swaying her hips enticingly as if she were Ms. Black America.

Charity sighed. Suddenly the evening had lost its enchantment.

Hands on her hips, Arika greeted her with a sickly sweet smile. "Hello. I was hoping you would come," she said, totally disregarding Tasha and Beverly.

Tilting her chin slightly, Charity gave her a direct stare. Irritation sizzled within her. She tried to conceal the anger and resentment running through her rigid body. While taking another sip of her drink to ease the tightness of her throat, she allowed herself a moment to compose her thoughts before replying. They hadn't spoken since the night she had found her with Donovan. Arika had tried calling her, swearing she had been manipulated into the relationship. That she'd tried to resist, but that Donovan had blackmailed her.

After an extended silence, Charity asked in a razor-sharp voice, "Why is that?"

Arika smoothed out imaginary wrinkles in her dress. "Now is not the time. Let's talk in private later."

Exasperation flickered across Charity's face. "What could we possibly have to talk about?" she replied with a cold edge to her voice, eyes sparking with fire.

"Us . . . of course," Arika answered with a dramatic toss of her honey-blond shoulder-length hair. "You couldn't possibly still be trippin' over that little incident?" Placing a dainty hand across her heart she pretended to look surprised before her brow rose innocently. She gave a soft laugh that carried through the air. "I already told you, Donovan threw himself at me."

Charity narrowed her eyes and struck an insolent pose; one hip thrust out and her arms crossed on her ample bosom. "It's funny you would say that, especially when I found you in the driver's seat." Her tone held a bitter twist.

"Looks can be deceiving."

"And so can friends," she countered, temper flaring.

Standing only inches apart, tension brewed between the two women. The glow faded in Arika's eyes.

Beverly exchanged a humorous glance with Tasha before slipping between the two women, "Are we missing something?"

Her words broke the spell, and Charity realized that this was not the time or the place. The music seemed to have faded. A hush had spread across the lounge and Charity realized that the words had been loud enough for everyone to get an earful. Frowning, she was growing inexplicably annoyed by the minute. She sent Arika another sharp stare before she hissed, "Nothing worth explaining." She then turned away only to bump into Donovan.

He curled an arm around her waist restraining her. "Sweetheart, where are you rushing off to?"

She jerked free of his hold. "Away from you and your little tramp," she said in a frustrated hiss. He watched her cut through the crowd without a backward glance with Bev and Tasha hot on her trail, their mouths wide open.

* * *

He had been watching her every move. Even from across the room Keelen could tell that something wasn't right. Charity's eyes had always given her away. She and Arika were no longer friends. *Amazing.* He'd waited a long time for her to take off the blinders. Keelen had always found Arika selfish and stuck up, the kind of girl who would send her own mother to jail if she had to. He didn't think Charity would ever see any wrong in "Arika the Great." She had grown up quite a bit.

Chuckling, he followed Charity's path. The cruise had proven to be quite interesting so far.

Five

"Where are you rushing off to?" Beverly asked as she scurried to keep pace with Charity's angry strides.

"To get some air," Charity huffed as she stomped in the direction of the deck. How could she have been so stupid?

It wasn't that Arika had slept with her husband. She had gotten past that betrayal and moved on a long time ago. What bothered her most was that Arika had thought she would show up and act as if nothing had happened.

Swinging her arms wildly, she increased her speed, anxious to put as much distance as she could manage between the two.

Talk about naïve! How in the world had she ever remotely considered Arika her friend? She had been a fool and even after all that time the stupidity still chilled her.

"Would you please slow down?" Beverly ordered.

Ignoring her, Charity pushed open the door and stepped out onto the cool deck.

"Girl, what's the deal with y'all?" Tasha inquired.

"Are you concerned or just being nosey?" Charity asked, speaking more sharply than she intended. With a raspy sigh, she sank onto a bench.

Tasha's eyes were filled with questions as she took the seat beside her. "Both."

At least she was honest. Charity glanced at the two who

were studying her carefully before she dropped her gaze to her lap.

"We had a fallin' out." She offered no further explanation.

"Apparently over your ex-husband," Beverly responded dryly.

"Whew! It was getting hot in there!" Tasha mockingly fanned herself with her hand.

"No doubt," Beverly mumbled. "I'm glad you're finally seeing the light where Arika's concerned."

"I was stupid!"

Beverly nodded in agreement. "You won't get any argument there, but I never held it against you so there is no sense beating yourself upside the head about it. We were young. We all made mistakes."

Tasha laid a comforting hand on Charity's forearm. "She's right. Is there anything we can do?" When Charity didn't respond, she tried for humor. "If you want me to beat her ass, I will."

Bev cracked up. "Wouldn't you love to get back at her for picking on us all those years?"

"Yes, I would," Tasha answered.

Despite herself, Charity had to smile. "I can just see you putting chocolate laxatives in her brownies again," she said, remembering a stunt Tasha had once pulled in Home Economics.

"No, that's high school stuff. I would like to do something worse than that." Bev's eyes turned glassy. "Something she would never forget."

Tasha rose and swayed slightly to the left. "Hmm, I don't know," she pondered. "Let me think about it."

"Are you drunk?" Bev asked.

"No," Tasha denied. "Are you?"

"Hell yes!" she cackled. "This is the best I've felt in a long time."

Tasha draped an arm across her shoulders for support. "Me too."

Charity gave a short laugh. "The two of you are just what the doctor ordered."

She looked up in time to see Keelen moving swiftly in their direction. Taking a seat on the bench beside her, he reached out toward her, his fingers gently cupping her chin and lifting her face so that he could look into her eyes.

"Are you okay?" he asked.

His touch felt warm and strong. He had not only touched her flesh but also a part of her heart with his genuine concern. She gazed into his perfect gray eyes that were overcast with worry.

Even though she nodded, it was obvious that she was far from okay. Keelen squeezed her hand.

Beverly glanced at both of them then sighed with relief. "I'm going to leave the two of you alone so you can talk."

Tasha nodded. "That's a good idea. Keelen, you're officially in charge of cheering Charity up while we find ourselves another drink." With that, they snaked their arms together and swayed back to the sliding door.

Keelen rubbed his chin sheepishly. "Excuse my cousin. I think she's enjoying herself." He inhaled her sweet scent. "Would you like to take a walk around the deck with me?"

Her lips softened in a smile. "I'd love to." Without hesitation, she slipped her arm through his.

It was a lovely moonlit night. A gentle breeze kissed her cheek. Having him so close, she suddenly felt chilly and wrapped her arms tightly across her chest.

"You cold?"

"Just a little," she shivered. "But I'm okay."

Removing his jacket, he draped it about her shoulders then drew her close to him.

"Thanks." With his arm around her waist, Charity rested her head comfortably against his arm. "It feels wonderful out here." It was dark on the deck except for the path lit by the moonlight. By the time they reached the end of the ship, her irritation had dissipated. Wrapped up in the tranquility of the moment, she moved to the railing. Her fingers curled around the bar as she stared off into the ocean while enjoying the moist, cool air. Despite the band and the sound of voices laughing and talking at once, she felt like they were the only two on board.

"I could get used to this."

"So could I," Keelen agreed. He could get used to seeing her face every day. He had been watching her all evening, noticing the admiring glances from her former male classmates, and the looks of envy from several females. Charity had come a long way.

The freshness of the outdoors swept over her; her hair tousled by the wind. "This is paradise." She held up her palm as if taking a sacred vow. "I promise to take another cruise before the next decade."

She looked so sad. He wanted to do something, anything to make it better. If he had his way, he'd make her every dream possible. "I'm still a good listener if you want to talk." He reached out and touched her forearm comfortingly.

She noted the hint of query in his tone. Glancing over his shoulder at the party just beyond the glass, she could still hear drowning conversations and soft music. Turning toward the horizon, she stared off in silence as if looking in the past. Then after several seconds of silence, she finally spoke, "Arika was considering having plastic surgery done on her nose. When she decided to fly in one Thursday evening, we made arrangements to have dinner following her consultation with Don. I arrived at the office and found my husband and Arika . . ." her voice trailed off. She briefly squeezed her eyes shut.

Keelen studied the wounded expression in her downcast

eyes. "I'm sorry." He allowed his hand to slide from her forearm up to her shoulder where his fingers squeezed gently.

"Things happen. I just never expected that to happen to me. I had dreamed of having the perfect life, but I guess that's what I get for dreaming." Unable to stand still, she signaled for him to move along the deck beside her. Enjoying the closeness, she reached for his hand and was not at all surprised by the shiver of delight. Her words were unhurried and her eyes didn't quite meet his while she poured out her heart.

"You know, it's more than just that," she said in sudden anguish. "I had made so many enemies in high school that I didn't even want to attend our reunion. But I did hope to give everyone a chance to see that I had changed. I was horrible back then, just horrible. Because I wanted so bad to be part of the popular group I allowed Arika to dictate my life for four years. Then I let Donovan dictate my life for the next nine. They both had this uncanny ability of making me feel like I was incapable of making my own choices. Now I look back and ask myself what the hell was I thinking?"

"You can't blame yourself for the mistake your husband made. You did exactly as you chose to do; be a dedicated wife and a loving mother. There is no point in beating yourself over the head because you decided to put your family before your career. It was a very unselfish act. Not many people can do that. I admire that about you."

Keelen was right. She couldn't keep dwelling in the past. She had grown so much and learned even more. Life had been a painful lesson. His reassurance and the knowledge that she had overcome so much suddenly eased some of her anger.

She stopped walking and turned to him a weak smile tilting the corner of her mouth. They used to share everything, sometimes talking for hours at a time. Keelen had always been a good listener. Anytime she'd had a problem Charity knew she could always turn to him for comfort. The thought brought a frown to her face. Keelen said that she wasn't a selfish person. However, over a decade ago she had spent so much time worrying about her own feelings that she wasn't sure if she had ever thought about his. She had never been there for him like he had been for her.

"I'm sorry," she finally said.

He looked confused. "For what?"

"For the way I treated you," she declared without hesitation. "I was so stupid back then. I put popularity before friendship."

He shrugged. "We were young. We're supposed to make mistakes," he said reassuringly, trying to put her mind at ease.

Her eyes darkened with emotion. "I know, but there's no excuse for the way I behaved."

Drawing her eyes to his, he saw the old Charity he knew. The Charity he had fallen in love with. He clasped her hands in his. "It's all in the past," he said, cutting short any further argument.

She tipped her head back and gazed in his eyes. Beautiful eyes. Why hadn't she realized years ago how wonderful he was? After a prolonged silence, she blinked rapidly and smiled as she said, "Thank you."

Their eyes were locked for several seconds before a delicious shudder invaded her body. What was going on? Pulling the jacket tightly around her, Charity turned and leaned against the railing, watching the moon dance on the water.

"If anything I should be thanking you for cheering me up for years."

Charity swung around, puzzled. "How is that?"

"Let me show you something." Dropping her hands, he

reached into his pocket, pulled out an old wallet and flipped to a photograph.

She looked down at the worn picture, then back at him, eyes wide. "That's my fifth-grade photo!"

"Do you remember when you gave this to me?" She nodded. "I've carried it ever since. While I was away at college lying in my dorm, I used to pull this photo out and think about the good times we used to have." He looked into the past. "I remembered all of the crazy stunts we pulled on one another and would lie in my bed cracking up. My roommate thought I was nuts."

"We did have some good times," she giggled, the memories bringing an instant glow to her face and light to her eyes. "I remember when we tried to build a glider and you jumped off the garage and broke your arm."

Shaking his head, he grinned, deepening the dimples on either side of his face. "And the time you tried to dye your dog's hair and it turned orange."

They were cracking up.

"I even remember when we were ten years old and you were curious about how it felt to be kissed."

With a jolt, her laughter died and was replaced by a rush of heat to her face. "You remember that?"

He nodded; a smile tickled the corner of his lips. "I was so nervous. But I was willing to do anything that you wanted."

He was talking about the time she caught his sister, Kay, kissing in the bushes. Wanting to follow in her idol's footsteps, she had later pulled Keelen behind that same bush demanding that he also kiss her.

"Yeah, you busted my top lip with your big front teeth." A nervous chuckle came from her throat. Smiling, she looked at him and saw the tenderness of his gaze. Even in the darkness she could see the sparkle in his eyes that had widened under the moonlight. Her curiosity

swelled up inside her about the boy who was now a man.
He was standing so close she could feel his warm breath
against her nose. Her senses surged with heat from his
masculine scent and the alluring glint of his gray eyes.

Keelen almost shook from the growing heat spreading
through his loins. He took her hands in his and inhaled.
Her rose scent was driving him mad. Her face was only
inches from his. The light dancing in her tender eyes mesmerized him. His eyes slid from hers and fastened on to
her lips. They were the most sensuous lips he'd ever seen.
Red kissable lips. Lips that he had never forgotten. Lips
that were right in front of him. After all these years he had
never forgotten how her lips molded with his or the desire
that had spiraled within him. He wanted to kiss her. His
eyes lingered on her mouth; he could also taste the heat
of her lips on his.

Taking a moment to try to calm the urge, he raised a
hand to smooth away a wisp of hair from her cheek. She
had been the first woman he had ever kissed and although
the kiss had only lasted a matter of seconds, it had always
carried a special place in his heart.

Now the time had come again.

"I had always wondered if your lips were really as soft
as they appeared." He looked down at her and Charity
swallowed. "And they were," he murmured, moving closer.
He slipped his arm around her waist and pulled her close.
How many times had he fantasized about holding her like
this? "Now I'm interested in finding out if they are still
just as soft." The provocative tone of his words was barely
above a seductive whisper.

Charity felt her throat go dry at the flare of interest in
his eyes. Her heart was thumping madly as he moved in
closer, aiming for her mouth. For a moment, she thought
of pulling back or turning away, telling herself this was
wrong, that she was jeopardizing their friendship again,

but instead her trembling fingers inched their way up to his shoulders where they finally curled around the back of his neck. When he dipped down and brushed his lips against hers, a warm feeling similar to an ocean breeze washed over her.

Charity took a deep breath, trying to control her excitement. What she hadn't expected was the flood of sensations that overtook her. Parting her lips, she raised her chin to meet him halfway. Again the kiss was soft and surprisingly gentle. When he nibbled and teased her lower lip with erotic urgency, she thought she had gone to heaven.

"Open your mouth," Keelen growled, his lips a fraction of an inch from hers.

Charity obeyed without hesitation, allowing his tongue to slip inside. Since Donovan had never cared for this type of kissing she had never properly learned how. Lacking in experience her tongue moved awkwardly at first, but eventually she relaxed and imitated his gestures. She felt her control slip another notch with the hunger of each kiss as he sought and tasted the sweet liquor on her breath and grew bolder as she succumbed to temptation with every stroke.

She was unprepared for the heat vibrating through her as his large hand caressed her back and then moved down to cup her behind. With his other hand he angled her head back, giving him complete access to every corner of her mouth. Each kiss was longer and deeper, robbing her of all resistance.

The heat of his fingers penetrated through her dress and seeped into her skin causing her body to sizzle. Her heart pounded rapidly as the desire moved beyond anything she had ever experienced. Her nipples hardened as his chest brushed against them. Her knees weakened as she allowed her body to rest against his. The kiss that had started out gentle continued to increase in intensity.

Straining against him, she welcomed his touch and longed for much more.

Overwhelming desire flared deep, his arousal straining against his slacks. Keelen hungered for much more, which made stopping almost impossible. However, with a ragged breath Keelen finally ended the kiss. Burying his nose in her hair, he planted his lips close to her scalp while Charity laid her cheek against his chest.

He wanted to say so many things, he was feeling so many things, but he would wait. They both needed a chance to think about what was happening between them.

"Will you spend tomorrow with me in Nassau?" he asked in a breathless whisper near her ear.

Charity struggled to find her voice while her lips continued to tingle. "I would like that very much."

"Good." He continued to hold her close until their heart rates returned to normal.

What was happening here? Pulling back slightly, Charity peered at him through her lashes. "I'm suddenly very tired. I think I'll go to bed now." She was only slightly tired but anxious to put some distance between them so she could think.

He met her chestnut gaze. Charity looked confused and more beautiful than ever before. Drawing her close one more time, he pressed his lips against her forehead then forced himself to move away and reached down for her hand. "Let me walk you back to your cabin."

Knowing sleep was out of the question, Keelen returned to the lounge to find that the crowd had begun to thin. He moved to the bar, ordered a drink then stood near a window. Raising the drink to his lips, he couldn't stop smiling.

He had kissed Charity Rose.

Keelen had imagined this moment hundreds of times

while lying alone in his bed watching shadows dancing on the ceiling. He would always savor their first kiss, but the second time was priceless. He had never tasted anything so delectable before.

While taking another swallow, he took a few moments and allowed the kiss to wash over him. It was everything he dreamed of and more. Even though it had been several minutes since the kiss, he still felt her touch as if their lips were still locked. Warmth splintered inside his chest, sending heat dancing through his body.

His body throbbed and ached, reminding him of just how long it had been since he had had intimacy in his life.

Keelen didn't have a girlfriend until his junior year of college and that relationship had lasted until graduation when she dumped him for a guy who she believed to have a much more promising future. From that point on, his romantic life had progressed from one disappointment after another; gold diggers, chicken heads, you name it.

And although it had been almost two years since he'd been with a woman, right now no other would satisfy his need but Charity. Her delicate scent clung to his jacket. He had known passion before but never like what he'd experienced with her.

Her lips were soft and aroused a part of him that he had not known existed. He had almost lost control with the overwhelming need to take her to his room and bury himself deep inside of her. He had felt weakened by the desire to caress her through a dress that brushed all of her feminine curves. When she had wrapped her arms around his neck and demanded more, he was certain he was about to explode. He managed to maintain his composure. Now that he had tasted Charity, he couldn't wait to do it again.

He wasn't even going to lie to himself. He wanted Charity and had every intention of making love to her.

He took another sip, swallowed it and silently admitted that it wasn't just lust. He found something, a connection with Charity that he hadn't found with any other woman. She was very special to him, she had always been. Modest, beautiful, caring and sincere were the best ways to describe her. Now he could add passion to the list. In those ten years, she had matured into a fun-loving and sincere woman whose beauty was more than skin deep. Instead it was rooted not only in her personality, but in her emotions. The short time around her renewed those feelings. After only a few hours, he not only wanted her in his bed, he also wanted her in his life. This time he was determined to win her heart.

"Hello, Keelen. It's so good to see you," Arika said, quietly stepping next to him.

He tore his gaze away from the ocean to find the beauty by his side. He didn't return her warm greeting, in fact, he had to grit his teeth in order to manage a smile.

"And you, Arika," he answered, while looking down at the dainty woman who barely reached his shoulder.

"I wanted to tell you that you have a beautiful ship," she informed him in a soft feminine voice.

Keelen stiffened at her words.

Seeing his discomfort, Arika chuckled. "Yes, I know you're the CEO. I'm the one that approved the contracts, remember." She pushed her hair away from her eyes where a light twinkled in their depths. "Why else do you think we decided to use your cruise line?" Her fingernail traced circles on his arm. "I won't tell if you don't," she purred. She leaned closer with a secret smile on her curved lips.

Anger mounted inside him at the implication of her words. He had gone to great lengths to keep his identity a secret and somehow the most manipulative woman on board had found out. Arika had always had a way of finding out the truth and he should not have underestimated her attempts at wiggling out the information.

He didn't know anymore why he was keeping his business a secret. He was no longer looking to prove his point; triumph was no longer a factor. Once he told Charity he was the CEO he could care less who else found out.

Feeling a growing annoyance at her innocent expression, he uncurled her fingers from his arm.

"What do you want, Arika?" His question held a note of impatience.

She laughed softly, delighted that she was getting a rise out of him. Being in control was what she did best. "I don't want a thing . . ." she paused delicately, batting her long lashes innocently, "except to get to know you better. If I'd known you'd grow up to look this fine, I would have tried to be your friend in high school." Then she frowned, remembering his appearance. "Well . . . maybe friends from a distance."

Keelen didn't find any humor in her joke and decided it was better not to comment. He looked the woman over from head to toe. She still managed to be beautiful, a flawless complexion, not a hair out of place. Her dress and shoes had to have cost several hundred dollars; her perfume, though expensive, was too strong after being around Charity's light floral scent.

He had encountered many women like Arika over the years, self-absorbed, beautiful and selfish. He had even fallen in love with a couple, but life was his biggest teacher, and after falling head over heels for a conniving gold digger, he'd learned a valuable lesson.

"Arika, let's cut the crap. You made it quite clear that you never liked me. Why start now?"

"I was young and a victim of peer pressure," she pouted, her full lips drawing attention to their sensual curve. "Can we be friends?" Watching her blink away false tears, Keelen groaned at the dramatic impression.

His eyes were expressionless, and his smile tight. "Sure,

Arika." He held out a hand so they could shake, but instead she flashed a confident smile then threw her arms around him and kissed him on the mouth. When her lips lingered, he disentangled her arms and stepped away.

Arika didn't appear the slightest bit fazed by his rejection. "May I buy you a drink?" she offered with a seductive smile.

Before he could respond, a staggering Olivia joined them. He sighed as his gaze traveled to the woman swaying unsteadily beside them.

"Hey, Arika." Olivia reached them and he could smell the booze on her breath.

"You're drunk." Arika's lips thinned in barely concealed outrage.

She pointed a shaky finger at them. "Iknowhowtocontrolmyliquor." A hiccup escaped.

After rolling her eyes with all the disgust she could muster up, Arika hissed. "Obviously you don't." She cast Olivia a warning frown. "As you can see I am busy right now."

"Oh," she hiccupped. Stumbling on her feet, she spilled the contents of her drink on Arika's dress.

"You stupid klutz!" Arika screeched.

Keelen scratched the top of his head and tried his best to contain his laughter at the scorching frown Arika was sending her friend.

"Why don't I help you to your cabin?" he offered, glad for the diversion.

Jealousy flashed in Arika's eyes before she could hide it behind a fake smile. "She can find her own way." Glaring at her friend, Arika grumbled under her breath with displeasure.

Olivia hiccupped. "Soundsgoodtome."

Arika crossed her arms beneath her breasts with a huff. "She's always drunk."

Raising a hand to her forehead, Olivia mumbled, "I don't feel too good."

Keelen reached her just before she fell. He tried to steady her and turned to Arika, his expression serious. "Can you give me a hand? She is *your* friend."

She looked as if he had just grown a horn. "No way! She might throw up."

He shook his head, not at all surprised by her answer. Olivia was weaving from side to side. He placed an arm firmly around her waist, fearing that she would collapse. "You have a good night."

Arika stamped her foot with frustration as she watched them leave. "You can run, but you can't hide," she mumbled, her voice dripping with disappointment. She had seen him out on the deck with Charity and had not liked the way he had looked at her. "She's nowhere near as beautiful as I am. If I can't have you, then neither shall she."

Charity woke and it took her a few moments to remember where she was. Then she recalled the kiss that had rocked her world to the core. A shiver raced up her spine as she remembered the sensation of Keelen's tender lips and the warmth of his body against hers. She had never experienced anything so passionate. The kiss had overwhelmed her senses and sent a heat that started at her toes and worked its way to the core of her body. Keelen's kiss had been so arousing that it had awakened feelings in her she hadn't felt since . . . since, never. God, she felt like a schoolgirl experiencing her first kiss. She hadn't known that anyone could make her feel that way. Keelen made her believe that anything was possible. *Wait until I tell Tia.* The big-headed boy that used to live next door was now a man.

She hugged herself as she remembered how wonderful it felt having his arms wrapped around her body holding her tightly against his taut frame. She didn't want to admit it, but she was attracted to Keelen, so attracted it scared her. *It's the ship, nothing else. You're both just wrapped up in the moment.* Fantasy, she reminded herself, it was all an illusion. But she knew that wasn't true. There was something more going on between them.

As a shiver coursed through her, she swallowed hard. Now that it had happened there was no turning back.

But what would happen after the cruise was over? Would they stay in touch or go their own merry ways? She shook her head. It was too soon to think about that. After all, it had only been one kiss.

Stretching her legs out she sat up in her bed and noticed that Bev was still not in. A glance toward the clock indicated that it was almost twelve-thirty. She had been asleep for almost two hours. The social hour was long over. She shrugged. Beverly and Tasha were probably at the casino.

Lying back on the pillow, Charity closed her eyes, anxious to return to her dreams.

Olivia staggered back down the hall. Who took a cruise to sleep? Not her! She had still quite a bit of juice left. She climbed the flight of steps holding on to the rail, ignoring the looks of criticism she was receiving. She was a paying customer. A rich customer at that. So what if her fiancé never paid her any attention and was only with her because it was cheaper to keep her. She didn't care. She had a beautiful son, a hefty allowance, a large home and a new Lexus. What more could she ask for?

She reached the fifth floor and decided to take the elevator the rest of the way. What floor was the party on? She racked her brain but couldn't remember.

"May I help you?"

She turned in the direction of the strong Jamaican accent to find a porter eager to assist her.

"No. I am fine." *All he wants is my money.*

Pushing the button to the top floor, she staggered off and followed the Latin tunes out onto the pool area. There were several people surrounding a midnight buffet, but none were familiar.

Holding on to the rail, she moved toward the stern. Fairly close, she heard the sounds of laughter. Swinging around, she found no one. She strained her ears trying to pick up any signs of movement. After several silent seconds, she folded her arms across her chest and moved toward a bench several feet away. Hearing the tread of footsteps behind her, she turned just as someone stepped out from the shadows.

"I thought you went to bed," the oncomer said.

Olivia reared back at the lone figure standing in front of her. "What business is it of yours?" She spat before turning away and moving toward the stern again. What nickname did they used to call her during high school, four eyes, bucky beaver? There were so many she couldn't tell them apart anymore.

A wave of dizziness swept over her and after catching her balance she decided it was probably time to go to bed after all. She staggered around the deck and found herself beside a winding staircase going down. *I wonder where that goes?*

She stooped down to take a closer look and saw nothing. However, while leaning over she felt a hand at her back. Startled, she tried to stand, but instead lost her balance and stumbled down the stairs.

Six

Charity rose early the next morning to find sunlight streaming through the porthole and Beverly lying flat on her back snoring up a storm. Despite the ruckus, the lullaby of the ship across the waves had kept her in a deep, uninterrupted dream state of sleep. She stretched her body beneath the sheets, feeling wonderfully relaxed and looking forward to her day.

Parting the curtain, she stared out the window and sighed at the beauty of it all; nothing but miles and miles of blue-green ocean. Already she longed to feel the cool air against her skin. With her chin resting in the palm of her hand, Charity felt the corner of her lips turn upward. However, it wasn't the beautiful ocean view in front of her that had her smiling this morning.

It was Keelen.

Half the night she dreamed of the heat of his kiss that melted her like hot candle wax. If she closed her eyes, she could still taste him on her lips . . . smell his sultry scent . . . feel the strength of his body against hers. She still had trouble putting to words what had happened to them out on the deck. The only thing she was certain of was that their friendship had moved to the next level.

Charity couldn't wait to see him. As anxious as she was to see his handsome face, she was surprised she had been able to sleep at all. Already she missed him, and she found it amazing that she was looking forward to the next several days. It was an opportunity for the two of them to get to know each other better.

While staring out the window, she wondered how she would react when she saw him today. Would Keelen cause her pulse to race, would she be tongue-tied? "There's only one way to find out," she said out loud. They had made plans to spend the day together. This would be their first date, one she looked forward to, and hopefully the start of many more to come.

Not to disturb Beverly, sleeping beauty, she quietly took a shower and washed her hair. Toweling it, she removed any excess water and decided to let it dry naturally with a little styling mousse. She smoothed sunscreen over her face and arms then decided on a simple cotton sundress. Slipping into a pair of matching undergarments, Charity found herself pleased that her sister had insisted that she treat herself to something special. The lacy red set looked and felt fabulous against her skin. Moving away from the mirror, she slid the dress over her head and lowered it over her hips. Then she reached into the side pocket of her bag and removed a pair of small diamond studs, and placed them in her pierced lobes. As an afterthought, she dabbed a little of her favorite toilette spray, *Beyond,* behind each ear.

Hearing her stomach growling for food, Charity reached down for the newsletter labeled DAY TWO that had been slipped under her cabin door during the night to find that a buffet was being served on the seventh floor until ten. After a quick glance at her watch indicating that she had less than an hour, she stepped into a pair of yellow flip-flops, retrieved her key card from the desk and left the room.

As she moved down the narrow carpeted hallway, she acknowledged her porter with a friendly smile and informed him that her roommate was still fast asleep. He would wait until the two had left for the island before he took the liberty of cleaning their cabin.

Five minutes later, she exited the elevator. The murmur of voices and the aroma of fresh brewed coffee led her into a room completely encased by glass.

Finding several other classmates in line, she engaged in chitchat about the previous evening until she reached her place at the front of the line. She was loading her plate with generous helpings of fruits and pastries when she realized that she was absentmindedly looking around the room hoping to run into Keelen. Not finding him, she felt a tinge of disappointment, but after she reminded herself that they were supposed to spend the day together on the island, her smile returned.

Charity moved to sit on the deck outside the glass walls. It was a beautiful morning. Stepping out of the air-conditioned room, she was met by a tropical breeze. Warm air flowed over her face. It was nothing like the humidity she was subjected to in Missouri this time of year. Drawing in a lungful of air she inhaled the smell of salt from the ocean. *I could definitely get used to this,* she thought to herself with a smile.

She spotted the Forest twins sitting at a table close to the railing. As she moved to join them, something out of the corner of her eyes caught her attention. She looked to her right and found Keelen waving at her. Realizing he was eating breakfast alone, her heart skipped a beat. She stood there feeling like a foolish teenager as the memories of last night came flooding back tenfold. She hesitated, not sure if she should share his table, but to her relief he signaled for her to join him.

She examined her childhood friend sitting leisurely at the table before her. Keelen was wearing a Bahamas T-shirt and a pair of denim shorts. The relaxed look impressed her and was a complete contrast to his distinguished attire the night before. She watched his eyes as they journeyed the length of her. Suddenly, she felt self-conscious. The dimpling grin and the sparkling eyes left little doubt as to what he was thinking.

As Charity strolled over to him, Keelen took in every inch of her, drinking in the essence of her beauty. She looked sweet and pretty with damp wavy hair framing her face. Her chestnut eyes shimmered against the light from the sun. The yellow knit dress hugged her figure with precision; her breasts were high, her waist narrow, her hips voluptuous. The dress stopped inches above her knees, displaying what he considered her best asset: her legs. Even now the memory of their kiss still aroused him in a way that no other woman ever had.

He couldn't wait to see her this morning. The entire night her lovely scent surrounded him making it almost impossible to sleep. Now that he'd tasted and touched her, he couldn't stop thinking about doing it again. He'd even had to resist the urge to call her this morning and instead had hurried to the deck eager to see her smiling face.

"Good morning, sleepyhead," he greeted after a bite of bacon. "How did you sleep?"

She carried her tray in one hand and an empty coffee cup in another. With a smile she set both down onto the table. "Wonderful! Absolutely wonderful," she sang merrily. "I had thought it would have been virtually impossible to sleep with the ship moving at such a high speed. I thought I was going to have motion sickness, but instead I didn't feel a thing."

Keelen nodded knowingly. "I know what you mean. I thought the same thing the first time I took a cruise."

Looking toward the sliding glass doors he asked, "Where's Bev?"

Taking a seat beside him, her senses spun at the scent of

his freshly showered body. *Irish Spring.* "She's still sound asleep."

A soft chuckle escaped his lips. "She never was a morning person. I'm surprised she didn't keep you up with her snoring."

"I managed to sleep through it." The two shared a laugh.

While chewing on a cinnamon roll, Charity felt the rays of the rising sun warming the sky, however, there was still a gentle enough breeze to tickle her nose.

Keelen studied her profile, her nose raised toward the horizon, her mouth open drawing in the freshness. The same mouth he'd ravished only hours ago. The mouth he longed to taste again. A delicious shiver heated his body.

A server arrived carrying a carafe of hot coffee. "Good morning, ma'am. Would you care for some?"

Looking up she smiled easily at the young man who looked barely out of his teens. "I would love some." As she extended her mug, he filled it with the fresh black brew. "Thank you." When he departed Charity reached for a small pitcher of creamer on the table.

It wasn't until she was adding sugar to her cup that she noticed the vertical line of Keelen's mouth. She saw him gnawing on the inside of his right cheek and she knew him well enough to realize that he was bothered by something. "Is something on your mind?"

After another sip, Keelen nodded. He looked directly at her. She was right. Something was bothering him. It was evident by the lines furrowing his forehead.

He lowered his mug to the table. "Olivia fell down a flight of stairs last night."

Charity drew in a sharp breath. "What!"

Seeing her alarmed reaction, Keelen hurried to explain. "She said someone pushed her, but . . ." he paused, skepticism apparent on his face, "she was pretty drunk last night."

She stared numbly at him. "When I saw her she wasn't any more drunk than any of the rest of us."

Keelen took a forkful of eggs before muttering, "After I walked you to your cabin, I returned to the lounge and was talking to Arika when Olivia staggered over reeking of booze."

Charity didn't hear anything after he uttered Arika's name. Her heart sank at the thought of them being together. She should have known Arika would find him attractive.

As Charity regarded him with a speculative gaze, she tried to let go of the hot rush of jealousy that ran through her blood. Was Keelen flattered to have Arika interested in him after all these years?

After mopping his mouth with a napkin he continued, "Anyway, I made sure she made it back to her cabin safely. She couldn't find her key card so I had to wake Kimora up to open the door. I thought she had gone to bed, but I guess after I left she slipped back out."

Lifting the cup to her lips, Charity couldn't help wondering if he had then returned to resume his conversation. Her blood boiled. If Arika had had her way, she had spent the night in his room. The thought nauseated her. But rather than embarrassing herself further by asking, she took another long sip from her cup.

"Your friend obviously has a thing for whiskey," he said invading her thoughts.

For no apparent reason at all, Charity felt like she needed to defend Olivia. She inhaled, then let out her breath slowly. "Olivia's been battling alcoholism for years. I imagine living with a professional football player isn't easy. Not to mention the fact that he is frequently featured in numerous tabloids which tell about him being with one woman after another." Sitting her cup down, she noticed Keelen was watching her with interest. "I think Olivia was even using cocaine for a while even though she wouldn't admit it. She has spent more time in treatment centers than she has at home with her son."

"She has a son?" Keelen asked, brow arched with surprise.

She nodded while stabbing a slice of fresh pineapple with her fork. "Jesse, he's seven," she confirmed before bringing the fruit to her mouth.

His eyes grew round with concern. "Wow, I didn't know it was that bad."

She nodded back at him without speaking. For years Olivia had been denying that she had a problem and blamed it all on Tim's infidelities.

After sipping his cooling coffee, Keelen said, "Well, she's flying home as soon as we dock."

Her eyes narrowed questionably. "How do you know all this?" she asked as she toyed with the handle of her glass. She was curious if Arika had told him.

Keelen cleared his throat as he realized he had said too much. "I spoke to her right before I came down to breakfast."

If anything happened on the ship he was one of the first to know about it, especially now with him trying to impress several investors. The success of the cruise was vital to Enchanted's future. Olivia's history with alcoholism and a high level of alcohol in her blood would probably save him from a lawsuit. However, he felt obligated to pay for her transportation home.

Glancing up at him, Charity could still see a shadow of uncertainty in his eyes and tension around his jawline. There had to be something other than Olivia's fall on his mind, she thought inwardly. Could he be thinking about Arika? *Quit being jealous,* she silently scolded. She shook her insecurities aside and steered the conversation to more pleasant topics.

They talked through the rest of their meal about a cookie bake-off being held next month in Chicago that Charity was planning to compete in.

A soft smile softened the worry lines on Keelen's lean face as he assured her confidently, "I know you'll bring home the blue ribbon."

She smiled. "Thanks."

Looking down at his watch, Keelen removed the napkin from his lap. "I have a couple of things I need to do this morning, so why don't we meet on the top deck, say . . . around one?"

"Sounds good."

Charity returned to her cabin to find Beverly still sound asleep. When she closed the door, Bev stirred slightly but resumed her heavy breathing. Charity flopped down on the bed beside her then shook her vigorously on the shoulder. "Bev! Get up!"

"Leave me alone," she mumbled.

"Beverly, you've got to get up," she insisted while shaking her again. "Something happened to Olivia."

Rubbing her eyes, Beverly rolled over onto her back and mumbled. "What happened to your big-boob friend?"

"She fell down a flight of steps."

"What!" Beverly sat upright, micro braids swinging in every direction. "What happened? Quick! Give me the details," she urged with amusement gleaming in her eyes.

Dropping a hand in her lap, Charity replied, "Keelen says she fell down a flight of steps, however, I just talked to Olivia and she swears she was pushed." She then explained how after she had left breakfast she had gone in search of Olivia and found her in the ship's infirmary with a temporary cast on her left arm. The bone had been broken in two places. Her top lip was cracked and her right eye swollen shut. After a brief discussion with the hysterical woman, who told her own version of the story, Charity still wasn't sure what to believe.

Beverly folded her arms and gave a slow lazy grin. "Fantastic."

A knock was heard. Charity rose to answer it and had barely opened the door when Tasha dashed into the room.

"Did you guys hear the news?" she asked by way of a greeting.

Beverly glanced at Charity. "See, didn't I tell you she was worse than the ten o'clock news?" Lowering her head back to the pillow, she said with a yawn, "Charity was just telling me."

Chuckling, Tasha flopped down on the floor in front of her bed. "I sho' hate it."

Wearing skintight blue shorts, Charity wasn't sure how Tasha was able to squeeze her healthy hips and thighs in the pair let alone be able to sit cross-legged and breathe.

Charity lowered onto her own bed and shrugged. "Maybe someone did push her." She was trying to give a reason for doubt.

Beverly raised up on one elbow. "And maybe she was drunk and stumbled over those big boobs of hers."

"I know that's right," Tasha cackled and reached over to give her a friendly high five.

The two were like a pair of hyenas. Charity had to catch herself from laughing along with them. "You both are terrible."

"Whatever, girlfriend," Bev's shoulders were still shaking with laughter. "I apologize for talking about your home girl but everyone knows Olivia's a lush."

"True that," Tasha agreed with a laugh.

"Yeah," Charity mumbled in a distant voice. "I guess you're right. Maybe she did fall."

The comment was followed by prolonged silence, each

of them lost in their own thoughts before Beverly exclaimed, "Oh, my God!" She scrambled into a sitting position then leaned against the wall with a hand cupping her mouth. "Do y'all remember that girl our sophomore year who fell down the steps? You know the one who said Olivia pushed her but no one believed her?"

A light registered in Tasha's eyes as she gaped, "I remember that! Who was that girl?"

Beverly tapped her forefinger lightly against her chin. "Hmmm. I don't remember."

Charity's lips thinned as she answered in a quiet voice. "It was Rhonda Lawson."

Two pairs of eyes turned to her in surprise.

She occupied herself with smoothing out her bedspread so she wouldn't have to meet their probing stares before she continued. "Rhonda was on her way to class when Olivia stuck out a leg and tripped her." She stopped to draw in a long breath then looked up at the two waiting anxiously for her to continue. "She busted her lip and broke an arm."

Beverly nodded. "I remember it was Rhonda's word against hers and since she couldn't prove it Olivia wasn't suspended."

"That's right." Tasha looked up at Charity again. "How do you know Olivia really did it?" she asked as if she didn't already know the answer.

With a feeling of guilt, Charity swallowed a huge lump that had lodged itself in her throat. "I was there when it happened," she admitted sadly. She had seen it all; however, her sisterhood had sworn her to secrecy.

Beverly sucked her teeth. "Dang, girl."

Tasha shook her head. "Girl, y'all Cutie Pies were treacherous."

"Yeah . . . we were," Charity said simply. If they only knew all the things she had witnessed; all the things she felt responsible for happening.

While the other two looked at each other as if to be saying I-told-you-so, she lowered her haunting gaze to the floor. Dark memories pushed to the surface of her mind that she had buried so long ago. With all her heart, she wished she could take back one event—Senior's Night. If she had only insisted, if only . . .

". . . Did you hear me?"

Charity blinked and saw the two gazing expectantly at her. Shaking her head rid of the thoughts, she answered apologetically, "I'm sorry my mind wandered off. What did you say?"

Beverly couldn't understand why she looked so distraught, but went ahead anyway and repeated the question. "I said, I wonder if Rhonda is on board?"

Frowning, Charity shook her head. "I don't remember seeing her last night."

Tasha leaned leisurely against the mattress, legs stretched out and crossed at the ankles. "I don't even remember what she looks like."

"You'd remember if you saw her," Bev said.

The words were met by silence.

Looking from one to the other, Charity said in a low voice, "We shouldn't let our imaginations run wild, but what if there is some truth to Olivia's story? What if Rhonda or someone else did push her?"

"Then we should give them a medal," Beverly snorted. "After all the things Olivia's done, being knocked down the stairs should be the least of her worries."

Tasha nodded. "And like we said earlier, maybe she fell. She was wearing high heels." She paused then added, "However, you know her better than we do. She is your friend."

Charity shrugged with indifference. "I don't know what to believe." She forced her thoughts away from the different scenarios, hoping that the fall wasn't intentional and was an accident after all. Any further discussion on the topic was interrupted by a heavy knock at the door.

"Dang, what is this, Grand Central Station," Beverly muttered before tossing the covers over her head.

Tasha rose from the floor and went to answer it. "Well, well . . . look who's here."

"How are you doing?" a familiar masculine voice asked.

"Obviously not as good as you," she crooned.

Recognizing the voice, Charity let her gaze wander to the door where she found her ex-husband. Subconsciously, her fingers clenched tightly on to the bedspread.

Tasha opened the door wider so he could enter. "Ooh, my my! Don, don't you look good," she mumbled appreciatively while staring at his backside.

Donovan smirked proudly at the compliment as he moved inside the cabin and leaned one elbow against the wall. Tasha slid past his massive body that was taking up a great deal of space.

Charity could see why any woman would feel proud to bring him home to mama. The reason he was appealing was quite simple. Don was fine and after all these years he still looked as immaculate as ever. His shorts and top were crisp and obviously freshly pressed. As usual, he had not left home without his travel iron. The things that had first attracted her to him in high school were his healthy thighs and calves and after all that time they were still in top condition. A pair of leather sandals revealed pedicured toenails. He was undoubtedly handsome, but she knew from years of experience his beauty was only skin deep.

Beverly peeked from under the covers long enough to say, "Hey, Donovan."

"Hello." He inclined his head in acknowledgement. "Sorry to disturb you ladies, but I need a moment with Charity."

"What do you want, Don?" Charity inquired coolly.

He lowered his gaze and looked as if he had just realized she was sitting there. "Can we speak in private?"

She glanced over to find Tasha and Beverly watching with gleaming interest. Excusing herself, she pushed off the bed, walked outside the cabin and stood in the hall.

She gave a dramatic sigh. "All right, I'm all ears."

Leaning against the door, he blatantly took his time to study her fresh vibrant look. Her face was clear and clean of makeup and her hair had dried in natural waves, taking away several years from her face. "I really like your hair like that."

"That's a surprise coming from someone who insisted that I never cut it."

"I was wrong. I'm sorry," he said with remorse.

Gritting her teeth, Charity counted to ten. Last night she had decided to curb her annoyance with him and try to come to some kind of understanding. After all, he was Taylor's father.

"I know you didn't ask me out here to discuss my hair." Her eyes flashed a familiar display of impatience.

He sent her a lazy grin. "No, I did not. I want you to spend the day with me in Nassau."

She shot him a withering glance. "I can't believe you even have the balls to suggest such a thing!"

Donovan stared at her a moment—her sharp tongue was amusing and it was so out of character for her to speak that way to him. It now seemed to be a habit of hers. He found the change arousing.

Arching an amused brow, he replied, "Why not? You're my wife."

"Ex-wife," she corrected.

"Charity, I think it's time you stop playing these games. When this cruise is over I want you and Taylor to come back home with me." The slow arrogant smile that curved his mouth irritated her. He spoke as if he were at a drive-thru window at a fast-food restaurant requesting that they hold the pickles on his cheeseburger. She wasn't an impressionable and naïve teenager anymore. Did he really believe she was going to forgive him and go back to living under his command? He was spoiled and used to getting his way. It didn't matter if he asked her tomorrow or even a year from now, her answer would still be the same. No.

Shaking her head, she tried to remain calm. "You are something else."

He took both her hands in his and spoke in a low voice. "I'll beg if I have to. I want my family back."

She jerked against his grip. "You should have thought about that before you slept with Arika."

"I'm a man!" he defended.

Charity fell back against the door, started laughing and couldn't stop.

His brow furrowed with wrinkles. "What's so funny?"

"You," she cackled. "You're so full of crap." It felt so good to laugh about something that a year ago would have turned her into a whimpering fool.

Not taking offense, Donovan tried to confuse her with the flash of his familiar smile. The same one as a giggling teenager she had found so charming. "No, I was weak and stupid," he pointed out.

"I can't argue that." Her eyes were twinkling with humor.

His fingers caught her upper arm and he pulled her to him. Stiffening, her laughter vanished as quickly as it had appeared.

Arika hadn't been the only one.

Like clockwork every other Friday, Donovan would return home in the wee hours of the morning smelling like booze and expensive perfume, expecting her to welcome him in their bed with open arms. She cowardly chose to ignore it and look the other way, not wanting to rock the boat. However, after she found him with Arika she had finally decided that enough was enough and stood her ground.

Swatting his hand away, she reached behind her and gripped the door handle. "Leave me alone, Donovan." She turned and reentered the cabin, shutting the door on his surprised face.

The three made it to the top deck just in time to watch the ship pull in near Rawson Square, the very heart of the city's shopping. Prince George Wharf where the ship's berth was located was already occupied by five other cruise lines including Disney, Fantasy, Royal Caribbean and Carnival. As they moved closer to the island, Charity was mesmerized. She shielded her eyes from the rays of sunlight that were bathing the ocean in breathtaking splendor and gazed appreciatively at the long stretch of white sand beaches. Her stomach churned with anticipation. She couldn't wait to see the city.

"It's beautiful," Beverly said while she snapped several photos.

"Yes, it is," Charity murmured appreciatively. "What's that over there?"

Looking in the direction of her finger, Tasha answered, "Girl, that's Paradise Island."

"Wow." She had read about it. For years the island had stood completely undeveloped, its beaches and tropical splendor unnoticed by the world. Suddenly, with the addition of several luxurious hotels and a grand casino, it was transformed into one of the most glamorous resort centers in the world, combining exclusive tranquility and lots of action.

Atlantis was the newest and finest hotel on the island and she could see why. The resort had adopted an ancient mythological theme. The building reminded her of something she would find underwater in the movie *The Little Mermaid*.

Removing a small disposable camera from the front pocket of her shorts, she shot several pictures of the hotels and its surroundings.

"There's Keelen," Tasha mumbled, drawing her attention away from the island.

Charity turned around and her smile faded. Keelen was standing against the railing at the top of the steps talking to Arika. Her hand was clasped on his arm while she looked up at him wearing an adoring smirk as if he were the only man in the world. She couldn't help notice that they looked good together. Arika was wearing a two-piece yellow bikini with a floral wrap tied around her tiny waist. Keelen had changed into a pair of khaki shorts, a polo shirt and walking shoes. Charity felt a wave of jealousy rush over her. Once again she felt annoyed by her reaction.

"What's he doing talking to her?" Tasha murmured.

"Who knows." Her voice was quiet. Now that she had had a chance to see the two together it was perfectly clear that Arika was interested in Keelen. She knew that gleam in Arika's eyes. She'd seen it many times before. Charity also knew she was liable of doing just about anything to get what she wanted, Keelen included. The big question was, how did Keelen feel about Arika?

Whatever Keelen had said made Arika laugh and in response she dragged a lazy finger down the center of his chest. He then leaned forward as she whispered something in his ear. Charity burned to know what the two were talking about. They had obviously become very chummy since last night. Seeing the two together was like a fist to her midsection. What hurt the most was that he was flirting back with her.

Charity forced her gaze away and tried to jerk her thoughts to something else as she stared at the island ahead. She didn't need this. Since last night, Keelen occupied her every thought. Now, seeing him with Arika filled her with an unwelcome but no less powerful rush of jealousy. She tried to convince herself that she had no right feeling that way. She had no claims on him. They were only two friends who had shared an innocent kiss. But even as she tried to convince herself that that was all there was between them, the ache at the pit of her stomach told her it was something else.

She pretended she didn't see him moving in their direction, and resumed shooting pictures of the sandy shore. Nonetheless, she continued to watch him from out of the corner of her eye.

"Hi, ladies," he greeted the trio, although his eyes were on her.

Charity said hello. Although she hadn't paused from snapping pictures, a tingling of awareness spread over her.

Leaning against the railing, Beverly called over, "Hey, Kee. What are you planning today?"

"I'm hoping to show Charity the city. You girls want to tag along?"

His cousin clicked her tongue. "Heck no. I plan on doing a lot of shopping and flirting." She turned to her comrade. "What about you, Tasha?"

"I'm with you, girl."

She looked to Keelen. "Sorry, Cuz, but I'm trying to have a one-night stand." Returning her camera to its case, she latched onto Tasha's arm. "Girl, don't look now, but there's a fine Hispanic waiter to our left." Pulling her along, the two left to see what trouble they could get into. Charity watched them as they walked off arm in arm.

"Anything special you want to see or do today?" Keelen asked, capturing her attention.

Their gaze held. Charity found herself falling under his spell again as she quickly forgot about Keelen being with

Arika only moments ago. "It doesn't matter," she replied softly. A slow smile eased the lines of tension surrounding her mouth.

"Tell me . . . what does matter to you?" he asked as the need to kiss her overpowered him. Trying to control his urge, he raised a hand and gently traced her cheek, but the velvety feel of her face only made matters worst. He couldn't take it any longer. He had to have another taste of her sweetness. "I'll show you what matters to me." Before he knew what he was doing, he had tilted her head back and pressed his lips against hers, increasing the pressure until she responded with a moan. While his hands rested on her forearms, he merely touched her lips to his. Their bodies weren't touching but the heat from her lips left him feeling feverish. When he finally pulled back, he looked down at her stunned expression.

"How about we take a historical tour and then visit the botanical gardens?" he suggested. "They even have a zoo."

Despite the tremors traveling to her heart, she found the strength to smile at his photogenic memory. He had remembered her love of animals. "A zoo?" The wind whipped her hair.

Brushing a strand away from her left eye, Keelen nodded. "They have a very unusual zoo. You'll never guess what their national animal is."

"What?" she asked, her eyes sparkling with interest.

"I'm not telling you." The grin deepened the dimples embedded in his cheeks. Bending, he whispered close to her ear, "It's a surprise."

With that, he slid an arm around her waist and guided her to the elevator.

Any thoughts of Arika fled her mind. All Charity could think about was the man by her side.

Seven

"Let me out!"

Charity hurried down the hall in the direction of the high-pitched scream. When she reached the end of the west wing, she found Kimora and Arika hovering in front of the janitor's closet. Sharp banging from the other side of the door had drawn several onlookers' attention.

"What's going on?" she asked.

"I locked the nerd in the closet," Arika answered, looking quite pleased with herself.

Kimora turned to her and smiled slyly. "She's only been in there for about five minutes."

"Someone please let me out. I'm afraid of the dark!" the girl pleaded through the closed door.

Arika appeared unmoved. "She's pathetic."

Being the most sympathetic of the bunch, Charity swallowed, "Come on, guys. Let her out."

Arika fashioned her lips into an artful pout while planting a hand on her left hip. "Are you growing soft on us?" Her eyes grew narrow and observant.

"N-no, but she's afraid," Charity stammered, feeling intimidated by her tone, not to mention the half a dozen students watching with childlike interest.

Folding her arms belligerently across her chest, Arika pouted, "She shouldn't have tried to get smart with me."

The girl continued to bang on the door. Soft whimpering

could be heard while the two ignored her pleas and made comments that lacked compassion.

"Aw, she's crying like a baby," Arika laughed mockingly.

Chuckling, Kimora added, "She probably pissed in her pants."

"Enough!" Charity snapped anxiously. "I'm opening the door." She took a step forward. Arika reached out and halted her action.

"Not yet," she stated firmly. "She deserves five more minutes." Releasing her arm, she looked to the right and her expression stilled. "Quick! Here comes Ms. Arnold." Seeing the no-nonsense gym coach heading in their direction, all but Charity scrambled away. She stood frozen, unable to move as she debated what to do.

Ms. Arnold stopped when she heard whimpers coming from inside the closet and glanced sharply at Charity. "Who's in there?"

"I don't know," she answered with hesitation.

With a stern look the teacher moved to the closet door and unlocked it.

The girl stepped out, chest heaving, tears staining her cheeks.

"Do we have a problem here?" Ms. Arnold demanded. Although her voice was stern, she looked down at the girl with concern, then pivoted her eyes to Charity; the look she gave her could have parted the Red Sea.

The girl shook her head; she had never been a snitch. Besides, if Arika found out it would only make matters worst. "No, Ms. Arnold," she answered, eyes deep pools of sorrow.

"Then both of you get to your classes immediately," she ordered, then turned and walked toward the gymnasium.

Looking at the girl, Charity's face softened with obvious sympathy. "I'm sorry about that."

"No you're not! You're just as bad as they are." She

pivoted and moved down the hall. However, when she
reached the corner she looked back at Charity and yelled.
"You tell your friends that I'm going to get them. You
just wait and see!"

Kimora and Arika were seated at the Crocodile Bar and
Grille located on the harbor front, each sipping a fabulous
island rum concoction.

Arika mopped her forehead with her napkin then glanced
down at an elegant gold watch on her wrist. "As soon as we
are done, let's head to the Coach store. I need a new purse."

"Don't you have enough purses?" Kimora growled.
Every time they went shopping Arika had to buy another
damn purse."

Arika crossed her slender legs. "You can never have too
many purses"—she paused to roll her eyes—"but then
some of us wouldn't know that."

Lowering her thick lashes, Kimora mumbled under her
breath, "Some of us have better things to do with our
money." As a registered nurse she earned an excellent
salary even though the job required long strenuous hours.
She knew she deserved to treat herself from time to time,
however, right now she was trying to save every penny. In
a few short months her sacrifice would pay off when she
would be able to begin building her dream house. After
two failed marriages she had come to the conclusion that
the only way she was going to have a home of her own was
to do it on her own.

The waitress returned with their food. They had both
ordered the Bahamian special, which consisted of craw-
fish, peas and rice served with johnnycakes.

Kimora stabbed her food with a fork. "I still don't understand why Olivia left. She could have stayed. I mean it
was only a broken arm."

Arika snorted. "I'm glad she's gone, 'cause she was getting on my nerves." She raised the fork to her nose and smelled it. Only after finding the aroma acceptable did she bring it to her lips. When visiting overseas she rarely ever ate outside her hotel. However, when Kimora refused to return to the ship for lunch she had little choice but to make an exception.

A probing query came into Kimora's eyes. "Do you believe what she said about being pushed?"

"Nope," Arika answered without hesitation. "I was talking to Keelen when she came staggering back on the deck. Olivia's a drunk," she hissed. "If you had any sense, you would stop hanging around her. I know I am."

Kimora clucked her tongue. "She's not that bad." Nobody was going to tell her what to do, not even Arika.

Arika looked up from her food. "She's worse. All that money and she would rather blow it on a habit than shopping." She shook her head. "I still can't understand why Tim is still with her. It couldn't possibly be cheaper to keep her." Pausing, she added with a sniff, "I don't remember if I had told you or not, but Keelen and I were trying to get to know each other better when Olivia rudely cut in."

Knowing he wasn't the least bit interested in Arika, Kimora compressed her lips to keep from laughing. "Girl, puhleeze! Keelen has always had eyes for one person and that's Charity."

Arika's gaze flew up to meet hers. "Charity?" She laughed a harsh sound of denial. "You've got to be kidding."

"No, I'm serious."

Her laughter quickly vanished and her expression stilled as she stared across the table thoughtfully. "We'll have to see about that." There was no mistaking the challenge in her voice.

Kimora shook her head as she slipped another forkful of rice between her lips. "He's cute, but he ain't all that.

Besides, what do you want Keelen for anyway? All you're going to do is pass him off like an old purse, the same way you did Donovan."

"What business is it of yours what I do?" Arika snapped. Donovan had actually been the one to end their brief relationship right after his wife filed for divorce, but she didn't dare tell Kimora that. "Charity isn't woman enough to hold onto a strong man. I don't know why she doesn't see that and get over her continuous need to stay angry with me. Who in their right mind would put a man before friendship?"

Kimora sent her a dark look. "I'd probably do the same thing," she said with her mouth full. "She has every right to still be angry. You shouldn't have been sleeping with her husband."

"Don't try to act innocent," she countered, her lips tight and grim. "You knew all along what I was up to." Arika reached for her glass and took a sip. "Charity can have him back if she wants. Don proved to be just as weak as the rest."

"Did I hear my name?"

Both heads snapped to find Donovan approaching. He pulled a chair up to the small round table.

With a huff, Arika dropped her fork onto her plate. "Of all the restaurants on the island you had to pick this one. What do you want?" she asked rudely.

He gave her a piercing stare. "I need a favor."

"A favor?" she mocked severely.

"You ladies owe me."

Pointing a fork at him, Kimora blew out an exasperated breath before replying. "I don't owe you anything."

His gaze shifted abruptly to the woman on his left. "Oh, yes you do," he stated before allowing his eyes to fall to her breasts. "You forgot . . . those aren't even paid for."

At the reminder, Kimora slumped back in the chair with

dismay. She and Olivia had been two of Donovan's first patients when he had first opened his practice. While Olivia desired several cup sizes bigger, Kimora had only asked to move from an A to a B. Refusing payment, he instead asked to someday call upon her for a favor, which she had gladly agreed to. That was one of the reasons why she had never mentioned to Charity that Arika was having an affair with her husband. Instead she had turned the other cheek.

Kimora finally asked, "What is it that you want?"

He reared back in his seat then said, "I want you to help me get Charity back."

Arika threw her head back and gave a throaty laugh. "Charity is not taking you back," she answered tauntingly.

Kimora nodded in agreement. "She's right. Keelen has her preoccupied."

A muscle quivered at his right jaw as he fought to control the jealousy that surged through him at the thought of Charity being with another man. "Then we'll have to do something about that."

Last night as he held his ex-wife in his arms while the two danced reminded him how much he missed having her in his life. His mind burned with the memories of holding her in his arms; the feminine scent that engulfed him and the way her dress clung to her every curve.

The flare of defiance in her eyes had showed him how much stronger she had become. He had liked what he saw. In fact, the idea of her telling him no from time to time was a definite turn on.

Charity had been his since she was sixteen. She had given him her virginity at seventeen and he took full responsibility for shaping her into the woman she was today. Just thinking about parting her legs and losing himself in her narrow passage caused a stir in his loins. He had been a fool to let her go and wasn't about to share her with anyone. Surely, she couldn't possibly be happy without him?

Nevertheless, he wanted what was rightfully his and the two women sitting across the table were going to help him.

He glanced over at Arika. "You should be more than willing to help me. I saw the way you were looking at Keelen last night," he reported to the honey-blond bombshell.

She met his sharpened gaze. She hadn't remembered seeing him after he stormed out of the lounge. "You came back on deck last night?"

Donovan answered with a smirk and a nod. "I even saw Olivia spill her drink all over you."

Arika leaned forward in her seat, confidentially. "You wouldn't know anything about her being *pushed* down a flight of steps, would you?"

He raised a hand to stroke her arm and allowed his fingers to slide down to her wrist where he tightened his grip. "If I was going to push her, she would have sustained more than a broken arm."

Shaking her wrist free, Arika eyed him long enough to know he meant every word.

"Now . . . unless you want me to share to the world how you stumbled across that damaging evidence on the Murphy case, I advise you to cooperate." Donovan leaned back in his chair with a malicious grin. He loved when he had the upper hand.

Arika clenched her teeth against an instant refusal. The malpractice suit against a local surgeon had landed Arika her current position at the television station. Thanks to Don, who had provided her with vital information he had obtained while attending medical school with Marvin Murphy.

Several medical students in the community had accused Dr. Murphy of unwanted sexual advances that he denied. As a prominent member of the community, the students didn't have a leg to stand on. But according to Don, the same incidents had occurred during his residency program at Washington University. Once again Marvin had been the accused. However, rather than bring attention to their school, the dean suggested to Marvin that he finish his residency program somewhere else. If the television station found out that Arika was handed the information on a silver platter after agreeing to sexual favors, she would be the laughing stock at Channel Eight.

Hatred blazed in her eyes as she looked up at Donovan's frosty gaze . . . the sensual lips she had insisted on tasting . . . the fine hair she had been determined to run her fingers through, and the face she had slapped when he ended their relationship. Instead of kicking him to the curb first, he had beaten her to the punch, which was a definite blow to her ego. She scowled, hating rejection.

She glanced at Kimora who was toying with her glass as she remained silent, leaving the decision to her.

"So . . . what's it going to be?" Donovan asked impatiently.

Combing her fingers through her hair, Arika contemplated his demand. Why would she want to help him get Charity back in his bed? But just as she prepared herself to tell him a thing or two, she remembered how good Keelen had looked last night. He was now rich, handsome and single. That was a potent combination. Why couldn't she also get something out of the deal? After all, all she had to do was get Charity out of her way, then she could have Keelen all to herself.

Finally, she pushed her plate away and mumbled, "What do you want us to do?"

"Very good," Donovan replied. Lacing his fingertips behind his head, he grinned. He had every intention of making love to his ex-wife before the cruise was over.

Keelen had hired a driver to take them through the streets of Nassau. Charity found the city rich with history. Even with the thousands of visitors each year, Nassau had retained its overlay of British charm. As she stared out the window of the taxi, she found old homes still standing, palm trees and hibiscus lining the streets. Police officers were seen directing traffic dressed in white jackets and helmets.

First they were given a reenacted tour of Fort Charlotte resurrected in the seventeenth century where they had the opportunity to explore the dungeons and touch actual cannons. Then they climbed the Queen's Staircase, which was probably one of the most famous sights in the city. The sixty-six steps had been carved into a sandstone cliff by slaves in the eighteenth century, linking Fort Fincastle to the Princess Margaret Hospital. At the top, Charity had a bird's-eye view of Nassau. She had gone through several rolls of films within two hours.

After soliciting several vendors on the streets, they drove through the village of Adelaide, which was believed to have been the first black settlement on the island after the abolition of slavery. The neighborhood was captivating; big houses with big breezy verandas faced the sea and showed the full flavor of the colonial past.

An hour later they departed the cab again, only this time instead of asking the driver to wait, Keelen instructed the driver to return in two hours.

"This is a zoo? It looks like a botanical garden," Charity commented while staring at a large sign that read Ardastra Gardens and Zoo.

"It's a special kind of zoo. You'll see." Taking her hand, he pulled her along beside him.

There were several dozen visitors. They followed the winding path, entering a lush tropical garden bursting with colors. Breathing deeply of the sweet summer air, Charity caught the scent of hundreds of different plants. The trail was draped with mosses and spectacular exotic fruit trees ranging from bananas to coconuts. There were even hummingbirds overhead feeding on hibiscus nectar.

Charity smiled up at him. "This is so peaceful."

Keelen nodded as if to say I-told-you-so.

"How large is the garden?" she asked with increasing curiosity.

"Five acres. About three times the size of our garden back home."

Charity smiled as she remembered the first time his parents had taking them to Shelter Gardens. They were still in elementary school. It was only a fifteen-minute drive from their home. She loved the plants when they were in full bloom and the little red schoolhouse. The gardens had become a popular spot for weddings. Without giving it any serious thought, she could name at least a dozen couples who'd said their vows under the rose-covered gazebo.

Making a right on the path, they reached the first cage. Charity dropped his hand to crouch down to stare in between the bars. "What is that?"

"It's a Vietnamese potbellied pig."

Looking back at him she asked around a chuckle, "A what?"

"A potbellied pig." Keelen moved down behind her, wrapping his arms around her, pulling her close. "Pigs need love too," he whispered before planting a kiss at the base of her neck.

Her eyelids fluttered close and she savored being in the comfort of his arms. Relaxing against him, his body heat penetrated her. *Man, he feels good.*

Patting her playfully on the behind, he replied, "We had better keep going before I ravish you in front of the pig."

It was a brief yet sensual experience. She tried to keep her body from quivering as he reached for her hand again. Taking the path through the trees, they crossed a small footbridge where swans swam in a small stream surrounded by freshwater turtles.

"Oh, look!" Charity exclaimed. Dropping his hand, she scrambled after a peacock. Removing the camera from around her neck, she stopped to capture a picture of the bird in action as he proudly strutted his feathers.

Keelen stood back and watched her childlike behavior. This was the Charity he remembered. Free spirited, joyous, and funny. Nevertheless, when she leaned over she reminded him of the woman she had become and caused the blood to flow to his loins. He enjoyed the bend of her waist and the shapeliness of her calves. Her smile made him want to find a soft secluded spot in the bushes and take her right then and there. He grew increasingly aroused as the fantasy continued to take shape in his mind.

With his head cocked to one side, he studied her standing in the grass while taking photographs of the peacock. As she raised the camera to her face an emerald tennis bracelet dangled from her wrist. Although the peacock was fascinating, he was captivated by the lovely picture she made. Under the warm sun, wisps of hair clung to her damp neck. A man would be a fool not to appreciate her beauty. She looked so tempting. He wanted to taste her lips . . . lick the sweat from her skin . . . hold her in his arms. He wanted to make his fantasy a reality.

Keelen had been observing her all afternoon. Hell, he couldn't stop watching her. The sway of her hips as she moved from one basket weaver to the next, her toned legs when she climbed the stairs, her laugh, the sparkle of her eyes as she listened attentively to what their guide was saying. Everything she did aroused him.

It was unnatural for him to desire someone as badly as he desired Charity. Yet he couldn't help himself. He wanted her all to himself.

Keelen grew increasingly warm as he recalled their

passionate kiss the previous night. It was like nothing he'd ever known. But it was more than just the kiss. He remembered the perfect fit of her soft curves in his arms. How nice it would have been to have held her in his arms all night. Images of her lying naked across his bed, her arms folded behind her head, her large breasts on display, invaded his mind. Shaking his head, he tried to rid himself of his adolescent daydreaming.

As if she knew he was thinking about her, Charity turned to him. Her face was blazing with excitement. Keelen felt an undeniable tightness in his chest, a feeling that was becoming all too familiar when he was around her.

"What are you doing over there?" she asked, bringing him away from his erotic thoughts.

Folding his arms, he simply answered, "Watching you." His voice had lowered to a whisper as he continued to gaze at her stunning features.

His words caused her lips to part in surprise. Every time he looked at her, her heart flip-flopped in response. They stared at each other in silence and electricity sparked between them. Keelen's gaze dropped to her mouth. Even from several feet away the desire in his eyes startled her. But before she could respond to his bold approach, Keelen closed the distance between them. Her body jolted when he pulled her snuggly against him.

Taken by surprise, she opened her mouth then closed it again. She couldn't even remember what she was going to say.

His right hand circled the back of her neck. His thumb stroked the delicate lines of her jaw. The light caress sent waves of tingle clear down to her toes.

Staring down into her dreamy eyes, Keelen whispered, "I've been wanting to do this all day."

He couldn't take it any longer. He had to taste her. He

dipped his head, claiming her moist lips with a kiss that was both long and deep.

Charity wound her arms around his torso and locked herself into his gentle embrace. The rise and fall of her breasts quickened. She hadn't realized how badly she needed to feel his lips until that very moment. A moan escaped as she welcomed his warm tongue which plunged into her mouth, tasting, searching then leaving her body weak and melting in his arms. His fingers traced her spine and brushed the curve of her behind, igniting a rush of heat beneath her dress. Passion inched through her veins and rang in her ears, stirring desire from the night before. Yesterday had only been a beginning, an initial intimacy, a taste of what was yet to come.

Faint laughter and footsteps coming up the path broke the spell. Keelen eased back slightly and their eyes met. She was entranced by the tenderness she saw in his eyes before he lowered his arms and released her. Charity stood next to him, chest heaving, her breath coming in pants and eyes dazed with hunger.

Keelen stroked her cheek with his thumb, trying to curb his desire. "I think that should tide me over for now." He draped an arm firmly around her shoulders and pulled her close to his side as they moved down the path together.

She was too emotion-filled to reply. Her heart was racing and her brain was spinning. His mere touch stole the very breath from her lungs. How could she be feeling these things for Keelen, her buddy?

For the next hour, Charity felt dazed. She couldn't remember when she had felt this happy before. She felt so alive, her senses were in sync with the magic of the afternoon. She had never expected Keelen to be so open with his affection, yet he dropped a quick kiss, a squeeze whenever allowed. She found she liked it . . . hell . . . she loved the attention. Donovan had never believed in public displays of affection. Now she realized she had been missing out.

They moved on to see a South American jaguar, a Bahamian rock iguana, boa constrictors, and several other endangered species. The zoo had almost 300 mammals, birds and reptiles.

They had reached the end of the trail when Keelen glanced down at his watch. "It's show time," he announced.

"Show time. What show?" she asked, her brown eyes sparkling. She scrambled to keep up with him as they neared a straw-roof arena. Taking her by the hand Keelen guided her to a spot beside him on the bleachers. One of the first to arrive, they moved to the lowest point. Keelen took a seat, dropped her down onto his lap then planted another tender kiss to her lips. "I can't keep my hands off of you," he mumbled when they came up for air. "I used to imagine us being together like this but I never imagined that it would ever happen." He smiled at his confession.

Looking at him, Charity smoothed several wisps of hair from her brow. "You used to think about me?" She saw the seriousness of his expression.

"Of course. You were every man's fantasy."

She gave an unladylike snort. "Arika had that privilege, not me."

He shook his head in complete disagreement. "She doesn't come close to you."

His compliment made her warm inside to know that he preferred her. Maybe he wasn't interested in Arika after all. The questions weighing on her mind lightened and eventually floated away.

Seeing several other groups enter the arena, Keelen lifted Charity from his lap and sat her gently in the spot beside him.

After her heart returned to its normal heart rate, she asked, "So, what are we about to see, lions, seals?"

He shook his head, being amusingly evasive. "Nope."

"Then what?" she asked again.

After turning her way so that he could see the expression on her face, he replied, "Flamingos."

"Flamingos?" she echoed.

"Flamingos," he confirmed with a dimple smile curving his lips. *"National Geographic* called them 'Ballerinas in Pink.' They've been trained."

Charity folded her arms across her chest, unconvinced even though her eyes sparkled with amusement. "This I've got to see."

She didn't have long to wait as a woman moved to the center of the arena announcing the beginning of the show. After giving a brief history of the zoo and how close the Caribbean flamingos had come to extinction, a native drill sergeant marched out into the arena followed by a flock of flamingos.

If Charity hadn't been there she would never have believed it. The birds which stood almost six feet marched to his command and dutifully obeyed his instructions when he asked them to stop and take an about-face. They were a magnificent sight with their thin graceful legs and long delicate necks.

"Can we have a volunteer from the audience?" the MC asked.

Waving her hand wildly in the air, Charity pointed boldly at Keelen.

"The gentleman in the front row."

Charity giggled when he rose. She laughed even louder when he stepped past her and mumbled, "I'm going to get you for this." Keelen moved out into the center of the arena as the flamingos marched around him.

The drill sergeant moved to the front of the line. "On my command I want you to raise your right leg, our volunteer included."

Charity practically fell out of her seat with laughter when Keelen raised his right leg like the flamingos and tucked it behind his other leg. She made sure to take several shots. *Wait until my mother sees these.*

Watching him imitate the flock of flamingos flapping their arms, her jaws ached from so much laughter. Tall and athletically built, his boyish smile was so refreshing. With that in mind, her thoughts traveled to the tenderness of his kiss, the strength of his warm embrace. Her heart did a flip-flop. What could be happening between them? Her smile faded as she quickly sobered. God, if she wasn't careful, not only would she find herself in his bed but she would be giving him her heart. She shook her head, not quite ready yet to explore that possibility.

Her smile sprung back in place when she saw him returning to his seat. "You were great!" she greeted.

"Thanks a lot," he murmured sheepishly. Charity's face was bright and glowing. Seeing her like this was well worth the embarrassment.

"You are so welcome." She planted a kiss on his cheek. Keelen wasn't a little boy anymore, nevertheless the gesture caught him by surprise. It was the first time Charity had initiated the advance. He hoped it was a sign that she also shared what he was feeling.

When the show came to a close, the two rose. Sliding an arm around her waist, Keelen steered Charity up the path to the end of the garden.

"Look at that lady."

In front of them was a native woman wearing a straw hat with a large green parrot perched on top. Charity moved to take her picture. "Keelen, stand next to her." He followed her directions.

The woman smiled, increasing the wrinkles around her eyes. "Here, you can wear my hat."

Before he knew what was happening, she removed the hat and placed it on top of his head.

"Now hold out your hand."

He did just as the lady instructed, palm down, and within seconds the parrot moved to sit on his hand.

"Oh, my God!" Charity laughed hysterically as she snapped several photographs.

When she was finished, Keelen thanked the lady and handed her several bills from his wallet.

After thanking him, she turned to Charity. "Okay, ma'am, it's your turn."

"What?" she asked, dumbfounded.

"Oh, yeah. It's your turn." Keelen stepped forward and grabbed for her wrist.

Charity quickly jumped out of his reach. "I'm scared."

Keelen flapped his arms. "Come on, chicken."

"Pretty lady, he won't bite," the woman said reassuringly.

She sighed and handed Keelen the camera. With the lady's assistance, Charity allowed her to put the hat on her head and sure enough the bird perched on top.

Laughing, she soon felt at ease as Keelen took her picture. Then the woman took a picture of the two of them together.

Keelen thanked her and slipped her another bill before he moved on with Charity hand in hand outside the gate.

Charity smiled up at her friend. "That was wonderful. Thank you so much for bringing me."

"My pleasure. I knew you would enjoy it." It made him feel good to know she was pleased. He considered himself lucky to have spent the afternoon with her. She always had appreciated the simple things.

Their cab driver was waiting for them. They climbed inside and headed back to the ship, holding hands the entire ride.

* * *

They parted at the lobby and Charity took the stairs down to her cabin. As she rounded the corner near the theater, she found herself face-to-face with Arika.

Oh, brother, here we go again.

Arika had stopped. With deliberate nonchalance, she smiled. "Hi, Charity."

Charity didn't even bother to hide her displeasure. "Why do you keep trying to talk to me?"

Arika smiled as if Charity had just said something funny. "Because we used to be friends. Women have to stick together. I don't understand how you can let a man come between us."

"That man was my husband," she countered, lips twisting with anger.

Inclining her chin like she was a queen, Arika replied, "Men are weak. Donovan had been trying to get with me for years."

Sniffing in an exaggerated fashion, Charity retorted, "And you finally agreed."

"It wasn't like that," Arika denied.

With her hand parked on her right hip, Charity gave her a cool penetrating look and asked pointedly, "Then tell me, what was it like?"

"It just happened that one time."

"And that makes it okay?" Charity spat. "You know . . ." she started then gave up, throwing her hands in the air in disgust.

Arika looked at her as if she had lost her mind. "Your animosity is way out of hand. What else can I say, except that I'm sorry?"

Charity felt a wild urge to hit her in the mouth, but she thinned her lips grimly instead and retorted with, "What you can do is stay the hell away from me," she replied tartly. Satisfied with herself, she bounced down the hall humming, leaving Arika standing there. She had finally stood up for herself. She giggled. Boy did it feel good.

Once in her cabin, she stripped off her sticky clothes and took a shower. As soon as the hot water hit her skin, the tension slowly began to leave her body while bringing her temper under control. She wasn't going to let Arika ruin her vacation. She'd had a wonderful day with Keelen and nothing was going to spoil that. Tonight Keelen was taking her to dinner on the island.

Still wrapped in a towel she climbed into her bed and curled up under the cool sheets. Beverly was still on the island and she was grateful for the peace and quiet. She needed a few moments alone to make some sense out of what was happening between her and Keelen.

Never in a million years would she have expected the attraction between them, yet being in his presence she found herself giddy and happier than she'd been in years. When he touched her his warm flesh caused her skin to tingle. When he kissed her, he caused a quake in her that she had never experienced, not even with her own husband. She couldn't explain it but it was like they had never lost touch, as if he had always been a part of her life. Their relationship had not only continued but also transgressed into something that she could not quite put into words.

Snuggling comfortably on her pillow, she smiled. Already she missed him and anticipated the night to come. She didn't want to make more of the relationship than it really was and tried to tell herself to slow down. She had to remind herself that it was only a romantic fling that would end in less than two days. Somehow she needed to hold back her feelings and try to stay in control. She couldn't allow herself to fall into the same emotional trap that she had been in before. The last time she had given her heart it had been torn out of her chest and she had felt like dying. She hadn't come on the cruise for a relationship.

She had come to make amends, and renew old friendships, nothing more.

Rolling onto her back, she groaned. Now if only she could find a way to communicate that to her heart.

Keelen returned from his meeting with the investors and was pleased to know the additional financial backing was almost in place. He smiled. It was just the type of news he needed after a fantastic day.

Moving down the hall he was heading to his room when he found Arika standing outside his door. *Now what does she want?* Earlier on deck she had invited him to spend the day together on the island before he had declined. Hopefully she wasn't about to try again.

"I didn't think you were ever returning," she whined as she thrust out her lower lip in a pout. "I've been waiting for you," she added in a breathless whisper.

He looked down at her with caution blazing in his eyes. "I had business to attend to in the city."

"Oh, I thought you were spending the day with Charity," she inquired. He didn't even bother to respond. Arika might be beautiful and ten years older, but he knew she hadn't changed a bit. He saw that same manipulative gleam in her eyes. She would do anything for attention. He found her sudden interest in him rather ironic since she used to look at him with disgust.

"Channel Eight is interested in doing a story on the reunion, however, I'd rather do a story on the cruise line and you. A local resident turned millionaire, that's news."

Keelen laughed inward. He was far from being a millionaire.

Sashaying closer Arika whispered, "May I come in so we can talk?"

Keelen slid his key in the door. "I have about five minutes before I need to get ready for a date."

Her lips curled into a sensual smile. "That's plenty of time for me to go over the preliminaries."

With a nod, Arika followed Keelen in the room. Five minutes would be time enough to put her plan into action.

After applying her lipstick, Charity checked her watch. She was to meet Keelen in the lobby in less than an hour. Dreaming of the possibilities, she felt a flutter of butterflies in her stomach at the idea of spending the entire evening together.

Zipping into her dress she heard a light tap on the door. She went to answer it and found Kimora standing on the other side.

"Don't you look nice," she complimented.

"Thanks," Charity said. She was wearing an off-the-shoulder, midlength dress made of sheer mocha satin.

"How was your day?" she asked as she moved into the room.

Charity couldn't do anything to control the flow of color to her cheeks. "I had the most exciting day."

"Why was that?" she asked inquisitively. "Did you spend the day with Keelen?"

Boy, word got around fast. "Yes, as a matter of fact, I did. How was your day?" she asked, purposely steering the conversation away from her and Keelen.

Kimora gave a bored shrug. "It was fair."

Even without asking, Charity was certain she had spent the day with Arika. Chances are they had stopped at every store on the strip that sold purses.

She reached for her cosmetic bag and moved to the mirror. "Have you spoken to Olivia?" she inquired.

"Oh, yeah," Kimora sang while she took a seat on the

bed. "She walked in on Tim and his boys in the swimming pool with a dozen half naked women."

Her eyes grew wide. "I guess he wasn't expecting her to return home."

"I guess not," Kimora replied knowingly. "But Olivia will do like she always does, go off on him, take a hit of coke today, and go shopping tomorrow."

What a life. Olivia was going around in circles. "Why don't you convince her to go back into rehab?"

Kimora's lips thinned and her green eyes narrowed. "I have and it's proven to be a waste of time. She is too worried about what Tim would be up to while she is gone. I don't understand the attachment he has on her. What's love got to do with it? Things have gotten so bad her mother has temporary custody of Jesse."

"I didn't know that." There was a brief moment of silence before she asked, "What are you doing tonight?"

"Arika and I are going to dinner and the casino." She glanced down at her watch. "I wish she'd hurry up. She went up to talk to Keelen an hour ago and I haven't seen her since."

Her pulse began to increase. Pretending to be engrossed in her hair, Charity asked, "What's she doing up there?"

Kimora shrugged. "They made plans earlier to have a drink."

Charity's lips thinned disapprovingly. Kimora didn't seem to notice or so she thought. What were they doing spending time together?

Kimora's eyes were bright and observant. She hadn't missed the flash of jealousy in Charity's eyes before she had tried to lower her gaze to mask it. "I ran into Don at lunch today and he seemed really sincere about making amends with you."

Charity's head jerked around to meet her calculated stare. "Girl, puhleeze, don't make me throw up."

"I'm serious. He was wrong and so was Arika, but girl, he's a *doctor*. Women don't divorce doctors, they get even instead."

Charity grunted. "And this is coming from a woman who's already divorced two husbands." Kimora's two marriages had lasted a total of three years combined.

She shrugged. "But I'm a nursing director, I don't need a man."

"And I do?" she countered.

"Well . . . you've always been the little homemaker. I have never been any good at that sort of thing."

Charity dipped her head briefly then looked up again with her arms folded across her middle and said, "Stop hanging around with Arika and I guarantee you your life will change. It sure as hell did for me."

Kimora shook her head as if she didn't know quite what else to say.

Eight

Thirty minutes later, Charity stepped off the elevator to find Keelen already in the lobby. He was talking to a graying red head working at the information desk and with his back turned he hadn't noticed her moving in his direction. Slowing her steps, a hint of a smile curved Charity's lips as she observed him from behind.

Leaning leisurely against the counter, Keelen was dressed in a pair of pleated charcoal slacks that outlined his muscular thighs while an eggshell-colored short-sleeved shirt spanned his wide back and shoulders. The combination was a compliment to his smooth pecan skin.

"You're early."

Hearing the alluring voice that was every bit as sweet as honey, Keelen turned to face her. His breath stalled in his chest as his gaze swept her, assessing, moving upward slowly. Charity's dress skimmed every luscious feminine curve on her body and fit her like a second skin.

"Wow!" He whistled between his teeth.

She didn't miss his obvious examination and was pleased he liked what he saw. Only days ago, she had complained when Tia had carried the dress to the register, but insistence prevailed. Now she was glad that she had.

In all his years, Keelen couldn't recall a more erotic sight than Charity in that dress. The way it clung to her, she might as well have been naked. The dress was cut very low with a deep scoop across the breasts, hiding very little of their shape and cinnamon color.

Charity's hair was combed back away from her face, drawing attention to a pair of diamond studs in her ears. With her lean neck exposed Keelen found something that caused him to chuckle.

Charity tilted her head slightly and frowned. "What's so funny?" she asked. She thought she had outgrown self-consciousness long ago, however, at that particular moment, she wondered what caused the sudden amusement. Thinking she might possibly have lipstick on her teeth, she swiped them with her tongue.

Keelen had to bite back a grin at her puzzled expression. "The mole."

She raised her hand to cover the small mark at the side of her neck. "What's wrong with my mole?" she shot back defensively.

Sensing her uneasiness, he removed her hand and laced her slender fingers with his. "Relax. There's absolutely nothing wrong with your mole. I just forgot that you had it." His smile deepened, making his eyes crinkle. "The moment I saw it I remembered the time you tried to get rid of it using wart remover."

Charity blushed with embarrassment. "I forgot about that." She then chuckled softly with relief. Keelen was just teasing, however, what he had said was true. For years she had considered it an imperfection. It wasn't until junior high after reading an article in a teen magazine that referred to it as a "beauty mark" that she started seeing the mole in a different light.

As Keelen continued to caress the back of her hand, warmth spread through her body. Their gazes met, and emotions crossed the other's face as they shared an intense moment of awareness. There was no denying the sexual attraction.

Her eyes were filled with awe and surprise. In a matter of hours Keelen had made her feel excited and more alive than she had in years. What she hadn't realized until now was that with Keelen her defenses were down and her heart exposed. His effect on her and the attraction she had for him was like nothing she had ever experienced.

She had to be careful.

Even though Keelen wasn't anything like Donovan, she had pledged after her divorce that she wouldn't take any chances, she wouldn't repeat the same mistakes. That rule needed to also apply to Keelen.

Still seeing the lines of worry across her delicate face, Keelen shook his head. "I was just teasing. So you can relax, sexy lady."

Tilting her chin, Charity wrinkled her nose. "Are you going to spend the entire evening embarrassing me?" His sensual teasing smile was driving her crazy.

"No." Keelen snaked an arm around her waist and dragged her gently against him. Leaning closer, he brushed his mouth over hers. "I'd rather spend the evening doing that," he whispered. Her lips parted and that was all the invitation he needed as he brought his mouth down on hers, kissing with a desperate passion, kissing her lips and parting them with his tongue. Then as quickly as it had started, Keelen ended the kiss and pulled back.

Her nose was assailed by the tangy scent of his cologne mixed with pure male essence. The man was one hell of a kisser! She could get lost in his lips for hours. Happiness was a warm bubble inside of her. The dazzling look in his eyes sent a message to her brain that promised a night to be remembered.

Her insides jangled with excitement as he escorted her off the ship to where a taxi was waiting.

Smiling, Charity sat back against the cool leather seat and stared out the window. The view was once again magnificent. The sun was setting on the horizon with the colors of orange and yellow bursting on top of the ocean.

Thirty minutes later they arrived at the Buena Vista, a historical mansion situated on five acres of tropical foliage that had been converted into the most elegant restaurant imaginable.

Keelen draped his hand loosely around her waist as they were escorted to a table out on the garden patio. Her heels tapped lightly on the Spanish tile as they entered a room with a greenhouse setting. Captivated by what she saw, Charity thought that maybe they were sitting outside until she looked up to find a skylight ceiling.

After the host departed, Charity raised her arms to the table and laced her fingers together. "This place is beautiful," she whispered as she continued to look around in awe.

Keelen was glad that she was pleased with his choice. He wanted everything to be perfect tonight. "I thought maybe you'd like it. I found this place a couple of years ago. Wait until you taste the food."

Her smile faded slightly as she wondered if Keelen had been in the company of a woman during his last visit, but she didn't dare voice her curiosity. *Stop it!* she scolded. This behavior was unacceptable. But in a short time she had developed a possessiveness toward him that bothered her. Jealousy was too new an emotion and she didn't like how she was handling it. She had never been a jealous person, so why was she starting now?

When their waiter arrived to take their drink orders, Charity allowed her eyes to travel around the room again. All the tables were elegantly covered in tasteful white linen. Small lit candles in the center of a floral centerpiece and the drift of soft piano music coming from the other room gave it a romantic setting.

The waiter returned shortly with a bottle of chardonnay.

He poured some in each of their glasses before asking if they were ready to order. Since Keelen had been here before, Charity gave him the liberty of ordering for both of them, certain that everything was going to be delicious.

She listened as he spoke to the waiter with a confident style that she was quickly growing increasingly fond of. It amazed her how much he had changed. Nevertheless, she had seen enough to know that deep down he was still the same ole' Keelen. Resting her head in her open hand, she watched the way the dimples materialized as his jaws moved, the way his sexy mustache twitched. She stared at his wavy hair that defined the close-cropped style. What was it about Keelen that made him so different now? *He's fine, girl, that's what,* her brain screamed. He was quite handsome, she thought as she took in his masculine beauty. The lines that etched the corners of his gray eyes only added to his appeal. But even though he was handsome, she knew that it was more than that. She liked him. Not just the new Keelen, but also the old. It startled her how much and she wondered if he could sense the extent of her feelings. The thought made her senses quicken and her blood warm. She wondered what it would feel like to lay beside him with his arms wrapped around her.

Once the waiter moved to another table, Keelen leaned back in his chair and focused his attention once again on the beauty sitting cross from him. Staring at her, he watched the light from the candle dance on her perched nose, while casting a sheen on her face that made her cinnamon skin appear to possess a bronze tint. She was wearing the giddy smile he'd adored since childhood. He thought to himself how wonderful it would be to have her look that way as she lay beneath him. God, the woman made him hard just by looking at him. He took a sip from his glass, trying to calm the thoughts that were swarming in his head.

Charity found him watching her and lowering her lashes, she blushed openly. "What are you looking at?" she asked.

"You," he answered without hesitation. "Does it make you feel uncomfortable?"

"No, not at all," she quickly denied.

Keelen knew she was lying, but he couldn't have stopped himself even if he had wanted to. He was drawn to her beauty. Reaching across the table he commenced to caress the inside of her palm. "Good, 'cause I can't help it." A faint smile curled the edge of his lips that made her knees melt. "I like what I see."

And I like what I see.

Their appetizers finally arrived. Bringing a spoon of the Bahamian lobster bisque to her lips, Charity took a cautious sip. "Mmm. This is wonderful." Laced with cream and cognac, she was pleased to find the soup rich, smooth and flavorful.

"I told you," he said with a broad wink.

She couldn't stop smiling. Being with Keelen made her feel alive without a worry in the world. He was adorable and had her nerves in a knot, but it did nothing to alter the happiness that he was back in her life.

He leaned forward in his chair. "I can tell you are enjoying yourself."

She blushed openly. "You're so right. I always wanted to visit the Caribbean but never got around to it."

Keelen frowned. "I can't believe Donovan never brought you here. Jamaica either?"

"We never went anywhere." Shaking her head, she saw Keelen's gaze widen. "It isn't fair to point the finger. It was no one's fault but my own. I was so busy working two jobs trying to put Don through medical school that there wasn't much time for anything else," she shrugged. "Then Taylor came along and . . . well, the rest is history."

He saw the pained look return to her eyes as she spoke about her marriage. His jaw twitched with anger that a man could take advantage of such a beautiful person. If he had his way he'd make sure that she'd never have to work again.

Leaning across the table, he cupped her hand in his and stared at her intensely. "We all live and learn. Life is too short."

She nodded, eyes sparkling with excitement. "I agree with you one hundred percent. That's why I am here, now, in the Bahamas enjoying a fabulous cruise and having dinner with a wonderful old friend."

Releasing her hand, he raised his glass. "I propose a toast. To living life to its fullest."

"Here, here." She raised her own drink to her lips.

Shortly after, the waiter returned to their table carrying a tray lavishly covered with scrumptious dishes. Everything looked wonderful. Keelen had ordered a Bahamian seafood platter, which consisted of lobster tails, conch, and yellowfin tuna with onions and sweet pepper sauce, accompanied by a steamed vegetable medly. After making sure they didn't need anything else, their waiter departed.

Charity brought the conch to her mouth and closed her eyes as she relished the heavenly taste.

Oh, she was like a kid in a candy store, Keelen thought as he watched appreciatively as she dug into her food, pleased with his choices; no qualm about trying new things or having to dab her mouth with a napkin after every bite. Charity was as real as it gets.

"Oh, I'm in heaven," she moaned, her brown eyes seemed to smile also.

Her response did something to his insides. "I'm with you, sista."

They passed the rest of the meal with idle chitchat, while deep in the back of her mind, she wondered how their evening would end.

Keelen suggested that she have dessert and she was not disappointed. He ordered them each a soufflé served with rich vanilla sauce.

When the waiter returned to see how they were doing, Charity leaned back in her chair, smiling as she rubbed her belly. "I can't handle another bite."

"You must have a cup of our finest coffee," he insisted with a strong Bahamian accent.

"He's right," Keelen agreed.

Unable to resist, she nodded.

While they both drank a cup of fabulous Calypso coffee, Charity talked about Tia's bookstore and the fabulous Blue Mountain coffee she served with her cookies.

Lowering his mug, Keelen replied, "I'm amazed at how you still manage to look so good after being around cookies all day long."

She blushed. Keelen wasn't stingy on the compliments. "It's a challenge in itself. Sometimes Tia and I sit and eat an entire batch in one sitting. Other days the thought of eating even one makes me sick. As long as I continue to exercise daily, I don't think I'll have anything to worry about."

He nodded. "I agree."

There was a prolonged silence as she stared wordlessly at him; their gazes fused and the air seemed to sizzle.

Dinner had finally come to an end.

Keelen leaned across the table and cupped her hand. "You ready?"

She nodded. Her pulse raced with anticipation of what was yet to come. As he signaled for the check, she felt ready for just about anything.

They drove away from the restaurant. The smell of hibiscus and fruit drifted in the warm breeze. Staring out the window, she watched the seashore and drew a long steady breath. "It is so beautiful here. I would love to watch the sun rise and set every day."

Keelen nodded. He knew exactly how she felt. "I'm thinking about purchasing a veranda here."

She couldn't help wondering again what kind of business he was in. She restrained from blurting out the question—there was plenty of time for that later. She didn't want him to think she was a gold digger. Besides, if he wanted her to know, he would tell her. "Isn't that expensive?"

"Not as much as one would think."

"They're beautiful. Are you planning to rent it to tourists?"

He nodded. "Maybe as a time-share. Otherwise, I plan on visiting Nassau quite often. How about coming back with me this winter? You can even invite Tia, her fiancé and your daughter. In fact, you can extend the offer to your world-traveling parents."

His last sentence caused her to giggle. "I'd like that."

He gently squeezed her knee, drawing her full attention. "I'm not saying this just to be saying something. I'm saying this because I don't intend for our relationship to end when this cruise is over."

Her heart swelled.

The cab pulled off at the beach. Keelen reached into the front seat and removed a tote bag.

"What's in the bag?" she asked, glancing down at the bag quizzically.

"You'll soon find out. But first, shoes off," he ordered.

"My shoes!" she cackled. "What are you up to?"

"I am trying to fulfill another one of your dreams. Are you going to trust me or not?"

"Yes . . . completely," she answered honestly. Never had she ever trusted anyone the way she trusted him right then.

Removing their shoes, they tossed them in his bag and slid out of the cab. After instructing the driver to come back in an hour, he draped the strap over his left shoulder.

"Let's go."

Linking his fingers with hers, they moved across the cool white sand and headed toward the ocean. Palm trees were blowing with the wind. The sun was just beginning to set. Together they stared out into the early evening sky that was bursting with colors of orange and gold.

They were silent as they strolled together, listening to the ocean splash along the shore. Holding hands felt right. Being together felt right and Charity found herself trembling with emotion. All she could think about was the kiss that they had shared and the anticipation that it would happen again. Soon.

"This looks like a nice spot," Keelen finally said. Releasing her hand, he slid the bag from his shoulder, reached in, and removed a blanket. After spreading it on the cool sand, he dropped the bag from his shoulder and revealed a bottle then signaled for her to sit.

She couldn't resist a smile. "You remembered."

He nodded. "How could I have forgotten?"

It was like she had told him so many times. Her dream of a moonlit walk on the beach barefoot, then sipping champagne while watching the sunset.

Reaching into the bag again, he removed two flute glasses.

Charity took a seat on the blanket and held the glasses while he proceeded to remove the corkscrew. With an explosive whoosh, the cork popped out and champagne bubbled down his arm and onto their clothes. He joined her on the blanket. Laughing, Charity put a glass under the bottle to catch the foam.

That's what he liked about her. Any other woman would have had a fit about her dress getting wet, but not Charity. She never cared about material things. She was still one of a kind. Desire surged through him, spreading fast. If he didn't get himself under control, he would try to take her right here on top of the blanket.

Charity did not notice Keelen raising her hand to his mouth until she felt his tongue lick the sweet liquid from her arm. Involuntarily, she gasped.

With a teasing smile, he kissed her on the lips then poured them both a glass. "We have quite a bit to celebrate tonight." He lifted his glass in a toast. "To lifelong friendship."

"To friendship," she agreed, clinking her glass against his.

"And to the memories this vacation will bring." He reached his other hand out to stroke her face. "Hopefully two friends can become lovers," he whispered.

She felt a rush of heat at his toast. Their eyes met and held for several seconds before her lashes lowered a fraction. She took a sip from her glass, the liquid sliding down her throat in a burst of bubbles.

Moving closer, Keelen slid one arm tightly about her shoulders, holding her tightly. Charity dropped her head comfortably to his shoulder. What was happening between them, she asked herself as a warm tropical breeze blew strands of her hair across her face and she brushed them out of her way so she could see clearly. Feeling at peace, she smiled to herself. They were quiet for quite a while, each lost in their own private thoughts as they sipped from their glasses.

Charity was the first to break the silence.

Closing her eyes briefly, she smiled. "I like this."

"What?" Keelen asked. Even though he knew, he needed to hear her say it.

"Being here, like this with you." She laughed as the bubbly froth slid down her throat. "It's so ironic. I used to talk with you about having this same experience, but I never imagined it being with you."

"I did," he confessed in a husky whisper.

His admission caught her off guard. She turned her head and looked at him, eyes narrowed. "You did?"

"Of course." Their gaze connected. "I've been crazy about you for years. You just never noticed."

The passion in his voice turned her heart over and emotions overflowed. Charity couldn't respond because her heart was beating far too fast.

Keelen moved his hand to cradle the back of her head, tilting her head back. His mouth was only inches from hers. She lifted her mouth to meet his lips. His lips pressed against hers then gently covered her mouth with his slow drugging kisses. Only this time the kiss was different. His lips were demanding, his embrace possessive. Dropping his glass on the sand, he used his other hand to cup her shoulder, bringing her even closer. Passion surged through him like blood. He challenged her with his kiss, wordlessly acknowledging the attraction between them.

He feared the intensity might frighten her, but Charity welcomed the urgency. She wanted—needed this. It was a desperate kiss as if he were searching for answers. A delightful shiver of wanting raced through her. Her hands came up to caress his body as their tongues twined a soulful dance. Wrapping her arms around him, she pressed her breasts tightly against his chest. She could feel the gradual tightness of her breasts and the hardening of her nipples. Desire shuddered through her so intensely that she felt as if she were floating.

He wanted unrestricted access to her mouth. Without interrupting their kiss, he lowered her slowly onto the blanket. He lay down beside her, planting a wet trail down one side of her neck to her shoulders before recapturing her lips. He could go on and on for hours but what he wanted right now he needed to do in the privacy of his room.

Pulling back slightly, he searched down in her eyes and

saw desire that mirrored his own. "I want you," he whispered. "Do you want me, Charity?"

Seeing the question in the tenderness of his gaze, her heart lurched madly. She needed this night with Keelen desperately.

Tonight they would make love.

Charity drew in a deep gulp of air then replied, "Yes."

On the ride back she placed her hand in his lap and rested her head on his shoulder. The feeling of his fingers caressing hers caused her blood to heat and surge through her, leaving a pool between her thighs. God, she found herself anticipating lying in his arms tonight after they spent hours bringing each other sexual pleasure. She found herself watching him and he her. It was unspoken but each of them knew what the enchanted night would bring them. Passion.

Emotions were running so high her head was spinning. Charity closed her eyes briefly. Hadn't she told herself that this trip was going to be all about what she wanted and needed? *This is what I want,* she told herself. She didn't care that it was only the second day of their cruise. Nor did it matter that she hadn't seen Keelen in almost a decade. Her body was talking to her, screaming for him. Right now nothing felt more right than being with him tonight.

As soon as the cab pulled in front of the ship, her heart flipped three times.

Keelen climbed out and held a hand out to her. "Ready?" he whispered, gray eyes fixed on her.

Taking a deep breath, Charity took Keelen's hand and allowed him to escort her to his room.

At the stroke of midnight, Charity moved out onto the balcony. The night was still and bright with stars shining in the moonlit sky. Closing her eyelids, she listened to the whispering of the breeze.

It wasn't long before Keelen came up behind her, his arms locking around her waist. Relaxing against him, she found his embrace almost unbearable in its tenderness. He rained light kisses on the sides of her neck and earlobe, each touch sending a shockwave of pleasure spiraling through her entire body.

Turning toward him, she wrapped her arms around his neck, her breasts pressed to his hard chest. She sought his lips with hers and Keelen felt her open to the thrust of his tongue. Charity wanted him. Wanted him as badly as he wanted her. Her tongue was urgent and exploratory with an intensity that made his head swim. His hands cradled her head and his thumbs caressed her temples. As his lips swept the curve of her cheekbones the fragrance of her skin filled his nostrils.

"Keelen," she whispered, feeling a throbbing in the passage below. Her body quivered for his touch. His hands slid up and down her back following the contours of her curves before finding their way to the front where he gently outlined the circle of her breasts, roaming intimately. Charity groaned, unprepared for the intense pleasure that radiated through her body. Welcoming his caress, she leaned back slightly allowing his thumb to tease the chocolate bud until it puckered.

Suddenly, she was in his arms being carried into the room where he laid her gently on the bed.

Taking a seat beside her, Keelen reached up and his hand easily slipped the dress from her shoulders, running his fingers over her smooth skin and revealing the firm rise of her breasts. His heart thundered against his rib cage.

Appreciation burned in his eyes. "You are beautiful." That was an understatement. She was exquisite and undeniably desirable. Keelen took her left breast in his palm.

He felt her tremble and heard the gasp of air as his thumb teased the nipple to hardness.

Charity was unable to silence her whimpers of pleasure. Keelen had a way of weakening her limbs while strengthening her desire. There was no way she could deny the inevitable. She yearned for him to make love to her. She knew it was too soon but it had been so long and it felt so right. Pushing her conscience aside, she followed her heart and leaned into him, not able to think rationally when he touched her like that.

Keelen urged her to lie down. He drank in the sight of her on her back. Her arms were above her head and her legs spread apart. Her full breasts were round and lush; her small waist flared at the hips.

He moved to lay beside her, supporting his weight on his elbow. His smile was promising as he kissed her lips, then her throat, and finally moved to her breasts. He kissed first one brown curve of flesh then the other.

"Keelen," she moaned, arousal burning in her eyes. She leaned into him, loving the feel of his warm lips caressing her hardened nipple. She cried out as he suckled her other breast, worshipping each equally.

His tongue traveled down her abdomen, kissing every inch and whispering a compliment for every part of her body. He dispensed any haunting reminders of how Donovan had enjoyed finding fault with her body. Instead, he reiterated his opinion that she was beautiful and her body flawless.

She continued to weaken as his mouth descended. Then with one skillful move, he slid the dress down the flare of her hips followed by her lacy panties.

Keelen swallowed as he revealed the nest of chestnut curls between her thighs. Charity aroused him in a way that no other woman ever had.

He resumed exploring her soft cinnamon flesh with his

tongue then moved to her parted thighs. With a low groan he kissed her most private place.

"What are you . . . Ohhh, my God!" Charity gasped. "Donovan never . . ." The rest of her sentence was lost as she was met by a wave of passion. Her gasps turned to broken cries as he found the moist petals of flesh between her thighs. He teased them open and stroked them with nothing but the desire to bring her as much pleasure as he could.

Charity wrapped her legs around his neck while he pleased her in ways she had never dreamed possible. The sensation was so pleasurable she cried out his name several times. He brushed her clitoris, which she discovered to be her pleasure point. He did things with his mouth that caused her to thrash on the sheets beneath him. He did things with his tongue that brought tears to her eyes. While he darted in and out of her warm center, her hands instinctively moving to his head, holding him there. Her breath came in long surrendering moans as he continued his exploration. She planted her feet firmly on the mattress while her hips rocked into his touch. She cried out, her head tossing violently on the pillow. She was losing herself in a sensual whirlwind. She moaned Keelen's name over and over again as the tension built in her body until she was overwhelmed by the inexorable rhythms of release. "Yes!" she cried out in ecstasy as he held her close.

Never had she experienced such joy. He held her close to him. The frantic hammering of her heart was as his own.

Keelen removed himself from the bed to discard his own clothes. He yanked off his pants, tossing them to the floor. He shrugged out of his shirt and Charity feasted her eyes on a work of art. Her eyes drank in the sensuality of his physique. *He looks so damn good,* she thought. Her eyes followed the sandy brown hair that traveled down and disappeared in his boxers. He slid them off and she found him fully aroused.

"See what you do to me?" he murmured, demanding that she take ownership of the state of his arousal.

The length of him caused her to gasp. His size made her eyes grow wide. She had only seen one other man naked. There was no comparison. She had no idea a man could grow so large. For just a brief second she wondered if her body could accommodate him. Then her body throbbed in preparation to be filled so completely.

Lowering himself back on the bed, Keelen grasped her hips and slid her to the center of the bed. "Your husband was a fool to deny you such pleasures," he commented as he positioned himself between her trembling thighs. "I don't want to hurt you." He placed his hand there; probing with his finger he found her wet and slick. "Are you sure you're ready for me, baby?" he crooned.

"Yes!" she gasped as she arched up to him, ready and waiting to be overcome by a tidal wave of pleasure. His fingers were driving her out of her mind. She could feel the heat of his manhood throbbing at the opening of her desire. In all the years she and Donovan were together, she never felt as consumed by as much passion as she was right now.

Her eyes were closed, a thick, lush curve against her cheeks. "Open your eyes," Keelen commanded.

Her lids fluttered opened. Her eyes held a mixture of desire and impatience.

"Say that you want me to make love to you," he whispered.

"I want you, Keelen," she whimpered, her senses scattered. "I want you to make love to me . . . *please,*" she begged.

Keelen needed no further prompting. He reached down on the side of the bed for a box of condoms. Tearing one free, he opened the foil envelope, and rolled it on.

Though she knew she would appreciate his wisdom

later, the fact that he was able to remember protection at such a time surprised her. Right now she needed to feel him inside her.

As he lowered himself, she heard him expel a deep sigh of pleasure as he slid inside, filling her completely with one single thrust. Welcoming him into her body, Charity trembled with pleasure and her legs rose locking around his waist. She grasped his buttocks wanting all of him inside her. As she eagerly met his thrusts, she murmured his name as if uttering a prayer. He began slowly moving back and forth between her thighs in an erotic rhythm. He buried his face in her neck, breathing and kissing her there. Her arms went tightly around him, stroking his back while the gentle movement of his body penetrated her soul. Her body arched upward in pleasure meeting his thrusts, matching his rhythm.

"Ah, you feel so good," he moaned, fanning her lips with his breath before reclaiming them. His lips grazed her ear, her cheek, and eyes, then returned to her neck. His kisses sang through her veins.

Moonlight spilled into the room allowing him to look down at her face and find her eyes closed. He was so excited, so damn aroused, he wasn't sure how much longer he could hold on. His pace became more demanding as he pumped even harder, pushing both of them closer to the edge. His control was slipping. Each hard stroke into her body was divine ecstasy.

Charity lay beneath him, panting, chest heaving, lifting her hips to meet his every thrust. Such pleasure was beyond her wildest dreams. Her cries of satisfaction echoed off the balcony and out into the breeze. Shortly after, Keelen erupted inside her and collapsed, pulling her tightly into his arms.

Nine

Keelen awakened early as usual. It was something he'd been doing since he was a child. Not that he had done much sleeping, he recollected with a smile. After the first intense round, he and Charity had made love again. They took their time exploring, arousing then building to another earth-shattering finish before falling into an exhausted sleep.

He glanced at the woman curled up beside him. The rays of the morning sun were already beaming in the room drawing attention to her face. She looked so beautiful, so innocent. Lying on her stomach with a white sheet draped across her naked body, he found her lovelier than ever. Giving into the urge, his lips feather-touched the top of her head. Charity stirred slightly, snuggling closer and sending desire stirring in his loins once more.

As he watched her, wanting her, he could feel a tightening in his chest yearning for something more than the physical. The emotion disturbed him and had been disturbing him for a long time. He had tried for many years to put her to the back of his mind but he never could.

Because of her you have never been able to love another woman.

It was true. Keelen had always found himself comparing others to the woman he had thought he'd lost. With other women he searched for the same radiant smile, smooth cinnamon skin and inner beauty. He had wanted to hate her but found he couldn't. Charity was in his blood.

He loved her.

It came as no surprise. He'd always known the extent of his feelings.

Unable to resist touching her a second longer, Keelen ran his index finger up her velvety smooth cheek then across her temple. Charity stirred again and the movement caused the sheet to slide off her shoulder, baring her back and a side glimpse of her left breast.

As he remembered lavishing the pair for hours, he felt himself harden. It pleased him to know that he was the first man to give her such pleasure. He shouldn't want her again so soon, he told himself. Yet he did. He wanted to climb back on top of her and slide into her warm passage. Aching for her, he squeezed his eyes shut, trying to block out the tempting sight. No point in waking her, Charity needed the rest.

But closing his eyes did little to ease his hunger for her. How could it when he could feel her warm flesh pressed against him? When he could smell her feminine scent? When he could all too clearly recall the taste of her in his mouth? Even now he could still hear the sound of his name coming from her lips as she came apart with him buried deep inside her.

"Damn!" he groaned. Thinking about it wasn't doing anything to curb his hunger.

"Keelen?" She touched his shoulder. "Sweetheart, what's wrong?"

Keelen snapped open his eyes and looked down at her concerned face. He hadn't realized that he had voiced his frustration out loud. "Nothing, baby."

Tilting his head slightly, he drank in the sight of her hair all mussed, curling around her face. Damn, she was so sexy, he thought. His gaze slid lower past the slope of her neckline running over her bare shoulders and then down to where she was clutching the sheet to her breasts. Remembering how good they had tasted, he quickly diverted his gaze to her eyes, which still held the softness of sleep. "I didn't mean to wake you." He leaned forward to kiss the tip of her nose.

"No problem. What time is it?" she asked around a yawn.

He loved her voice, deep and raspy with sleep. "It's well past six."

Charity groaned. "It's too early." She rested her cheek against the fine hairs that covered his chest. While listening to the soft beat of his heart, she pulled him even closer and lightly caressed his back with her fingertips.

His skin heated wherever she touched. Sweat began to bead across his brow with the effort it took not to give in to the urge to roll her on her back and join their bodies together as one. Stroking him, her hand slid down his buttocks where she kneaded and massaged. And when her hand traveled across to his inner thigh, he groaned with agony.

Discovering his state of arousal, Charity lifted on one elbow to gaze at him. "Mmm, what do we have here?" she asked, pausing, waiting.

"Nothing," he mumbled between stiff lips.

Giggling, she replied, "Oh, no, this is definitely something." With that, she curled her fingers around the length of his penis and began to stroke gently. Never had she felt so brazen or powerful as when her touch caused him to moan aloud. Until Keelen, she had been uncertain at her ability to please a man sexually, now she knew otherwise.

Her lips sought the hollow space between his collarbones. From there her tongue traveled down to his chest where she teased his body, tasting his skin, laving one nipple then moving to the next.

"You're starting something," he warned, voice strained, almost afraid he was going to die of pleasure.

"Am I?" she murmured innocently as her lips descended down his chest. She stroked him harder.

As his face convulsed, he muttered, "Hell, yes."

Keelen gripped the bed and almost came out of his skin when her lips traveled pass his navel, tracing the hard angles of one hip bone, and then circled his hard shaft. He flinched.

"What's the matter, sweetie?" she asked, her breath warm against the tip. He flinched again and she giggled, pleased at the effect that she had on him. Sliding across the bed, she slipped him inside her mouth.

How had he managed to get by without her all these years, Keelen thought as his eyes rolled to the back of his head. She licked him like a lollipop, moving up and down, sliding him partially out of her mouth and then bringing him back in. She continued to suckle, nibble and tease until Keelen was sure he would go insane from the combination of pleasure and frustration building up inside him.

"Enough," he groaned with frustration. Before he lost control, he slipped on a condom and instructed her to straddle him. Keelen held on to her hips as she lowered her warm, wet opening over his hard length. Welcoming her return, he shuddered as she accepted all of him. After taking a moment to pull herself together, she began moving slowly at first. The slow sweet rhythm was exquisite. So was allowing Charity to take control. She was magnificent as she rode him with fierce concentration, her knees braced on either side of his body, her breasts gently bouncing. Her head rolled forward, her lips parted and a moan escaped. Keelen lifted her up until only the tip of him was inside of her then pulled her down fiercely, filling her wetness with his heat. She cried out in sheer pleasure.

Clinging to her shoulders, Keelen bathed her nipples with his tongue as she rode him faster and faster bringing them both closer and closer to the brink. When the first spasm hit her, she shuddered and cried out his name. He watched the pleasure take her, send her up and over the waves.

He fought back his own release and urged her on until she was completely spent. Holding her so that he stayed locked within her, Keelen pulled her down, rolling over so that she was on her back and his body covering hers.

"Hold me, Charity," he instructed. "Move with me."

"Oh, Keelen . . ." she whispered.

He thrust deep inside with a delicious sensuality that spiked his hunger for her until it was all consuming.

"Tell me you want me," he demanded. "Tell me, Charity."

She locked her arms around his waist and kissed him with passionate intensity as she whispered, "I want you more than I can say."

He drove inside her moving in and out, again and again, faster and faster. He repeatedly cried out her name. Then to his gratification he sensed her own pulsation echoing his own and heard her cries mingle with his. When she cried out his name, Keelen exploded inside of her.

Her forehead fell to his shoulder. His throat was heaving, his heart was trying to force its way out of his chest.

Later as she lay in his arms with her head against his heart, he rained her face with kisses. He cuddled her close to him listening to the calming of her heart against his chest. Smoothing a strand of hair away from her eyes, he watched her until he drifted off to sleep.

Hours later, Charity woke up to find her leg resting over his and her body tingling from head to toe. She had read numerous romance novels and had always wondered what was meant by sexual fulfillment. Now she knew. She had missed so much and had learned such a great deal in a course of one night.

Charity rolled onto her back and groaned. Unable to hold it any longer, she climbed over Keelen's sleepy body and dashed into the bathroom. She sighed with relief as a smile curled on her face. How could she ever put the last few hours to words?

She felt alive and like a woman.

Cracking the door she found Keelen hadn't moved a muscle. He was still sound asleep so she decided to go ahead and take a shower. She was sore after hours of making love. Not that she was complaining.

Turning on the water, she adjusted the temperature and stepped into the shower stall. She allowed the warm water to beat across her sore nipples and all the other places Keelen had explored. Although the water was hot, she shivered as she remembered his hands stroking her body as well as the tantalizing feel of his tongue on her bare skin. Closing her eyes she relished the memories. He had been tender and gentle. Memories of him moving inside of her assaulted her senses. God, help her! She was falling for him fast. However, after last night, she was certain that the feelings were mutual.

Reaching for the shampoo she lathered her hair then turned her face into the spray and reached for the soap to lather her washcloth. The soap slipped out between her fingers. She reached down to pick it up and felt something else. Wiping the water away from her eyes, she cupped the object in her hand and looked down at it. Her breath stalled. She knew the exquisite gold piece anywhere.

It was a gold earring that she had bought Arika for her twenty-first birthday.

Wave after wave of shock slapped her in the face. Arika had been in his room. She didn't want to think about what had happened but it was quite obvious that Arika had taken a shower afterward. Why else would her earring be here? Now what?

She closed her eyes then reopened them slowly, hoping that this was a horrible dream. Instead, humiliation came crashing down on her. "Not again," she moaned.

She wasn't sure how long she had stood there staring at the earring. The water had turned cold. Tears spilled down her face as the impact of his betrayal stabbed at her heart. She dropped her hand to her stomach as she suddenly felt the urge to throw up. All the while he was making love to her Keelen had been thinking about Arika. Kimora's words came back to mind. Was that why Arika had been in his room? Or had it happened the night before on the same night Olivia fell down the flight of stairs?

Oh, my God! What a fool she was! She had let Keelen make her feel like such a fool! It was a humiliating, deflated feeling. Sadly, she turned off the water and stepped out of the shower.

"Charity, are you in there?" Keelen called through the door, breaking into her thoughts.

How she wished she wasn't there, that she could crawl down the drain and disappear. Lowering to the toilet seat, she took a deep breath and managed to calm herself enough to reply. "I—I'll be right out."

He didn't notice the strained tone of her voice. "Baby, take your time. I was just making sure you hadn't fallen in," he chuckled softly.

She managed a choked laugh, glad he could not see the pain etched on her face. *What a fool I've been.* How could she have been so stupid? Keelen had gotten back at her, leaving her with an inexplicable feeling of being used.

She examined herself in the mirror. She towel-dried her hair then took a moment to try and fix it with his brush. It was useless. Her heart was not into the effort. She inhaled deeply and silently counted to ten before she opened the bathroom door.

Keelen was sitting across the bed still in his birthday suit. He pulled his eyes away from the television when she stepped in. "Good morning, beautiful," he crooned.

Despite her best effort, she tremored in response to his greeting. Her gaze slowly slipped over his wide shoulders to the pattern of hair on his chest and down to . . .

She jerked her eyes away and forced a smile. It was awkward standing before him wrapped in a towel. She needed to put her clothes on and get out of his room as quickly as possible.

She reached for her clothes. However, Keelen was quicker. He reached out and pulled her in his lap. He rained a trail of kisses across her collarbone. Despite her inner turmoil her body chose to respond. A pulsing knot formed in the pit of her stomach. She was weakening and was about to give in when he gave her one final kiss on the cheek then he slid out from beneath her.

"Let me brush my teeth before I kill you with my breath." The smile in his eyes contained a sensuous flame.

When he turned and dashed into the bathroom, all her pleasure left her and suddenly changed to anger. She had almost given in. God, she was weak! Charity scrambled to put her clothes on. Her staying like this was dangerous. Her nipples had hardened in response to seeing him with nothing on.

Quickly, she slipped into her panties and bra then retrieved her dress that was laying crumpled in the corner and slipped it over her head. Her dress looked like she had slept in it. Great! Looking like this people would know she hadn't spent the night in her own cabin.

As soon as she slipped into her heels, Keelen stepped out of the restroom with a towel draped around his trim waist. No man should have such a flat ridged stomach, narrow hips and long powerful legs. She did not miss the look of disappointment that she had already gotten dressed.

Moving to her, Keelen pulled Charity in his arms and she found his breath was minty fresh.

"What do you want to do today?" he asked after he released her.

Unable to look at him she replied, "I need to go shopping for my family."

Keelen frowned, remembering yesterday's excursion. Charity had gone from one vendor to the next searching for a deal before buying anything. "Shopping? I think I'll pass."

Charity sighed with relief. She had hoped he would decline. Like many men, going shopping with a woman was a painful thing to do.

He reached into the closet for something to wear. "I'm planning to see a realtor today. You want to come?"

She quickly shook her head. "No, you go ahead. I think I'll spend the day with Beverly," she said quietly.

"All right." Actually it worked out pretty well. After his meeting with a realtor, he was scheduled to meet with an investor. "I'll see you at dinner."

Charity didn't answer. Swallowing hard, she tore her eyes away from his chiseled chest. Watching him was painful. It was too easy to get lost in the way he looked. However, the earring she was clutching tightly in the palm of her hand served as her strength.

Keelen realized that she was still standing. "Have a seat while I order room service."

She shook her head. "I really need to get going."

"You need to eat something. We had one hell of a workout last night." He smirked.

Her traitorous body tingled at his comment. "Really, I'm not hungry."

Hearing an edge to her voice, he stopped what he was doing to look directly at her. "Is something wrong?"

She shook her head. She couldn't speak. Not now, not while the humiliation was still fresh.

"Will I see you at dinner?"

She shrugged trying to ignore the tenderness of his gaze. "It depends on what time I get back from shopping. You know how women are."

He chuckled with agreement. "You'll get no argument there. Are you planning to participate in the auction tonight?"

She nodded.

"Any hint as to who you are bidding on?"

She saw the twinkle in his eyes and smiled despite herself. He was feeling for information. "No."

"Well, let me give you a hint as to who you need to spend your money on." He lowered the towel and reached for his shorts draped across the chair but not before she witnessed his state of arousal.

Charity tried to contain the heat that was settling between her thighs. Her attraction to him was much too strong. If she had any sense she would get away from him as quickly as humanly possible.

Keelen found her eyes on him and grinned wickedly. "As much as I'd like to make love to you again, I'm going to leave you alone. Besides, I have a surprise for you tonight."

And I for you, she thought as she clutched her fingers tightly around the jewelry.

"I'm going to return to my cabin," she stammered.

He saw something lingering in her expression. Was it regret? "Why are you running off? I would like to talk about what happened last night."

"What about it?"

He forced a short laugh. "What do you mean what about it? I want to know how you feel about me and where you'd like us to go from here."

She wasn't sure how to answer his questions. If he had asked her that last night she would have taken a chance of telling him how right their relationship felt. How happy he had made her feel. Last night she had thought that she was someone special.

"Are you going to tell me what's going on?" She was quiet as he slipped into his shorts. He glanced over at her strained expression and frowned. "What just happened here? This morning you were all over me but ever since you got out of the shower you've been acting strange."

She wrung her hands. Maybe she was wrong. Maybe there was a logical explanation. Then again . . . maybe she was correct at taking the situation at face value. "I'm not sure. Everything is happening so fast."

Keelen could tell something was bothering her but he wasn't going to pry. Was she having second thoughts about what had happened between them? The idea caused him to frown and he began to second-guess himself. Maybe he had misinterpreted her feelings. The vibes she had given him last night gave him the impression that the feelings were mutual. Had he really been that far off?

"I'll see you later," Charity said as she brushed past him. "Sure."

Charity returned to her cabin. As she walked through the door, Beverly was the first to glance her way. "Look who decided to come home."

Tasha looked up from her magazine and snorted. "There's no point asking how your night went."

Charity was startled by their assumption. Was it that obvious? Unable to meet their knowing stares, she moved to the mirror. She wished she could honestly say the coloring in her cheeks was from embarrassment, however that was not the case. She looked like a woman who had been made love to. Her hair was a mess, and her lips were swollen and bruised. She was surprised there were still signs after her humiliating blow this morning. Tearing her eyes away from her reflection, she glanced over at Tasha. "I see you slept in my bed."

She was spread out across the bed. Arms bent at the elbow, she rested her chin in her open palms. "I knew you wouldn't be using it."

If she had used it she wouldn't feel half as humiliated as she did now. Charity pulled in her breath and asked, "How'd you know that?"

Tasha gave her a knowing look and said with unconcealed envy, "Girl, as *fine* as Keelen is you'd be a fool to come back here and listen to Beverly snore."

Charity chuckled knowing her friend was telling the truth.

"I don't snore," Bev spat defensively.

As if on cue, the two answered simultaneously, "Yes, you do."

Beverly pretended to be annoyed. "Forget both of y'all."

"So do we get details or what?" Tasha asked, eyes burning with curiosity.

Charity's cheeks burned in remembrance. What started out as a memorable evening ended in embarrassment. With renewed humiliation she looked down at her shoes. "Well . . . I . . ."

"Uhhh, excuse me." Beverly covered her ears with her hands. "That's my cousin you're talking about."

Relieved, Charity smiled at her friends. "Don't worry. I don't kiss and tell."

She was glad that Beverly had intervened. As much as she was aching to share her discovery with someone, it would be unfair to make his cousin take sides.

Dropping her purse on the table, she flopped down in the chair. Trying to steer the conversation away from her, she asked, "What did the two of you do last night?"

Tasha's lips curled with amusement. "Girl, we went over

to Paradise Island and visited the casino. Beverly thinks she saw Michael Jordan."

"Really?" Charity asked incredulously.

With the quirk of her eyebrow, Tasha gave her an unconvincing look.

Beverly nodded. "He jumped into the elevator before I could get a closer look. I raced up the stairs but he was already gone."

Tasha raised her eyes to the ceiling. "And while she was chasing after a pipe dream, I won a hundred dollars at the blackjack table."

Charity smiled. The two women were too much, but without knowing they had put her mind slightly at ease. She could tell why they were such good friends. "What do you two have planned for today?"

"Sight-seeing, maybe a little shopping."

"I need to go shopping. If I don't pick Tia up a gift, she'll kill me."

Tasha nodded. "I've been to her bookstore. It is really nice to see a sista doing something positive for the community."

"Thanks. I'll tell her you said so." Charity rose. "I think I will hang out with you two. I saw some really nice shops on the Square yesterday." She opened the closet and removed her suitcase suddenly anxious to change into something else. She could still smell Keelen all over her clothes.

Tasha closed the magazine and sat upright on the bed. "I need a pair of shoes for tonight."

"Don't forget the Bachelor's Auction this evening," Charity reminded.

"How can I forget?" Beverly interjected. "Bobby Barnett is being auctioned off and you know I've always had a crush on him."

Tasha snorted. "So have most of the females in our class."

Parliament Square was within walking distance from the ship. Cameras in hand, the three toured the historical section of town where they found several government buildings that dated back to the 1700s.

After their sight-seeing tour, they walked back down Parliament Street to begin their shopping expedition. The bazaar ran from Bay Street down to the waterfront. Charity was amazed. The three explored one store after the next. She found Bahamian T-shirts for her entire family, a straw doll for Taylor, a bag for her mom and Cuban cigars for her dad. She would have enjoyed the outing, laughing and joking, if her mind wasn't on Keelen. She was trying to put on a front and so far neither Beverly nor Tasha had mentioned anything about her acting strangely. Why had she been so quick to jump in his bed? She should have learned the hard way but it seemed her desire for Keelen had taken over her common sense. The occurrence kept playing over and over in her head. She had allowed another man to use her.

Two hours later with each of their arms weighed down with bags they headed back to the ship.

"Oh, look!" Beverly exclaimed. "There are some specialty shops up this street." They had encountered a cobblestone alleyway with garretted storefronts. The strip looked like a European village. They browsed through several designer stores with outrageous prices before they embarked upon a perfume shop.

As she scanned the shelves, Charity found several fragrances that she had never heard of that were sold exclusively overseas and in New York. She still had not found anything for Tia.

A sales associate came up to her. She was a stout woman with a wide smile. "Here is something you might like." She removed a small diamond-shaped bottle of perfume called Wish and sprayed a little on her wrist.

Charity lifted her arm to her nose. "Ooh, that smells good." Tia had almost every fragrance imaginable but she definitely didn't have this one.

Turning, she held out her wrist for Tasha. "What do you think?"

She leaned in and took a whiff of her skin. "Mmm, give me a bottle."

A grin covered Charity's face. "I'll take one too."

Keelen shook hands with the realtor and moved to hop back in the awaiting cab. After seeing several properties for sale he finally saw a veranda that he was sure was exactly what he wanted. Plenty of amenities, lots of space, centrally located, the house even had it's own private section of the beach. He promised to get back with the realtor in a couple of days.

While heading back to the square for a meeting at the bank, he smiled as the memories of the previous night surfaced again. He summed it up with one word: fantastic.

However, he was bothered by Charity's behavior that morning. First her face was lit up like a Christmas tree then at the blink of an eye she looked as if she had lost her best friend. Something was bothering her that she had chosen not to share.

Tonight, not only was he going to announce he was the CEO of Enchanted, but he also had arranged a romantic evening for two. Whatever was bothering Charity, he planned to wipe all thoughts from her mind.

* * *

The crowd started moving into the auditorium that was quickly filling to capacity. Excitement was building as everyone was anxious for the Bachelor's Auction to begin. Not only the members of the class reunion, but also every passenger on board had been invited to the fund-raiser. Women were decked out in smashing dresses and men were in suits.

Tables were covered with red tablecloths and there were several cushioned benches. There was a big stage up front covered by a black velvet curtain.

Charity, Beverly, and Tasha were seated at a table near the front with another classmate, Latoya. She was a commissioned officer in the air force.

To Charity's relief, they had decided to have dinner on the strip before returning to the ship. She wasn't ready to face Keelen yet. She still needed time to prepare what she wanted to say to him. The outing had done a great job of shaking her recent humiliation. Now that she was back on the ship and Arika was sitting at a table across the way, the pain had returned.

Tasha looked radiant in a simple two-piece rayon outfit with the pair of gold sling-backs she'd found during their shopping excursion. Beverly had decided to wear the coral dress with her braids piled high on top of her head.

"You guys mind if I sit here?"

They looked up to find Kimora standing over them. For a long moment the group studied her intently. Dressed in a slinky royal-blue gown that set off her dark curls, she looked lovelier than ever.

Charity broke the silence. "Sure." She tapped the empty chair to her right. "Have a seat."

"Thanks." Kimora took a seat and crossed her legs. She glanced around the table for signs of opposition. She saw plenty.

"Beverly, your dress is the bomb," she said as an ice-breaker.

"Oh, my! You finally got my name right," she mocked, her voice dripping with sarcasm.

Awkwardly, Kimora cleared her throat. "No harm done."

"How come you're not sitting with Arika?" Latoya asked, making no attempt to hide her curiosity.

Kimora rolled her eyes heavenward. "Girl, she's been getting on my nerves."

"What else is new?" Tasha snorted.

Elbows on the table, Kimora propped her chin in the palm of her hand. "You'd think I would have learned after fifteen years. You know what they say about hard heads."

A waiter in a white coat came to their table carrying a tray of drinks. "Anything for the ladies?" he asked.

"Yes, Bahama Mamas for the four of us." Gnawing on a stale piece of gum, Tasha glanced to her right. "What would you like, Kimora?"

Kimora looked surprised that she was including her. "I'll have the same."

After the waiter left with their orders, Charity inquired, "Who are you bidding on?"

Kimora drummed her fingers lightly on the table in front of her. "I don't like any of the choices, probably nobody."

"That's 'cause she's already slept with half of them," Latoya joked.

There was a long beat of silence, then Kimora's eyes widened. Tasha and Beverly both had the nerve to laugh, even Latoya had a smile on her face.

"She got you there," Charity said with a grin.

"Forget y'all." Kimora broke down and joined in with a giggle.

The ice had finally broken.

She shrugged. "I dumped several men in my day. Being nice doesn't get you anything but a lot of broken hearts."

"True that," Tasha chimed in.

Charity nodded her head knowingly as disappointment stabbed at her.

Shortly after the waiter returned with their drinks, the lights dimmed.

Arika sashayed onto the stage dressed in a shimmering navy-blue gown. She moved up to the microphone, dazzling them all with her wide toothpaste grin.

"Good evening, classmates!" she welcomed. "We are about to be mesmerized by ten of the finest bachelors to have ever set foot at Rockbridge High School."

Catcalls came from women all around the room. She waited for the crowd to quiet down before she continued.

"Now, before we start our show, I would like to take a moment and share with you the reason behind the Bachelor's Auction. For those of you who don't remember, Tabitha White was valedictorian of our class. Unfortunately, she never had a chance to walk across the stage. Tabitha committed suicide the night before graduation. The reason is still unknown.

"Tabitha was a wonderful person, an asset to our class. She was active in cross-country, drama, and student council and still found time for a four-point-oh GPA. She was an honor student who had been accepted at Harvard University where she had planned to pursue a degree in medicine. All proceeds from this auction will be donated to the Tabitha White Scholarship Fund."

Tasha fell back against her seat and snarled louder than intended. "I can't believe she has the balls to say all those things, especially after the way she used to treat Tabitha."

Charity looked over at Kimora at the mention of Tabitha's death, wondering if she still remembered. Her strained expression told her she did.

"The scholarship fund was her idea," Kimora said,

quickly coming to Arika's defense. "Maybe guilt has gotten the best of her."

Everyone at the table looked unconvinced, but returned their attention to the stage as Arika delicately cleared her throat.

"Since I plan to have one of those fine gentlemen on my arm tonight, I'm going have to pass the microphone to our mistress of ceremonies, Samantha James."

The audience clapped as Arika relinquished the stage to a tall willowy blonde who was now modeling overseas.

"Hi, class! Are we ready to have fun?"

"Yes!" the crowd screamed.

"For years we've interacted with some of the handsomest men in the city. Like myself, you probably had a crush on one of these fabulous-looking gentlemen. They shared our classes or maybe we were lucky enough to have been asked out on a date while some of us just stood back and admired them from afar. Well, ladies, tonight is the chance to spend until the stroke of midnight handcuffed to the man of your dreams. Unfortunately, I'm already married." On her hand sparkled a diamond large enough to be seen across the room. Then she blew a kiss at her gorgeous husband sitting in the corner.

"Let the games begin!"

She had to raise the gavel to silence the cheers around the room.

"Our first bachelor has a degree in biochemistry from Texas State, and is currently living in St. Louis where he is employed as a chemist for Monsanto. He works out five days a week and is an amateur bodybuilder."

"Oooh!" was heard from the back of the room.

"Ladies, let's welcome Jeffrey Barnes."

With long powerful strides the tall, mocha brother stepped from behind the curtain. He strutted across the stage dressed in a sharp gray double-breasted suit. His arresting good looks captured all of their attention. The entire room fell apart.

Tasha's brown eyes rounded. "Holy moly, where the hell was he yesterday?"

"I thought he was married." Beverly could barely contain her excitement.

"Well, you thought wrong." The entire table fell apart with oohs and aahs.

"Take it off!" someone yelled from the back of the room.

"Sorry, ladies, this isn't a strip club," Samantha scolded the crowd in good humor. "The numbered flags on your tables are to be used for bidding. We will begin at one hundred dollars."

A lady in the corner waved her flag.

Tasha raised a flag in the air. "One-twenty-five," she yelled.

One-fifty was heard from the back, but Tasha wasn't giving up that easily and again bid. The lady countered and the bidding escalated until Tasha won with a final bid of $400.

Beverly leaned over and whispered, "Girl, he better be worth it."

There were several other handsome men to cross the stage. Bachelor Two brought in $500 and Bachelor Three, an exotic dancer, did something indescribable with his tongue that brought in another $700.

Samantha quieted the excited crowd. "Next we'll have Canadian basketball player Bobby Barnett."

Holding his head high and proud, he was dripping with conceit. Dark eyes, square face and a shadow of a beard that made him sexy, he knew women found him deliciously appealing.

"Bobby, Bobby, what am I gonna do," Beverly sang with appreciation.

"Lord, help us!" Tasha swiped her forehead. "Look at the size of his feet."

"You've been misinformed. It's the size of his hands that matter," Beverly corrected before waving her flag in the air.

A half hour later, Beverly had an evening with Bobby, Kimora with a former track star, Duane Davis, and Tasha with Jeffrey. They were having so much fun that Charity had almost forgotten about Keelen.

Tasha leaned forward. "Arika hasn't bid on anyone yet."

"I hadn't noticed."

Kimora pursed her lips prettily. "She's waiting on Donovan."

"Donovan?" Bev mocked.

Charity snapped to look at Kimora. Donovan? After finding her earring in the shower she would have thought Arika was interested in Keelen, but then . . . she had never been one to stay with one man for long. A well-known gold digger, a wealthy doctor was more her cup of tea.

Charity shrugged. "Who cares? They deserve each other."

Kimora leaned back in the chair with her legs crossed. "Wouldn't it be wonderful to bid against her?"

"No," Charity answered, not quite following her suggestion.

"No, no. I mean like whenever Arika bids, you counter her offer until she spends a ridiculous amount of money." Her green eyes twinkled with devilment.

Tapping her fingers on the linen cloth, Charity looked straight at her. "I see you're still as vindictive as ever."

Kimora had to sniff at that. "You should be too."

Hearing the entire conversation, Tasha commented, "The way Arika used to dog Tabitha, I think her donation should be the largest."

Beverly joined in. "Girlfriend, that's a good idea. Too bad I've already been eliminated."

Looking off to her right, Charity observed Arika sitting near the front, flag in hand, legs crossed and swinging with anticipation.

Tasha nodded eagerly. "It sounds like a plan to me. If she thinks you want to spend the evening with Don she is going to do everything she can to keep that from happening."

"Sounds like fun," Latoya chimed in.

Charity nodded as if considering her idea. The suggestion of making Arika spend her money was intriguing. "All right."

Two more bachelors strutted across the stage before it was finally time.

Samantha returned to the microphone. "Next we will have the former captain of our football team and now the best plastic surgeon on the east coast, Donovan Gross."

Don strolled onto the stage dressed in a black tuxedo that fit him to a "T." Whoever hadn't known he was divorced definitely knew it now. Wearing his come-hither expression with left brow slightly arched, he moved to the front of the stage. Dropping to one knee, he ran his tongue slowly across his lips. Screams were heard from around the room.

"Who would like to start the bidding?"

Arika raised her flag. "I'd like to start the bidding at two-fifty."

"Ooh! That bitch wants him," Tasha mumbled under her breath.

"Do we have three hundred?" Samantha asked looking around the room.

A bid for 300 was heard from the back.

"Three-fifty," another sister bid.

"Do we have four hundred?" Samantha asked. "Five . . . do we have five-fifty?"

"Five-fifty," Arika called.

Charity raised her flag. "I bid seven hundred dollars."

She was certain Donovan tripped over his foot at the exact moment Arika had turned in her chair. Surprise had siphoned the blood from her face.

"Nine hundred," Arika countered with a determined expression.

Charity raised her flag again. "One thousand dollars."

The crowd grew quiet; only a hush was heard across the room.

"We have one thousand dollars from Charity Rose. Do I hear one thousand one hundred?" No one responded. Charity turned to find Arika pretending to be filing her nails. "Going once, twice," Samantha slammed down the gavel. "Sold to Charity Rose."

With her body stiff from shock, Charity stared wordlessly at Donovan who was grinning as if he were saying, "She wants me." Falling back against the seat, she glanced from one to the next. "What just happened?" she asked with disbelief.

Kimora shook her head. "Girl, that was not the way it was supposed to end."

Beverly was cracking up. "I think that trick backfired on you."

"I'll switch with you if you'd like," Tasha offered between giggles.

Charity shook her head. "No need. I don't plan on being around Don any longer than it takes to write the check." Now she would just have to figure out where she was going to get a thousand dollars.

From behind the curtain, Keelen couldn't believe his ears. Why had Charity bid on Donovan? It didn't make any sense. First she was acting strangely this morning and later he had been unsuccessful in finding her for dinner. It was as if she was purposely avoiding him. Keelen frowned. What happened to all that stuff about how she was over her husband and the way he had mistreated her? He had come to believe that they had something special, so why had she chosen to spend the evening with Donovan instead?

Don strolled toward him wearing a confident smile.

"You lucky dog," Keelen simply said.

He gave a cocky grin. "I don't think luck had anything to do with it. Who else would Charity bid on but her husband." It was a statement, not a question.

As he moved away, Keelen mumbled, "Who else indeed."

Drawing order around the room, Samantha continued. "Our last bachelor is a man who excelled in several sports, then went on to pursue an MBA. He is now the CEO of this fabulous cruise ship. Ladies and gentlemen, let's give a warm round of applause to Keelen Brooks."

"Oh, my God!" Tasha cast an accusing glance at Beverly. "Girlfriend, you've been holding out."

Taking a quick breath, Charity's eyes grew wide with astonishment. She turned to face Beverly speechless. How come he hadn't told her?

Knowing what she was thinking, Beverly shrugged apologetically. "I'm sorry. He swore me to secrecy."

Charity glanced up at the stage as Keelen strolled onto the stage wearing a fabulous two-button single-breasted charcoal suit carrying a bouquet of yellow roses in his hand. He had never looked better. Their eyes met for several seconds. She was certain she saw a look of disappointment in his tender gaze. His expression gave her a warm rush inside.

Keelen was an ever-changing mystery. Just when she thought she had him figured out, he again surprised her. He wasn't at all what she had thought.

As he smiled and showed dazzling white teeth, she ignored the warm feeling that surged through her at the sight of him. She ignored the tenderness in his expression. Not only had he lied, but he had also used her. Blinded by anger, she didn't see that his smile was without malice. In fact, it was almost disappointed.

Samantha smashed the gavel, bringing order to the room. "We will start the bidding at five hundred dollars."

Arika rose from her chair and turned to look over at Charity's table wearing a triumphant smile as she said, "I'd like to start the bidding at two thousand dollars."

The entire room grew quiet.

"Do I hear two-thousand-fifty?" Samantha's eyes traveled around the room, but hearing no response she ended the bidding. "Going once, going twice, sold to Arika."

Tabitha broke the silence. *"Whoop!* There it is! She wanted your cousin bad."

"It looks like she got him," Beverly mumbled.

Charity watched as Keelen descended the stage and handed the bouquet to Arika.

Kimora rose from her chair, waving a check in her hand. "Well, it's time to join our dates."

Charity was at a loss. She caught Arika's pleased expression and quickly looked away.

"Girl, you okay?" Beverly asked, her voice mirroring the concern on her face.

"I'm fine," she replied. After one more glance, everyone but Charity departed to greet their dates.

She wasn't sure how long she sat there before Donovan came waltzing over to the table wearing a satisfied grin. "Come on, Charity, they're waiting for us."

Looking up at the smug look he liked to call a smile, Charity folded her arms and released a huff of displeasure. "I'd rather not."

"Too late. I had started to believe you didn't care anymore."

"I don't," she said with a bitter tinge in her voice.

"Then why did you bid on me?" he pointed out while studying her intently.

She regarded him with his arms crossed belligerently across his chest. "It was for a good cause," she declared while she struggled to keep her emotions under control.

He reached for her arms and tried to yank her out of the chair but she had already stiffened with resistance and was impossible to budge.

"Don't be a spoilsport. This will give us a chance to discuss our daughter's future."

"No," she said, cautiously aware of their audience.

He leaned across the table and spoke precisely. "If I offer to pay the thousand dollars, will you then reconsider?"

Donovan always did know how to say the right thing.

Her expression became thoughtful. Her voice faltered as she tried to think of a response, but instead she managed to rise from her seat and follow him to the treasurer sitting at a table up front. As soon as Donovan handed over the check, the handcuffs were locked.

Charity tried to pinch herself. It would have to be a bad dream for her to have to spend till the stroke of midnight with Donovan.

Ten

It wasn't a dream, Charity scowled inwardly as they left the auditorium. It was a nightmare.

"Charity, I was wrong. I know I made a mistake, but I want a chance to make things right again," Don said as if it killed him to admit it.

She didn't hear the slightest trace of emotion in his apology. Did Don even know what mistake he was apologizing for?

Throwing her free hand in the air, she hissed, "Don, I don't believe you! Why can't you just hang it up?" She swung around and pronounced each syllable slowly so there would be no misunderstanding. "Read my lips. It is over between us." Why was he so pigheaded? She then turned around and headed outside for some fresh air. Unfortunately, due to the handcuffs she had no other choice than for him to tag along.

"How can you say that?" He refused to believe it.

Charity halted long enough to erupt a bark of laughter as she replied, "We're divorced."

"That doesn't mean we can't work it out and get back together. Why can't you see that you and Taylor need me?"

"We are doing just fine."

"Taylor needs her father," he insisted.

"Taylor has her father," she retorted. "He is only a phone call away." She glanced down at her watch and groaned. It had only been five minutes and already it felt like a lifetime. *Who was it that came up with this stupid idea anyway?*

"I'm going to get you back," he vowed.

Seeing the determined look on his face, Charity knew he had every intention of trying. He would just have to find out the hard way that he was wasting his time. Her steps slowed as she looked over at the man she had once loved and all she saw was Keelen.

Their one night together had been more magical than her entire marriage. All she wanted to do was go and find him, to hear his explanation. There had to be some kind of explanation. How could he do something like that to her? She groaned with dismay. She had to know.

"Did you hear what I said?" Donovan asked, intruding on her thoughts.

She looked up at him and admitted. "No, I didn't."

Donovan was flabbergasted. He couldn't understand what could possibly be more important than them? "I said you're a bright and beautiful woman and it is a shame that it has taken me this long to realize it."

Lifting one brow, she eyed him suspiciously. "You better be careful with all those compliments. You might fall over dead."

"Well?" he prompted, impatiently.

"Well what?" She scowled. "What do you expect me to say?"

"I was hoping that you might consider giving me a chance to prove I have changed."

"No! Now quit begging."

"Begging?" He looked appalled. "Who's begging?"

She'd had more than enough of his arrogance. "If Arika had outbid me, you and her would be having this same conversation. I'm sure her body isn't anywhere near as *repulsive* as mine, but then you already know that from experience."

"I'd rather spend the evening with you. Now be a good girl and cooperate. I have a carriage out front waiting on us." He placed a hand on her shoulder and steered her back inside.

Her head spun around. "A carriage?"

He chuckled softly, not missing the interest in her eyes. "Don't you remember the trip to Kansas City we took on our honeymoon?"

How could she forget as it was the only time they had ever gone anywhere.

"Since we are handcuffed and I'm stronger than you, you have no other choice but to cooperate and follow me."

Who in their right mind would take a carriage ride around the square in handcuffs? This entire situation was getting more ridiculous by the second.

With her brow bunched in stubborn defiance, she allowed him to lead her off the ship where a surrey was waiting.

It would have been an elegant way to spend an evening with the one you loved if that had been the case. It was a traditional-style surrey with the fringes on the top. The horse wore a straw hat with a piece of dried hibiscus stuck in the brim.

"Well, it looks like we aren't the only ones in the mood for a romantic evening."

Charity looked in the direction of his pointing finger to find Keelen and Arika taking off in a carriage of their own. They were sitting very close. Arika talking animatedly, Keelen's attention focused on his beautiful date. Then Arika pulled his head down and kissed him, her tapered fingers caressing the back of his neck.

Charity quickly looked away as her heart sank. It had all been one big joke. He had never been truly interested at all. All Keelen had wanted was to get back at her for the way she had treated him and now Arika was his newest conquest. He never bothered to tell her he was the CEO of the cruise line, instead he had thrown it in her face. All the time they were together he never mentioned it.

It was then that Charity realized she had gotten herself in too deep. She should have stepped away and distanced herself emotionally from the start. Now it was too late. Did the pain in her heart mean that she had fallen in love? *Lord, please no!*

Even though they were several feet in front of them, Keelen's laughter vibrated in the air. He was obviously quite taken by Arika. Already their time together had become a memory.

"Arika seems quite interested in your friend." Donovan gave a throaty laugh of his own. "Who would have ever guessed?"

"Yeah, who would have," she mumbled.

She allowed him to assist her into the carriage. With a sigh she asked, "Where are we going?"

Donovan smiled as he took the seat beside her. "I thought we'd go over to Paradise Island and see the surroundings."

"Okay," she agreed. She knew she wouldn't have a chance to see the resort, but with plans to return to the Bahamas again with Taylor she hoped to stay at the popular resort.

His brow rose. "No argument?"

She shook her head in defeat, trying to make the best of a bad situation.

As they moved past several villas, her mood deflated even more. *I guess the invitation to stay with Keelen at his veranda was also a lie.*

She was quiet most of the ride as they crossed the bridge to Paradise Island. Even while staring at the sugar-white sand, her thoughts were still on Keelen. Had their night together truly meant nothing to him? More than likely he had already forgotten. It hurt that she had fallen in the same trap again.

They toured the luxury hideaway. Not to draw attention, Don suggested they hold hands and he then draped his jacket over the handcuffs. She was in no position to object.

They ended up spending an hour in the casino. Charity tried her luck at the blackjack table and walked away with an extra fifty dollars.

Afterwards, they went through the viewing tunnel at Predator Lagoon. There were eleven exhibits holding thousands of gallons of water and home to over 50,000 sea animals. Through panoramic windows and underwater viewing tunnels, she was able to see hundreds of different species including sharks and piranhas. A colorful handout told her the marine habitat was the largest in the world.

"Taylor would enjoy this," Don replied.

She glanced up at him with a faint smile. "I have to agree."

Once around the square, Keelen and Arika returned. Then at Arika's insistence they danced several sets in one of the ship's many discos. Afterwards, Keelen allowed her to lure him up to the deck.

"I don't bite," she smirked. She reached for his hands and laced their fingers together. "Thanks for the interview."

"My pleasure." After the shock of having to spend the evening with Arika, he hadn't seen any sense in canceling the carriage ride and had decided to use the time to conduct their interview. She was more than happy to oblige him.

She moved to take a seat. With the handcuffs, Keelen had no choice but to follow suit.

"Who would have ever guessed that the two of us would be like this together?"

He nodded. "Yes, it is amazing."

"I have made a lot of mistakes in my life, but now I am

trying to get it right. I've put my career first in my life and now that I'm where I want to be, I am ready to settle down. Only thing missing from my life is a man." She batted her eyes. "I think we would be good together." They would be better than good, but she wasn't one to brag.

"Oh, you do?" Keelen was amused.

She smiled up at him seductively. "I do and I would like the opportunity to show you." There was no mistaking the warm invitation in her eyes.

"Arika, I'm interested in Charity."

She was quickly losing her patience with him. After spending two grand on him she sure better get her money's worth. She suppressed her annoyance with him and said, "I hate to see you get hurt, but I think I need to tell you that she and Donovan are trying to work out their relationship. The trip was supposed to be a second honeymoon for them. Your interest in Charity is making that almost impossible."

"Oh, really?" He didn't believe a word she said.

"Why else do you think she bid on him tonight?"

His brows drew together as he considered her words. She did have a point. Why had Charity bid on Donovan? The thought of her loving another man—Don included— bothered him in ways that burned inside.

Handcuffs off, Charity allowed Donovan to escort her to her cabin. She had to admit that the evening was not quite as bad as she had anticipated. Despite her disappointment in Keelen, she had enjoyed herself tonight once Donovan laid off the charm.

"I'm glad we're getting along for once," he commented as if he had read her thoughts.

"We'd get along more often if you'd accept the fact that we are divorced and concentrate on your daughter."

When they reached her cabin, she turned to face him. "Thanks for the check."

"No problem. It was worth every penny." He paused to lick his lips. "I guess there is no way to get you to share my room tonight?"

She rolled her eyes at him. "We were getting along. Don't push your luck."

His expression turned serious. "You know I do not like to lose."

With an upward curl of her lips, she placed a hand to his chest. "There's a first time for everything."

Donovan took the intimate gesture as a sign that she was finally weakening. In one fluid motion, he pressed against her and gyrated his hips, rubbing his pelvis against her suggestively. "Quit playing games, you know you want me," he whispered, his lips brushing against her ear.

"Let me go!" she demanded as he continued to press her against the door.

His other hand cupped her face so that she couldn't turn away. "Let's cut the crap. Your snappy tongue is a turn on, but I've had enough of your playing hard to get." Before she could retort, he pulled her to him. "Give up that chocolate cookie dream of yours and come back home where you belong."

She tried to pull away but he caught her arm. "I want you now more than ever. Please listen to me. Arika means nothing to me. It was—"

"Let me go!" she interrupted.

Charity fought him, twisting her face and struggling, but Donovan held her hands behind her back as his mouth came down hard on hers.

Keelen had finally gotten rid of Arika and hurried down the hall toward Charity's cabin. They needed to talk. He needed to find out where they stood. He turned the corner and what he saw made him stop in his tracks.

Charity was kissing her husband.

Rage boiled inside. Before either of them had a chance to notice him, he turned around and walked away.

"Ouch!" Donovan yelled and bent over cupping his groin protectively. "Why'd you kick me?"

"You should have listened." Charity was breathing hard from resisting. She rubbed at her lips with the back of her hand, trying to erase the pressure of his mouth over hers. Sliding her key in the lock, she moved into her cabin then hastily shut the door behind her.

Donovan hated rejection. With a scowl, he moved down the hall and boarded the elevator. He found Arika on board. "I guess you struck out."

She snorted. "You got some nerve. Doesn't look like you will be sharing your bed tonight either."

Donovan caught her shoulders and pinned her to the wall. "Maybe we can do something about that. I mean there's no reason why *we* have to spend the rest of the evening alone," he said, running one hand seductively across her breasts. Leaning down, he kissed the beauty, long and hard. While plunging his tongue into her mouth he slipped one hand between her legs pushing her thighs apart and rubbing her there.

Arika fought against her weakness for him, but instead of pushing him away, she reached for him, her hands gripping his forearms. As he bathed her with his tongue and caressed her curves possessively all she could do was cling to him, panting, wanting, forgetting that he'd cast her aside at the drop of a dime, forgetting that only minutes ago she had tried to seduce Keelen.

Arika gasped when he slid a strap off her shoulder. He lowered his lips, skimming her cheek and chin before he grazed her shoulder with his wet tongue. Despite her determination not to respond to him, his touch aroused her. She thought he was going to release her breasts and her nipples hardened, yearning for the contact. He knew her body, knew the combination of caressing her to bring her to the brink. But he didn't. Instead, when the elevator doors parted, Donovan released her momentarily and gazed down at her smooth shoulders and the lipstick he'd smeared across her lips. He smiled wickedly then reached for her hand and pulled her along beside him in the direction of his stateroom.

Charity couldn't sleep.

The ship was swaying harder than usual. Beverly wasn't in and the cabin was extremely quiet. However, the stillness wasn't keeping her awake. She couldn't get Keelen out of her mind.

Frustrated, she threw off the covers and made herself pull off her dress. After she had kicked Donovan she had thrown herself across the bed hoping to cry herself to sleep. Only sleep never came.

Sighing, she shuffled into the bathroom. Turning on the light switch, she stared at her reflection in the mirror. She looked like the same woman who had boarded the ship a couple of days ago. But she realized that something about her was different. Something that could not be seen on the outside.

She had fallen in love.

Charity had sworn after her experience with Donovan that she would never fall prey to that emotion again, but somehow she had. And with that realization, she could now admit that what she'd felt for Donovan was nothing compared to what she was feeling for Keelen.

She didn't know when it had happened. Maybe she had always loved him. All she knew now was that her thoughts and emotions had begun to pivot around the man.

She reached over and turned on the hot water. Stripping out of her undergarments, she climbed into the shower. She needed to clear her head, try her hardest to rid the memories. She hoped somehow the water would help to erase some of her humiliation.

How could Keelen have treated her that way? He had really made her believe that he truly thought she was special. She had believed the way she felt for him was mutual. But instead it had all been lies. How stupid she was!

Fresh tears streamed down her cheeks. There was no way this could be happening to her again. She reached for a washcloth and scrubbed away the makeup from her face then proceeded to wash the rest of her body.

Sniffling, she climbed out of the shower and reached for a towel and dried off. She felt refreshed but the shower did nothing to ease the pain in her heart.

A part of her urged her to go and talk to Keelen while the other half told her to just let it go. She didn't know what to do. All she knew was that what she felt was not about to go away.

She slipped her arms through her nightgown and returned to the emptiness of her bed. Lying in darkness, she gazed up at the ceiling, reflecting on her relationship with Keelen. In a few short days she had been flying high then came crashing down.

She reached for the phone and dialed his room. There was no answer. So where was he? She chewed on her bottom lip and confronted the notion that had persisted in the back of her mind. He could only be with Arika.

The certainty left a heavy lump in the pit of her stomach. Obviously he enjoyed the woman's company so much that the lateness of the hour escaped him. Arika might be the lady to keep them apart.

She imagined the two of them together perhaps sharing a meal, conversing quietly or lingering over a drink. Or had they already slipped up to his room where Keelen would hold her in his arms, supplying her with gentle kisses.

The tears began again and she tried to contain her sobs. She didn't want to think of Keelen kissing Arika the way he kissed her or making love to Arika the way he had with her. Had their time together meant nothing to him? Did he make up all those things he had said to her?

Her ragged sigh echoed in the quiet stillness of the room. Even though Keelen had told her she was special, he had never told her he loved her. Charity now knew she had been just someone for him to spend time with. Nothing more.

She was hurt. Deeply hurt that he would treat her that way. Maybe she was throwing things out of proportion. He hadn't made her any promises. They had never spoken about what was going to happen after they got off the ship. She just thought that maybe . . . maybe he felt the same way she did.

How could she have been so naïve? Twice she had misjudged a man. She thought she had learned from the first mistake. After wasting nine years with Donovan she should have known better than to fall in the same trap twice. But she had. Keelen was no better than her ex-husband.

Charity lay on her side cradling a pillow as a lone tear fell from her eye, making its way down her cheek.

The gentle rocking of the ship lulled Charity. Her lashes fluttered against her cheeks as the heaviness of sleep touched her.

* * *

Kimora exited the shower wrapped in a large peach bath towel. As she sat on her bed, rubbing her legs generously with baby oil, she noticed that there was a bottle of Asti Spumante on the desk. *Where did that come from?* She rose to read the card. *To Kimora, from a secret admirer.* She smiled. They only person she could think of was Duane.

They had passed the evening doing something she never imagined doing. *Talking.* For once she'd met a man who was interested in getting to know her instead of trying to take her to bed. She talked about her nursing career and he had actually listened. Plans were made to spend the day together in Freeport.

Removing the bottle from the bucket of ice, she noticed that it had already been opened. *Damn, Arika.* She always had to be the first. It had been a mistake letting Arika move into her cabin.

Kimora reached for a glass and filled it with her favorite bubbly. She would make certain to finish the bottle's contents before Arika returned.

Eleven

"Girls, I'll be right back. In the meantime, swim two more laps then head to the locker room." Their coach moved around the pool and disappeared in her office to take a phone call.

She was barely out of the room when Arika hissed, "Look at her, she thinks she's something else."

Charity didn't need to follow the direction of her eyes to the other side of the Olympic-sized pool to know she was glaring at the new team captain. "Don't hate, Arika. She won fair and square."

Arika's expression suddenly grew savage. "Fair, how was that race fair! If I hadn't caught a cramp I would be the new captain."

Kimora snorted then spoke bluntly. "Even if you hadn't caught a cramp you still would have lost. Her legs are stronger than yours."

"Oh, shut up, both of you!" she sputtered. With a side-long glance, she signaled for Olivia to follow her. They dove under the water and swam to the other side.

"What's she up to now?" Charity mumbled.

"I don't know," Kimora answered. "But let's go watch." She dove in behind them. Charity planted both hands firmly on her hips and observed as their captain bounced once on the diving board and dove in. As soon as her body sliced the water, Arika and Olivia disappeared.

"*Ohhh, no!*" Charity groaned. She lowered her goggles over her eyes and at the count of three she swam after them. Sure enough, they were up to no good. She found the girl struggling under the water while Arika and Olivia were holding her at the bottom. In a panic, she had let out the air in her lungs and was now fighting to get back to the top.

Charity swam as fast as she could. They were going to drown her if she didn't get there in time. Reaching out, she seized Olivia's hand and yanked it away long enough for the girl to free herself and swim quickly to the surface then escape to the locker room.

Charity knew Arika was going to be angry, but for once she didn't care. She returned to the top. Several other members were still practicing their laps. None of them seemed to have noticed how close their captain had come to drowning.

When the three finally surfaced they found Charity floating leisurely on her back. Kimora climbed out, followed by Olivia and they moved to the wall to retrieve their towels.

Arika rose out of the water and took a seat on the ledge. "*What did you do that for?*" she demanded, chest rising rapidly as she tried to catch her breath. "*I was just playing.*"

"*You're always playing,*" Charity snorted. "*One of these days it's going to catch up with you.*" With that, she dove back in and swam to the other side.

Charity was just getting out of the shower when Tasha came barging through the door.

"Did you hear the news?" she asked, eyes sparkling anxiously.

Charity let out her breath in an audible sigh. "I'm afraid to ask."

Curiosity pulled Beverly away from some George Clooney movie on the tube. "What happened this time?"

"Someone shaved Kimora's head," Tasha said, looking quite pleased with herself.

Beverly's mouth was open so wide, she could have caught flies. Sitting down beside her, Charity reached over and shut it.

"I-I can't believe this! Somebody is definitely getting back at them," Beverly said, tossing braids over a shoulder.

Tasha nodded. "That seems to be the case."

"What a minute, guys! That *them* includes me." Nervously, Charity combed her hair away from her eyes.

Beverly shook her head. "You were never really one of them. You just never knew who your real friends were."

"Thanks a lot," she muttered, still unconvinced. Leaning forward, Charity propped her elbows on her knees. "Okay, Barbara Walters, tell us exactly what happened." She wanted to put all the pieces together.

Giggling, Tasha began, "Well, rumor has it—"

"Whoa!" Beverly cut in. "Hold up a minute." Using her hands she gestured a football time-out signal. "What do you mean rumor? This is a cruise ship."

She waved her hands. "Okay, okay, I mean I heard Arika—"

"Now we're getting to the source," Beverly groaned.

Tasha turned to glare at her. "Are you going to quit interrupting?"

Beverly brought a finger to her lips. "Go ahead."

Lowering into the chair, Tasha continued. "I spoke to the twins this morning, who ran into Arika in the hallway, and according to her she returned to her cabin this morning to find Kimora lying in bed with her head wrapped in a towel. Well, she had thought that maybe ole' girl had washed her hair last night but when Kimora rose, the towel fell away and so did all her hair."

"I can't believe this." Charity rose from the bed shaking her head in disbelief.

Beverly leaned against the wall, legs out in front. "Like I said, someone is out to get them fools back."

"I sho' hate it," Tasha mumbled.

Charity stopped pacing and lowered onto her own bed. She was dumbfounded. What in the world was going on? There was no way this could be another coincidence.

"Dang, I wonder if Kimora is going to come out of her room?" Beverly asked.

With a whistle Tasha added, "I'm sure she's not going anywhere until someone runs out and buys her a wig."

Charity glanced from one smug face to the other then arched an eyebrow. "I know you both are dying to laugh."

Beverly clicked her tongue. "We aren't that insensitive."

Charity knew better.

Tasha shook her head. "I just can't believe that Ms. Thang got her hair chopped off."

"Where was Arika when all this was happening?" Beverly asked.

She hesitated. "They said Arika didn't sleep in her room last night."

Beverly and Tasha looked at each other then glanced over at Charity, thinking the same thing. *Keelen.*

Trying to play it off, Beverly said, "She's always trying to tell her business."

Charity barely managed to cover her astonishment and struggled to keep her composure. She had hoped that she had been wrong. "It appears that way," was all she could manage to say as her heart cracked in two.

"Trifling," Beverly muttered.

This was not happening. Charity felt as if someone had kicked her in the stomach, not once but twice. Deep down she had thought that maybe if she talked to Keelen he might have had a believable explanation for yesterday, but the truth of the matter was that she had been a one-night stand. This was his revenge. How could she have been so stupid to think that after ten years, they could continue where they left off? She had truly believed that he really liked her. She had believed that he had felt what she had felt, but in actuality he had just used her.

Now he was with Arika.

She didn't want to believe it, not after their night together. The way he looked down at her with his handsome gray eyes as if she meant the world to him, the way he held her tightly in his arms all night. And the story he told her about carrying her picture around in his wallet since the fifth grade. Had it all been lies?

Charity rose from the bed. "Y'all excuse me, I think I'm going to take a swim." She reached for her bag, removed a swimsuit and disappeared in the bathroom to change. She exited shortly after to find their heads together.

Bev looked up, eyes bright with concern. "Charity, I think there's some kind of misunderstanding. Keelen wouldn't be with that tramp."

"I agree," Tasha nodded. "I think Arika is making it up." It was obvious to both of them that she was having a hard time dealing with the unexpected news.

With false self-control, Charity regarded them. "It really doesn't matter."

The phone rang and Bev reached for it. "Sure, just a minute." Covering the mouthpiece with her palm, she whispered, "It's Kimora."

Charity hesitated for a second, not sure if she wanted to know anymore than she already did before she took the phone from Beverly's outstretched arm and put it to her ear. "Hey, girl. I heard you had an accident," she said, forcing cheer in her voice. There was a prolonged silence and Charity thought maybe she had hung up.

"Can you come and see me?" Kimora finally said.

"I'll be right there." After she asked for her cabin number, she hung up the phone.

"So, what did she say?" Beverly prompted.

Charity looked at them again, their eyes wide with curiosity.

"I'm going to talk to her." She replied being deliberately evasive. The two were fishing for something else to gossip about and they weren't about to hear it from her.

Reaching for a towel and her key card, she headed out the door.

After dodging Donovan and a couple of other students standing in front of the elevators, she descended the stairs and knocked on Kimora's door. She had to have been waiting behind the door because she answered before Charity had even lowered her arm. She peeked around the door with her head covered with a silk scarf. Without saying a word she moved aside so Charity could enter.

"Please have a seat."

Charity moved over to the bed in front of the window and sat down. Several suitcases were packed and sitting behind the door. "You're leaving?" she asked.

She nodded. "As soon as we reach Freeport. But I wanted to see you first." Standing over her, Kimora was silent for a moment before she spoke. She had a look on her face that warned Charity she wasn't going to like what she was going to say. "I have a confession to make. . . . Your bidding on Donovan was a setup."

"What do you mean?"

"Donovan ask me to do it," she admitted, not meeting her eyes.

Charity stared with complete surprise on her face. She felt like the rug had been pulled out from beneath her feet. She had to have heard Kimora wrong.

Kimora hesitated as she watched Charity battling to

keep control. "I'm sorry but we didn't know how else to get you to talk to him."

"We?" she asked, her eyes cautious, her expression guarded.

She dropped her shoulders. "Arika and I." Her voice was husky with regret.

Charity sat there shaking her head.

"Ummm, I also want to warn you that when Arika was in Keelen's room conducting an interview, she purposely left an earring in his bathroom."

She missed out on an evening with Keelen because of a scheme. She had spent the night tossing and turning yearning for his touch for nothing.

Charity struggled to calm her mounting anger. A long uncomfortable minute passed before she asked, "Is there anything else you need to tell me?"

She shook her head. "I'm sorry. I was just trying to help."

Arms folded across her chest, Charity was unconvinced. "When are you ever going to learn to be your own person? A true friend wouldn't have done that."

She pierced her lips regrettably. "I'm sorry," she said again.

Even though she saw traces of remorse, it was kind of late. "Well it's a little late for that," she returned, her eyes unforgiving. After hanging around with Tasha and Beverly, she had learned what real friendship was about.

Kimora wilted onto the bed across from her. "You're right. I haven't been a good friend. I haven't been a good person. I guess that is why someone decided to get back at me." She raised her hand to remove the scarf from her head.

Charity gasped. Kimora's head had been butchered. Several sections had been cut to the scalp while others were whacked unevenly. Putting her animosity aside she couldn't help feeling a hint of sympathy. "How . . ." Her voice faded, she didn't know what else to say.

She dragged a shaky hand across her head. "I have no idea. All I remember is drinking a bottle of Asti Spumante and when I woke up this morning my hair fell onto the pillow." She took a deep breath. "I think someone drugged me."

Charity glanced around the room. "Where's the bottle?"

She shrugged. "It was gone when I woke up."

She looked unconvinced. "It couldn't have just walked away. What does Arika have to say?"

"She wasn't here last night, she spent the night with—"

Charity held up a hand. "I don't even want to know." The thought of Keelen making love to another woman bothered her in ways she wasn't ready to admit.

"You know Arika has always wanted what you had. I've watched the way she acts and I've even asked myself do I really act like that? Don't tell anyone, but I hate myself when I think about it." A darkness of regret glittered in Kimora's eyes. "Now it has come back to haunt me. It's just like something out of the movies."

"It could be a lot worse."

Lines of concentration deepened along her brows. "What could be worse than someone trying to get us back for everything that we have ever done?" Clutching a pillow, Kimora started rocking back and forth uncontrollably. "My sister warned me that it was going to catch up with me sooner or later and it has," she whispered around a knot of fear filling her throat.

Charity tried to reassure her. "It's going to be okay."

She shook her head vigorously. "No, it's not. Don't you see? Olivia tripped Rhonda down a flight of stairs and someone knocked her down a flight of stairs. I cut Elaine's hair off and someone cut my hair off. What is going to happen next? This isn't an accident. Someone is actually out to get us."

"But who?"

Dark memories pushed to the surface. Things that

Kimora wasn't sure Charity fully understood. "I can only think of one person who'd have a reason"—she paused and met her directly—"but she's dead."

Leaving her cabin, Charity couldn't help but think about what Kimora had said. What if someone was out to get them? Did that mean she was next?

She looked up in time to see Arika sauntering toward her wearing a blue two-piece bathing suit that barely covered anything.

"Don't tell me she's still at it," she drawled.

Charity glared at her. "Wouldn't you be if someone cut off your hair? Kimora thinks someone is after us and I agree. We better watch our backs."

"For what?" She gaped. "If I were to worry about everyone who hated me, I'd be looking over my shoulder all the time." She sniffed. "I was a bitch, still am. That's how high school students act. So shoot me! If Kimora wants to hop on a plane and go home then let her, but I'm not going anywhere."

"Then I guess you'll deserve whatever you get," Charity declared irritably. She pushed past her and moved down the hall.

"Charity?" Arika called.

She swung around. "Yeah?"

"Tell Keelen I said hello." Arika chuckled as she entered the cabin.

Charity stood out on the deck with her fingers curled around the railing as she gazed out at the paradise of Freeport Grand Bahama Island. The ship had docked over an hour ago in what was known as one of the most beautiful cities in the world.

But it was all a blur.

She was leaning against the railing, utterly still, the strong wind whipping her hair into dishevelment, her face without emotion. She tipped her head back and gazed at the sun trying to clear her mind. She had been wrong about the earring, but it did not change the fact the two had slept together. *Why couldn't you have waited to sleep with him,* she scolded. But while the breeze lifted her hair from her shoulders, Charity knew that it wouldn't have mattered if it had been a day or a year, she still would have given in to her desire. Making love had been inevitable since the day Keelen moved to her neighborhood. Without knowing it they had been working up to it for years.

Closing her eyes, she could still taste him on her tongue and smell the scent of his body. The thought tortured her with memories of his kiss, his arms drawn around her tight . . . him positioning himself between her parted thighs as she anticipated their union.

A long uncomfortable minute passed before she gave a shaky sigh. Keelen had shown her and taught her things that she had never known possible and if nothing else, she would always be grateful for that. However, it did nothing to calm the waves of emotion flooding her, both of yearning and humiliation. Gosh, she felt stupid. She scowled as she clutched the railing and stared off at the ocean. Now what was she going to do? Even after all that he had done, she still longed to feel his arms around her, his lips on her lips. The tenderness of his kiss still lingered with her. She wanted his touch, to feel him bury himself deep inside of her.

It was agony knowing that those few priceless memories of him would cling to her heart with almost unbearable pain once she returned home. Damn, she didn't need this kind of pain again. She'd had already had more than enough. But it was too late. Keelen had already stolen a piece of her heart, Her mind was filled with images of his face, his smile, his kiss. Each would haunt her for the rest of her life. Somehow she had let Keelen into her heart and now she had to find a way to get him out again.

Almost everyone had gone ashore and the ship was the quietest it had been since she'd arrived. Trying to shake her gloomy mood, she moved over to the pool and removed her robe. Even though it was the start of the lunch hour, the pool was surprisingly empty.

She stiffened herself against the burst of cold as her body hit the water. Diving down deep into the water she swam hard to the other side and then back to the other end. With each lap she released a layer of anger and humiliation. After several minutes she rose to the surface and clung to the edge while she caught her breath. Somehow, she felt better. Wiping the water out of her eyes, she found Keelen sitting in a nearby chair.

"You looked good out there," he complimented with a smile.

She despised the twinge of desire stirring inside her. Her heart leaped, but she didn't give in to his smile. She was weak around him. It was going to be virtually impossible to see and be near him and not reveal her feelings to him.

It took a great deal of effort for her to smooth her hair away from her face, and reply expressionlessly, "Thank you."

"I thought you were still afraid of the water." He remembered those fine summer days when they took swimming lessons at Macher's Swim School. She had lost hold of her kickboard and immediately went under. By the time the instructor had pulled her out, Charity had already declared that she would never swim again.

She frowned at the reminder. "Taylor's already a fish in the water. There's no way her mother could be afraid. Besides, I learned how to swim my freshman year."

Nodding, he rose from the chair and removed his towel draped across his shoulders. She stood frozen. He was wearing nothing but blue swim trunks. Muscles rippling, his skin glowed. His body looked so much more radiant under the sunlight. Charity tried to force her eyes to his eyes, but she couldn't stop her gaze from straying all the way down to his calves. His legs were dotted with sandy hairs, matching those on his chest and head. He slid into the pool until he was submerged to his chest. She could feel her breasts tightening and her legs weakening. Keelen was definitely a distraction.

Resenting his effect on her, she closed her eyes and dove deep down in the water, quickly backstroking away from him.

By the time she reached the other end, he was swimming toward her. Heart pumping fiercely, she dove in and swam another lap. They swam side by side for several minutes without saying anything. Yet her body tingled from his nearness. She needed to get away from him—fast.

She started to climb out when he emerged, water dripping down his powerful bare chest.

"Where are you going?" he asked, his brown eyes watchful.

"I suddenly don't feel like swimming any longer." Being around him was just too much for her to handle.

Keelen reached for her arm, stopping her from climbing out of the pool. "Why?"

She saw the question in his magnificent eyes. Speechless, all she could think about was the pressure of his body against hers and their bodies united. Her body was quivering for his touch. Unless she wanted to be tempted into falling into his arms, she needed to get away quickly.

A band of rage tightened around his chest. *She must be thinking about Donovan.* They were getting back together and she didn't want to tell him. Yet even knowing that,

Keelen still wasn't ready to let go. Despite the fact that she had used him, he still felt drawn to her. His control declined each passing second, overcome by the rise of desire. "What if I don't want you to go?"

His contact elicited a tingling sensation, but she ignored it. Glancing up at him she didn't quite meet his eyes before she dropped them again. This time when she spoke anger colored her words. "I'm sure Arika is looking for you."

He gave a harsh bark of laughter. "Don't hate 'cause she bid on me. You chose to spend your evening with your ex-husband."

She didn't look up nor bother to explain. He was standing so close she could feel the heat of his body and smell the heavenly scent of his skin. His closeness seemed to penetrate through her leaving her exposed and vulnerable in a way she hated.

He pinned her against the wall. Taking in every detail of the way the suit hugged her curves. Jealousy brewed in him to think that she had spent the evening with her ex-husband after spending the previous night with him.

He had had a long and difficult night away from her and was aching to hold her in his arms and kiss her again. His gaze moved to her mouth. He knew he should leave well enough alone. He was getting in way over his head. His heart was on the line. However, he couldn't take it any longer. He had to taste her sweetness again.

His fingertips brushed lightly over her bare throat then came up to cup her chin in his palm and brought her face closer to his. "I missed you in my bed last night. It could have been so good."

His body heat enveloped her, spreading through her body and quickened her heartbeat. Feeling slightly disoriented, she swayed slightly. "I heard Arika did a good job of—" Her last words were smothered on her lips as he covered her mouth with his.

Charity knew she should pull away, slap his face. But for the life of her, she couldn't do any of those things. Despite her attempt not to be affected by his presence, her body responded to him against her will.

She wanted his tongue in her mouth.

Keelen curled one hand around the small of her back, bringing their bodies flush. When his tongue stroked her lips, she felt a hot tendril of pleasure unfold low in her belly. Her lips parted and he slid his tongue inside. Something confusing overtook her, desire drowned out any lingering voices of caution. Unwillingly she recalled their blissful lovemaking. She brought her hands up to cup his head. The blood sang in her ears as she allowed him to grind his manhood against the most vulnerable part of her.

Raising his head slightly, he muttered, "I wasn't with Arika last night." Her eyes told him that she didn't believe him. "How could you think that after the time we spent together? I thought it meant something to you." He reached for her hand. "Do you feel that? That's what you do to me. Have you already forgotten how good it felt having me buried deep inside of you . . . you crying out my name? Did all that mean nothing to you?"

"I . . ." Those moments were too unforgettable to deny. Unwillingly she recalled the blissful passion.

"I don't have time for games." He raised her hand to his heart. "Either you want this or you don't." With that he climbed out of the pool. Reaching for his towel, he tossed it over his shoulder and left.

Her lips still burned with him. Could he be telling the truth? After all, Kimora had confessed Arika's deception.

With that question in mind, she floated lazily on her back staring up at the deep blue sky.

* * *

Thirty minutes later, Charity returned to her room to find Bev gone and almost slammed into the cabin steward who was behind the door changing the linen in the bathroom. "Oops, sorry, Everton. I didn't see you." She turned to walk back out of the room.

"No, mon, I can come back later," he said. He quickly gathered up the dirty towels and threw them in a bag.

Standing there shivering with a towel draped around her shoulder, Charity gave him a weak smile. "I hope it's not an inconvenience."

He shook his vigorously. "No problem, mon, I come back."

Talk about hospitality.

She took a seat on her bed that had already been changed. Later her covers would be turned down and like every night a single chocolate mint would be left on her pillow.

The Jamaican steward had been going out of his way for them since they had arrived. But then that was how he earned his tip. When they first arrived, she had found out that almost all his money was sent to his wife and kids back in Kingston.

Charity decided a quick shower was in order, anything to rid the thoughts of Keelen. She didn't want to think about him and Arika. Not now. Not after wasting the last twenty-four hours thinking about them. Enough was enough. If she was wrong then he would have to prove it to her because all she was thinking about right now was taking a nap before supper.

Keelen finished up a ship-to-shore call. His meeting with another investor was scheduled as planned. Everything was slowly falling into place. He wished he could say the same about Charity.

What had happened between them? Two nights ago they had lain in each other's arms making loving until the sun rose, then everything changed. She had spent the evening kissing her husband while he winded up spending the romantic evening he had planned for Charity with Arika.

Didn't she also believe that what they had shared was special or was he the only one who thought so?

Why was she playing games with him? Had their time together meant nothing to her?

What made her think he spent the night with Arika?

He flicked through the channels while he pondered over the question. If Arika hadn't stayed in her room, then where did she spend the night? Then he remembered that he had seen Arika and Donovan at breakfast. Could they have spent . . . then if so, Charity spent the night alone. In her own bed. A smile curled on his lips.

Dropping the remote on the bed, he moved to the bathroom to prepare for his last meeting, chuckling along the way.

Tonight the two had a lot to talk about.

Twelve

Charity felt someone shaking her. "Let me sleep," she growled as she turned to face the wall.

"No, it's time for dinner," Beverly ordered.

Charity opened one eye and raised her head. "I'm not hungry."

"Girlfriend, you don't have to be hungry, but there's no way anyone can pass up a spread like they serve upstairs." Beverly pulled the covers off of her roommate, exposing a blue nightshirt that read All About Me. "If you don't want it, then give your food to me, but you're not missing dinner. It's the Captain's Champagne Night."

"All right, all right," she moaned as she sat up in the bed. Dropping her feet onto the floor, she sighed before focusing on the crazy woman standing in front of her. "Where have you been all afternoon?"

"Shopping, girl!" Beverly pointed to the number of bags on top of her bed. "Tasha and I went up and down the streets and I think we stopped and bought something from every last vendor," she giggled. Reaching in a bag she started pulling out T-shirts and several unique souvenirs including an ashtray made from a coconut shell.

Charity looked at the items with interest. "Who's that ashtray for?"

"Kee."

"Keelen smokes?" she gasped then wondered why she was even surprised.

Beverly nodded. "He sometimes smokes cigars, the expensive kind in his private office at home."

Through her surprise Charity drew one word. "Oh."

"See! There's something you didn't know."

"It appears there is a lot that I don't know." Her tone held a bitter twist. "And since we are on the subject, how come you didn't bother to tell me he was CEO of this ship?"

Beverly shrugged. "It wasn't my place to tell you. Keelen didn't want to announce it until the auction."

"I wonder what else he's keeping from me?" she murmured.

"Nothing, now quit trippin'." Beverly moved to the closet. "Dinner is formal. So quick, find something nice 'cause I'm hungry."

Thirty minutes later the two sashayed into the dining room just as the appetizers were being served. Dim lights flowed from the chandeliers overhead. Tables were covered with beautiful ecru linen with formal place settings including china and sterling silver pieces.

"We thought you weren't going to make it," Tasha commented when they reached the table.

"Girl, please, you know I'm not missing a meal," Beverly said reaching forward and helping herself to a hot buttery roll. "Where else can I get a meal like this?"

"I know that's right," chimed former track star Eunique Mahan. She had been a regular at their table since day one. "I'm in no rush to get back and cook for my husband."

"Me neither," Latoya added, while stabbing a shrimp from her cocktail with a fork. "On second thought, I'm just not in a rush to get back. I could stay like this forever."

"True that." Tasha exchanged high fives with Beverly and Latoya.

Charity couldn't help joining in on the fun as she listened to Latoya's high-pitched laugh. All through high school her laughter had gotten their class through some of the toughest situations with their math teacher, who could never resist a smile at the infectious sound.

"Excuse me, ladies. Are you ready to order?"

All eyes turned to the handsome waiter standing at the head of the table.

"Felipe, dear, it's so good to see you again." Beverly replied, salivating at the mouth.

His cheeks reddened under their intense stares. "It's a pleasure to serve all of you beautiful women again."

"Lordy Lordy." Tasha started mopping her forehead.

Charity shook her head in silent laughter. They had been going through the same scenario each night. Felipe Hernandez was from Puerto Rico. Dressed in an elegant white jacket and black slacks, he was a dream. Dark sensual eyes, bronzed skin. He was something else.

"What will you ladies be having tonight?"

"You, if that's possible," Tasha answered smoothly.

Loud cheers were heard around the table.

"You lovely ladies are making me blush."

"Behave," Charity ordered. Reaching for her menu, she noticed it was International Night. "There are so many delectable choices it's hard to decide. Felipe, what would you recommend?"

He smiled, pleased that she had asked for his help. "I would recommend fresh salad with Italian vinaigrette dressing, chicken breast with sage and wine sauce and spaghetti with pesto and peanuts."

Lowering her menu, Charity smiled. "Sounds fabulous."

"Can I offer anyone some wine or champagne?"

The women glanced at one another, but remained silent.

"I have a fine Italian vintage."

Tasha cleared her throat. "I think we'll pass." She reached for her glass of water and took a long swig.

Felipe gave a slow bow and then departed.

After he left, Beverly leaned forward. "I can't believe we are all afraid to drink the wine."

Sitting across from her, Eunique huffed before saying, "After what happened to Kimora, I don't think any of us are willing to take chances."

"Who do you think drugged her champagne?" Latoya asked after a long pause.

Beverly snorted. "Probably Arika."

Eunique leaned forward in her chair. "Do you really think she would stoop that low?"

As one, they turned to Charity for answers. Unaware that they were waiting for her, she looked up from her glass to find all eyes staring at her rather oddly.

"What?" she muttered from around a roll.

"Do you think she's capable?" Latoya prompted.

Charity shrugged. "I don't know."

"Don't forget about Olivia," Eunique added. "Do you think Arika pushed Olivia down the stairs?"

Resting her chin in her hand, Latoya commented, "I heard she was trying to make a move on Keelen when Olivia interrupted and she was not too happy."

Beverly nodded. "Tasha and I discussed this earlier. I think someone is out to get them." She turned to Charity, sensing her discomfort. "I know you don't want to talk about this, Charity, but what if this is a vendetta?"

Eunique inclined her slender face. "She's right, Charity, what if someone comes after you?"

Charity rolled her eyes from side to side to find the group watching her. What did they want her to say? Admit that her life was in danger? She wasn't ready yet. She still needed time to sort through all of the possibilities. As far as she was concerned anyone could be a suspect. Arika as well as anyone else sitting at the table.

Her expression gave no clue to her thoughts as she forced a smile. "You guys need to stop. This is not a vendetta. I think that what happened to Olivia was because she drank too much and slipped." She paused and fingered her glass. "As for Kimora . . . it was an isolated incident that has no bearing on the other."

"Whatever," Beverly responded, unconvinced.

"What she said could be true. Kimora's hair has always been thin and occasionally she wears a weave. I've even seen her with tracks at work. How do we know she had any hair at all?" Tasha said.

"Oh, brother," Beverly mumbled.

Latoya rolled her eyes in disbelief. "The girl is half Chinese."

"And her other side is Nigerian," Tasha retorted with a raised brow, "and you know how nappy their hair is."

Charity choked on her water.

Beverly clamped a hand over her mouth and the entire table fell apart.

As soon as he entered the dining room, Keelen quickly scanned the area until he found his target sitting near the window with her friends.

Charity looked beautiful this evening dressed in a two-piece blue rayon pantsuit. Her hair was pulled back away from her face, revealing a pair of gold loops.

He had reboarded the ship only minutes before it had set sail for Sunset Island. He had hoped to have a chance to talk to her before dinner, but there wasn't enough time. After dinner, he planned to pull her away long enough to talk. He was going to make sure that she understood that he had not spent any time with Arika, that he was only interested in her.

"Good evening, Keelen."

Speak of the devil.

He glanced to his right. Arika was leaning slightly forward so he could catch a glimpse of her cleavage peeking out of her animal print wrap dress. "Hello, Arika."

"I've been thinking about our discussion the other day about your cruise line." She moved in closer, running a finger down the front of his white dinner jacket. "I think I might know of someone who'd be interested in investing."

He removed her hand. "Don't tell me, you're interested."

"Of course not," she said as if his question was ridiculous. "But I'm almost certain my father would be."

Even with a look of skepticism the mention of Andrew Anderson caught his attention. Her father, a self-made millionaire, was a huge investor in black-owned corporations around the world.

With the crook of her index finger, she signaled for him to follow. "Come, I want to see your five-year plan."

He turned and followed her toward the door.

Digging into her pasta, Charity looked to her right just in time to see Arika and Keelen leaving the dining room. Bringing the fork to her lips, the noodles lodged in her throat.

"Girl, what's wrong?" Bev whispered. She had also seen Keelen leave the room with Arika. As soon as she had a chance, she was going to have a long talk with her cousin.

Charity shook her head. "Nothing."

She was silent as the others chatted with one another while she tried to ignore the sudden stab of jealousy. Keelen almost had her believing that he hadn't slept with

Arika. She picked at her food. All it was was sex, nothing more. So why was she wondering where the two had gone?

Somehow she made it through the meal. The women made plans to attend the Follies show at ten. Outside the dining area near the staircase was a photographer taking pictures of the passengers in front of a backdrop painting of the ship.

"Come on, y'all, let's take a picture," Eunique encouraged.

Everyone agreed it was a wonderful idea and headed to the back of the line.

"We still need to go to the photo gallery and look at the pictures they took of us the other night at the party," Tasha reminded.

"They are fabulous," Latoya said. "Eunique and I looked at them just before dinner."

The line moved up. Beverly hit Charity on the arm. "Girl, look! There's Rhonda Lawson."

"Where?" Tasha asked, eavesdropping on the conversation.

Beverly pointed. "In front of the backdrop, taking a picture."

Charity looked over at the girl they used to call Spook Baby. *Boy, has she changed.* She was tall with legs that appeared a mile long. Her flawless mahogany skin set off large luminous eyes and high cheekbones that Charity had never noticed before. She looked model thin in a slinky gold dress that showed off her tiny waist and ample breasts.

"Why haven't we seen her before tonight?" Beverly asked curiously.

Charity shrugged. "I have no idea."

"She's been in her cabin with motion sickness," Latoya informed them.

Tasha stared in her direction. "Ole' girl looks good."

"Yes, she does," Charity returned while trying not to stare.

Finished with her photo, Rhonda moved their way with the grace and poise of any high-paid model.

Beverly was the first to make a move. "Rhonda, is that you?"

Rhonda blinked several times as if she didn't recognize Beverly before she broke out in a butter-sweet smile. "How have you been?" She pulled her in a friendly hug.

"I've been good," Beverly returned once they parted.

Rhonda turned her eyes in their direction and waved and exchanged greetings with each of them. When her eyes fell upon Charity, her lips formed a thin grim line. After all these years, her anger was still there lashing out at Charity.

Moistening her lips she said, "Hello, Charity, I'm surprised you even know who I am."

"Of course I do," Charity smiled, hoping to break the ice. "How have you been?"

"Fine. Just fine." She ran a slender hand across her short moussed hair. "How are your friends? I heard they've been having a little trouble."

There was something evil lurking in her eyes, something that made Charity suddenly uncomfortable.

She shrugged. "I wouldn't know."

"If you don't, I'm sure you will find out soon enough." Rhonda turned away. "It was good seeing you guys." Heading for the stairs, she moved away.

"Oooh, she has rage," Tasha instigated.

"What was up with that?" Eunique asked.

"I'm not sure." *What did she mean I'll find out soon enough? Was she warning me?*

Charity pondered over the possibilities until it was their turn in line. Even then she had to force a smile for the camera. Something just wasn't right with this trip. First Olivia, then Kimora, and now Rhonda's warning—did this mean she was next? She felt a wave of increasing uneasiness. Hundreds of miles away from shore, Charity suddenly felt trapped. The cruise just couldn't end soon enough.

As soon as the photographer was done Charity felt someone grab her hand. She turned to find Keelen standing next to her. Despite the fact she was upset with him her heart pounded rapidly in her chest.

Keelen nodded greetings to the other women before returning his gaze to Charity. "Will you take a picture with me?" he asked.

She shook her head, ready to pull away. "I don't think so."

"I would like to finally replace the photo in my wallet."

She shook her head again.

"I insist." He lifted her off the floor and carried her to stand in front of the photographer.

"Aw, sookie sookie now," Beverly called.

"Put me down, Keelen," she demanded.

"Only if you promise to take a picture," he challenged.

"Oh, all right."

He pulled her close to him in an embrace pose. "You're not getting away from me tonight," he whispered just before the photographer said, "Cheese."

Her pulse quickened as she tried to remain perfectly still. "What do you mean?"

"Just what I said. Tomorrow is our last full day on this ship and I plan to spend the next thirty-six hours by your side."

As soon as the photographer finished, he hustled her up to the ninth floor to a sixties lounge. The Temptations were playing and he pulled a reluctant Charity onto the dance floor.

"Can you two-step?"

"No, I can't. Donovan never cared for dancing."

"Then follow my lead." She stumbled over his toes a couple of times, but before the end of the song she had caught on.

"I always wanted to learn how to do this." She laughed, feeling like herself again.

The music changed to a slower tune. Keelen pulled her close to him. "I always look for an excuse to hold you in my arms."

She found herself forgetting that she was angry as she draped her arms around his neck. "You are a flirt."

His dark gaze was gently affectionate. He responded in a husky, hypnotic voice, "Only with you."

Her smile dropped.

His steps slowed as he asked, "What did I say?" She was quiet. "Talk to me."

"Arika. I saw you leave with Arika." She said, unable to help herself.

"We need to talk." He took her hand and led her off the floor and out the sliding glass doors. Still standing, they both leaned against the railing.

"Okay, talk to me." He was desperate to have her in his arms again.

"Are you . . . sleeping with Arika?" There, she'd said it. Keelen took a step closer just short of touching her. Everything in her ached for him to reach out and touch her again. How she missed his kiss and his strong lean body pressed against hers. However, to make certain it didn't happen, she took a step back.

"I will answer that question only if I can ask you the same."

"Deal."

"No, I am not sleeping with Arika. The only woman who has shared my bed is you."

"But last night—"

He put a finger to her lips silencing her. "I sent Arika away."

"Oh."

He allowed his hand to slide from her forearm up to

her shoulder where his fingers squeezed gently. His touch felt warm and strong. He wasn't just touching her arm, but her heart. She looked up and gazed into his perfect gray eyes, which were overcast and worried. Her pulse raced.

"Now, my turn. Are you and your husband reconciling?"

"Don't be ridiculous."

"But I saw him kiss you."

"And if you hung around a second longer, you would have watched him get slapped."

The corner of his lip twitched. He would have loved to have seen that. "Then why did you bid on him?"

Charity explained the scam.

Keelen chuckled. "You mean we lost an evening together because of a misunderstanding?"

A return smile tickled the corners of her mouth. "It appears that way."

They stared at each other in silence as currents sparked between them.

He pulled her into his arms. "Promise me that you will spend the rest of the cruise with me."

"Yes," she answered without hesitation.

"Promise me you'll spend the night in my bed."

Her heart was beating unnaturally. "Yes."

Nuzzling her neck, he whispered against her ear, "Promise me you'll scream my name at least a dozen times before morning."

Her gentle laugh rippled through the air. "I promise."

"I've missed you," he said, heat searing his body.

"So have I," she admitted honestly. She met his lips halfway. Shutting her eyes, she savored the closeness of his body, the sweetness of his kiss. Keelen's mouth was moist and warm as it nibbled and teased with an expertise that nearly dropped her to her knees. He explored her mouth and stroked the soft underside of her cheek.

A moaned escaped her. If he took her right there on the deck she would not have objected. Indeed, she wanted him to do just that.

He dragged his mouth aside and rubbed his jaw against hers, dropping little nibbles to the sensitive skin behind her ear. Charity clutched his jacket, needing his strength to stay afloat.

When they finally came up for air, Charity pulled away slightly and met the dazed look in his eyes. "Before you pull me away to your room, I would really like to see the Follies show tonight."

His mouth twitched in a grin. "I guess I can share you for now."

She laced her fingers behind his head and drew him closer. Her sweet breath brushed his chin and teased his nose. She tilted her head, her mouth now only inches from his, flirting with him. He kissed her once again long and hard then decided to save the rest for later.

"Come on, let's go get some good seats."

Charity had to hold her stomach. The comedian had her in stitches.

The theatre was exquisite. The huge stage was draped with large black curtains. The room seated 500. The lower level had several hundred red seats and, at the back of the room, several booths and tables. In the balcony, there was half as many. She and Keelen were sitting at a table next to Beverly and the rest of the clan.

There were several dance numbers including snippets from several off-Broadway productions and a chorus line. One of Patti LaBelle's backup singers stole the show with her rendition of "Over the Rainbow."

As soon as the curtains were drawn, Charity and Keelen raced to his room.

* * *

With a wiggle of her hips, the gown fell to the floor. Keelen reached forward and slid her panties down her hips to her feet where Charity kicked them away.

She now stood before him beautiful and naked. A low animal sound tore from his throat.

"Sweetheart," she purred as she stepped over her dress and moved closer. She splayed her fingers over his shirt and under the lapels of his jacket. "What's wrong with this picture? Why is it you still have your clothes on?"

"Probably because I am waiting for you to take them off."

She pushed the jacket down his shoulders and he shook it free, dropping it to the floor next to her dress. Charity then loosened his tie then unfastened the buttons on his shirt one after the other.

Both were added to the pile.

She unbuckled his pants and slowly lowered the zipper, allowing his pants to fall to his ankles. Keelen stepped out of them and kicked them over with the rest.

She stroked her palms across his chest in a slow circular motion, exploring, discovering then lowering to skim his belly and come around his ribs and finally to his back. His heart beat rapidly beneath her hand. Leaning forward, she rubbed the tip of her nose against his skin and inhaled deeply. Her black lashes fluttered shut and her tongue slid over flesh, hot, wet and glorious.

He felt weak with anticipation.

Succumbing to impulse his hands spanned her waist and drew her roughly toward him. He could feel her luscious breasts flatten against his chest. Shivers buzzed along his spine. He struggled for control and Keelen thought he'd die from wanting her.

Bending, he scooped her up into his arms and strode to

the bed. He managed to jerk back the covers and lay her down then slipped out of his boxers and lay beside her.

He lay still while she explored him with her mouth, stringing soft kisses over his shoulders, his throat and his face. Charity gave so freely that it moved him.

As she bent to feather her lips across his cheek, her hair brushed against his chest sending tingles across his skin. One of her hands caressed his cheek. The other stole down until she reached the source of his sexual frustration.

Rolling Charity onto her back, Keelen covered her with his body and claimed her mouth with all the tender violence of love unleashed. The kiss was hungry and demanding. She gasped with pleasure and returned his kiss with velvet strokes of her tongue that drove him to the brink of madness.

Without taking his mouth from hers, he reached down between them and found her hot, wet and ready. She moaned his name and spread her legs in the sweetest of invitations. He reached for a foil package and, with one glorious push, found his rightful place within her.

Bodies united, Charity moved her hips beneath him. She wrapped her arms around him. Her hands slid along his back and grasped his buttocks. All conscious thoughts erased as she was met by wave after wave of ecstasy. He sank deeper and she met his every thrust.

"You belong to me," he whispered against her lips and received no argument. His blood raced. His pulse pounded. Faster he moved within her. God, but he couldn't get close enough.

He quickly brought her to climax. Charity's cries of ecstasy bathed him in glorious heat and several jerking spasms delivered him into the brilliance.

He would let her sleep and then he would make love to her again before the sun began to set on the sea.

* * *

She glanced around to see if anyone was looking before she slid the card into the lock. Quickly, she shut the door behind her. Without turning on the light, she broke into action.

Using her house keys she removed a small screwdriver from her key chain then climbed onto the mattress and began loosening the screws.

By the end of the cruise all four would know what pain and humiliation meant.

Thirteen

Charity rose the next morning to find Keelen sitting up in bed beside her. Propping herself up with her elbows, she looked at him out of sleepy eyes. He was staring down at her.

Shyly, she lowered her eyelids again and laughed self-consciously. "What are you doing up?"

He lowered his lips to the side of her neck, nuzzling a delicate tender spot behind her right ear he'd discovered just yesterday gave her pleasure. "Watching you sleep."

With a moan, she leaned into him before lowering her lashes again. "Why would you do that?" *I probably look a mess*.

"Because I like looking at you," he answered with a devilish smile. "You are so beautiful."

She raised her lashes and laughed. "Quit! You're making me blush." The intensity in his gray eyes was igniting a slow heat within her. Reaching a hand under her pillow, she returned with two peppermints. She popped one in his mouth then hers. "Morning breath ain't nothing nice," she grimaced in good humor.

"True that." Lowering his head, he captured her lips in a deep kiss. "How's that taste?"

"Mmm . . . better . . . much better," she moaned against his lips between kisses.

Keelen reluctantly pulled away then growled. "If I don't

stop now I won't leave this room until we reach Sunset Island." With his finger he seared a path across her shoulder and down her arm as he spoke. "I need to go talk to the captain. Then I have a nine o'clock meeting with the marketing team. Would you like to join us for breakfast?"

She shook her head, smiling lips still warm and moist from his kiss. She never dreamed hands could feel so warm, so gentle, and so arousing. She was still amazed by her own eager response to his touch. "No, go ahead. I need to go back to the room and change then I'll just eat with Bev."

His body hungered for another taste of the feast she gave him last night. "You're sure?" His finger moved around to her breast where he gently outlined her nipple.

"Positive," she gasped, feeling passion rising inside her. "I can't take up all your time."

"Why not?" He rolled her flat onto her back and grabbed a condom. "I don't want to share you any more than I have to." She lifted her arms, inviting him to lie on top of her. Spreading her legs, he entered her.

Let them wait. After all, he was the boss.

Charity knocked on the door to her cabin. Tasha answered it before she had a chance to drop her hand.

Stepping aside so she could enter, Tasha asked curiously, "Girl, where were you?"

"Tasha, girl, that's a stupid question," Beverly said while looking over at her as if she had lost her mind. "Where do you think she was?" She realized her best friend just couldn't help herself. Tasha had to have the inside scoop on everything.

After searching on the desk and around her bed, Charity asked. "Have either of you seen my key card?"

"Nope." They answered in unison.

She dropped a hand to her waist, wearing a puzzled expression. "I can't find it."

Tasha let her eyes travel to the left side of the room. "It's probably somewhere in that mess."

Nodding, Charity had to agree her side of the room looked hazardous. "I don't mind if you borrow my things, but why are the entire contents of my suitcases all over my bed?" Her lips twitched with humor.

Beverly shrugged. "It was like that when I came in this morning. I thought you did it."

"No, I . . . wait a minute." Realizing what Bev had just said, Charity noticed Tasha had on shorts and a halter-top while Beverly was sitting on the bed in the same dress she had worn the night before. She gave a short laugh. "Where have you been?" Her eyes drilled her.

Tasha's amber eyes were sparkling with excitement. "Uh-huh. She was just getting ready to tell me."

"Why y'all all up in my business?" Winding a braid around her finger, Beverly dropped her lashes to her lap.

"Girl, don't play!" Tasha warned impatiently. "If we have to beat it out of you we will."

Beverly glanced over at her, brow raised in amused contempt. "Dang, you're violent."

Forgetting about her suitcase, Charity pushed some of its contents aside to make room to sit on the bed. Seeing the change on Beverly's face, she was suddenly curious to find out herself.

Tasha resumed her favorite position on the floor, crossing her legs beneath her. "Okay, spill it, girl."

"I spent the evening with my bachelor," Beverly confessed. A flush rose to her cheeks.

Charity's eyes grew wide. "Bobby Barnett?" Astonishment flavored her words.

"Yes," she shrieked with a dreaming smile.

"You go, girl!" Tasha shouted as she reached over and gave her five.

"Oh, my God! He was all that and a bag of chips." Beverly fell back on the bed and the three giggled like teenagers.

Charity cupped her mouth with her hand. "You didn't?"

Tasha knew the look and confirmed. "She did."

Beverly propped herself up on her elbows and gave them a wicked grin. "Yes, I did."

The three arrived at the dining room to find their group sitting together outside on the deck. It was a beautifully warm morning. Sunset Island was already in range.

"This is our last breakfast together," Charity expressed, saddened at the short time left. She realized she was going to miss them. In five short days they had developed a bond that she was not yet ready to let go of. This time she would make sure she stayed in contact.

Beverly frowned as she munched on a slice of wheat toast. "I can't believe it's over."

"I know. Where has the time gone?" Tasha said while sipping a cup of coffee.

"Hold up!" Eunique held up an open palm. "It's not over yet. We still have an entire day in store on the island." Sunset Island was a private island exclusively for Enchanted Cruise Line passengers.

Tasha's eyes were sparkling with anticipation. "Yes, and I heard there are going to be some fine brothers serving us this afternoon."

"Oh, I can't wait," Beverly chimed in.

"What happened to Bobby?" Tasha asked.

"Bobby, what about Bobby?" Latoya asked.

Beverly rolled her eyes. "Remind me to never tell you anything again," she managed between clenched teeth.

Tasha shrugged and finished eating her eggs.

While Beverly explained, Charity looked to her right in time to see Keelen stroll outside followed by a man and two women, all carrying briefcases. They must have been the marketing team he had told her about. He looked over at her and winked. The man could cause shivers through her by something as innocent as eye contact. She sighed, then rose and walked over to their table.

Keelen was still standing and draped an arm comfortably around her waist. "Guys, I'd like to introduce you to the woman in my life, Charity Rose."

"It's so nice to meet you." She shook each of their hands.

A tall blond man stepped forward and shook her hand vigorously. "I see Mr. Brooks has an eye for beautiful things." He looked down at her then winked.

"Thank you. I'm looking forward to seeing the travel brochures." She excused herself, allowing Keelen to kiss her softly on the cheek before she returned to her group. *The woman in his life.* Charity was certain she floated all the way back to the table.

Charity and Bev returned to their cabin to change into their swimsuits and relax for a few minutes before it was time to catch a water shuttle over to the island.

"Turn on the television. We've got time for a movie," Beverly called from the bathroom.

Charity reached up to switch on the television and jumped out of the way just as the television came crashing down onto her bed. It then bounced off the bed and landed on the floor barely missing her feet. She screamed.

Bev raced back into the room. Her eyes traveled up to where the television mount was dangling from the wall to Charity's stricken face. "Girl, you okay?" Her face was full of concern.

Shaking, Charity finally found her breath and slowly lowered herself onto Bev's bed, nodding her head. "I—I'm okay. My heart's just stuck in my throat."

Bev stepped around the television, reached up, examined the iron mount and frowned. "How the heck did this fall?"

Charity dropped a hand to her queasy stomach. "I don't know. I—I reached up to turn it on and it fell."

"Well, I'm calling the front desk." She stepped around the smashed television and reached for the phone.

While Beverly spoke, Charity tried to catch her breath. Her heart was still pounding so hard her head was spinning. Closing her eyes, she settled back on the pillow while trying to calm her erratic heart. What if she had been lying in the bed? She tried to swallow the lump again.

"They're sending our steward," Beverly informed her after she hung up.

All Charity could do was nod.

A knock was heard at the door. "That was quick." Beverly went to answer it. It was Tasha.

"Hey, you'll never guess . . ." The laughter that crinkled her eyes suddenly vanished. "What happened to your television?" Seeing Charity lying on the bed, she stared at Beverly baffled.

"It almost fell on Charity's head."

"What?" She moved and took a seat on the bed, eyes wide and steady on Charity. "You could have been lying in that bed," she said softly.

Charity opened her eyes. "I know," she finally mumbled.

Beverly had left the door open and Everton entered. Taking one look at the television on the floor he let out a loud whistle. "Are you lovely ladies okay?" he asked, looking from one to the next.

"We're fine," Beverly assured him. "But that television certainly isn't."

Everton scratched his salt and pepper Afro. "No, mon. I guess it isn't. Why don't I clean this up for you?"

Beverly nodded. "We're going to get out of your way."

"Come on, Charity. You need a drink." Tasha and Beverly helped her up. She managed to stand on shaky legs.

They were sitting on the deck sipping their second drink when Keelen found them. He openly studied her. Charity was hunched over in her seat, arms resting on her thighs, head almost between her knees.

"Are you okay?" He pulled up a chair next to her, placed a comforting hand to her shoulder and leaned in close.

She nodded. "I'm fine now." By the time she had finished the first drink, she had begun to feel better. Her pulse was finally back to normal.

Keelen clutched her hand. He hated to tell her, but he had to. It was only fair. He raised her chin so she was looking at him and clutched her hand with both of his. "Sweetheart," he said carefully. "Someone loosened those bolts."

Charity pulled back. "What?" she said as if she was trying to assimilate the words.

He nodded. "I just had maintenance examine the bolts. There is no way the television could have been that loose."

"Who could have done something like that?" Beverly asked.

"How would they have gotten in?" Tasha added.

Keelen met the concern in their eyes. "I was just going ask all of you the same question."

Beverly and Tasha wore identical puzzled expressions.

Charity stared wordlessly across the table as the shock at the discovery hit her full force. *Someone is trying to kill me.* She already knew why. The big question was who. As far as she knew the only other people who had been in the room besides her were Tasha and Beverly. How else would anyone have gotten in? And then she remembered.

"My key . . ." Charity blurted, unaware that she had spoken out loud. "I lost my key."

Keelen's gaze snapped to her. "When?"

She was momentarily speechless. "Some time yesterday. I'm not sure when." She felt her first stab of real fear.

"When could someone have gotten in?" He turned to his cousin for answers.

Beverly was spooked by the possibilities. "I didn't spend the night in my cabin. Someone could have gotten in last night." She gasped. "Oh, no! When I returned this morning her things were spread all over the bed."

Charity's head whipped to her right. "You really didn't do that?"

She shook her head regretfully. "No."

They exchanged a glance. "I thought you were kidding earlier."

Tasha pushed her drink away. "This is getting scary."

"Someone is after me, too." Charity's voice was soft and distant. Keelen watched her eyes grow haunted.

"Don't say that," Beverly scowled.

"It's true."

If you don't know, you'll find out soon enough.

Her blood turned to ice. "Oh, my God!" Panic stung her. She dashed off.

Keelen hurried after Charity and grabbed her arm. Turning her toward him, he pulled her close. "Baby, it's going to be okay." A surge of protectiveness coursed through him. Right now she needed his strength.

The shock brought tears she'd been holding in. "No, it's not," she whispered, choking back a sob.

He reached out and tipped her head back. He made sure that she could see his eyes, that she found them burning with deep affection as he gazed down at her.

"I'm not going to let anything happen to you. At this moment my staff is investigating this incident. In the meantime you're going to stay by my side until we get off this ship." He looked directly at Charity, willing her to relax and believe that everything was going to be all right. An intense feeling of emotion flooded him. He took her by the shoulders and hoped that she would trust him. "We are going to enjoy the island today just like nothing happened. Tomorrow we're going to get off this ship and I'm flying back to Columbia with you."

"You are?" she asked softly, heart beating as if she had just run a mile.

"I'm not letting you out of my sight," he promised.

She cradled his waist and she felt the warmth and inhaled what had become a familiar masculine scent. She was safe in his arms.

Nestled against his wide chest, she wrapped her arms around his waist. She clung to him as if he were a life preserver tossed in an angry sea. She hung on to him for a long moment. She needed his strength. She knew it didn't change the fact that someone was trying to hurt her. But it still felt good knowing that he cared.

Keelen felt as if he had been appointed her protector. It was something like out of a whodunit movie. She was the victim, he was her protector, with the cameras running and the producer saying action. And the emotions are on until the director says cut then it's back to your dressing room for water and makeup. Only this wasn't a movie. What had happened was real and serious. Someone was trying to hurt his woman and until that person was found her life was in danger. There was no way he was going to allow anything to happen to her.

"I love you," he murmured, his mouth brushing hers.

Tilting her head, Charity saw the words clearly reflected in his gaze as she looked into the face of the man who made her feel more desirable than anyone ever had before. She smiled, her first real smile since the incident had occurred. Her gloom suddenly turned to glory. "I never guessed."

"I've loved you since the day you threw a mud ball in my face." His mouth quirked with humor. "In the past couple of days I've come to the realization that I want to spend the rest of my life with you. I know you probably think it's too soon, but a year from now my feelings will be the same."

Keelen kissed her then as if he had never kissed a woman before. When he pressed his lips to hers again, all was forgotten except the love and security. As though his words had somehow released her, she held on tight. He had appointed himself her protector and deep in her heart she believed he would protect her from whatever harm would come her way.

Fourteen

When they arrived on the island, passengers were already occupying the several dozen rows of white chaise longue chairs along the shore relaxing, reading, drinking and laughing.

Although Keelen's revelation still rang in her mind, Charity was determined to enjoy her last day without wallowing in fear. She was going to hold herself together. Besides, there were too many people around for anything to happen.

They were fortunate enough to find two unclaimed seats under a tree that provided shade from the intense summer rays.

After removing his sunglasses, Keelen slipped out of his T-shirt. Charity's admiring gaze lingered on his solid chest. It had tanned and was the color of roasted nuts. His blue swim trunks molded to his solid thighs and slim hips. Tearing her eyes away, she slipped out of her own cover-up to reveal a red two-piece tankini.

"Wow," he whistled appreciatively.

She glanced up to find his focus was feasted on everything below the neck. "Does this mean you like what you see?"

"Most definitely," he answered as he took in the way the suit fit like a second skin. The top stopped just above her belly button revealing a trim middle while the bottoms were low riders that tied on both sides of her waist.

Drawing his gaze to the softness of her eyes, he found her smiling at him. Keelen cradled her chin with his left hand and brought a kiss to her cheek. He was relieved to see the pain had faded from her eyes. He didn't want her to worry about who was after her. He would worry enough for the both of them.

They discarded a tote bag and their towels and hand-in-hand moved toward the ocean. The water beckoned her to come closer. Together they frolicked in the blue-green water like children.

They swam for almost an hour before they headed over to participate in a volleyball game on the cool white sand. They played on separate teams. When it was Charity's turn to serve, she slammed a ball over Keelen's head then squealed with laughter.

They had been playing for almost an hour when the smell of barbecue wafted in the tropical afternoon air, bringing the game quickly to an end. Keelen's team won 24-12.

"Sorry, sweetheart," he greeted her with a sheepish grin. "I'll make it up to you later." Draping an arm loosely around her waist, he pulled her close as they walked toward the picnic area together.

Charity was feeling a lot better since Keelen convinced her there was no point in letting the incident ruined her day. As long as she kept her thoughts occupied she would not have time to reflect on what had happened. Her lips curled. Keelen was doing an excellent job of occupying her thoughts. Nevertheless, she was just going to have to make sure that whoever was trying to get her didn't have a second chance.

Charity had stopped to engaged in conversation with Latoya when she looked over to find Arika flirting with Keelen. Lips curled in a sensuous smile, she was clutching his arm. She was dressed in a purple two-piece covered by cotton shorts. Leaning closer she said something that brought a smile to Keelen's face.

Amazingly, this time it didn't bother Charity. She wasn't jealous. Maybe knowing Keelen loved her made all the difference. With that in mind, Charity moved toward him with confidence. Reaching him she draped an arm around his waist and smile slyly over at Arika.

"Hello, Charity," she greeted with a stiff smile. "Keelen and I had a little unfinished business to attend to. I think I now have everything I need."

Charity looked at her. The double meaning behind her words was obvious.

"Are you talking about the interview for Channel Eight or your father investing in the cruise line?" she remarked, pleased at how nonchalant she sounded. Arika's lips drooped a fraction. "My man told me all about it," she informed her possessively.

Without another word Arika rolled her eyes and moved toward the DJ booth.

Charity chuckled.

Keelen smiled down at her. "Sorry, she wanted—"

Shaking her head, she placed a fingertip to his lips. "Sweetheart, you don't need to explain. I know where I stand with you." She leaned slightly into him, moved her mouth to his and kissed him soundly. The mere touch of his lips sent a delicious shiver through her.

When they came up for air, Keelen gazed into her eyes. "Staking your claim was definitely a turn on." Putting a large hand to her waist, he drew her form against him.

She patted him playfully on the chest. "Down, boy, plenty of time for that later."

He couldn't seem to help himself. Everything about her drew him to her.

Taking his hand, they moved to the end of the line.

There were already about fifty other people ahead of them. The rest filled up the wooden picnic benches under shelters around the area, drinking ice tea and licking barbecue sauce from their fingers.

She filled a plate with ribs and hamburgers, coleslaw and baked beans, handing it to Keelen before repeating the process for herself. Everything smelled wonderful and she couldn't wait to dive in. Returning to their seats they ate and laughed while listening to Shaggy flow from the stereo.

Passengers were snorkeling, parasailing, jet skiing and swimming in the blue-green water.

"You sure you don't want to try any of those?" Keelen suggested.

"No way," Charity declined around a bark of laughter. "I was lucky that I learned to swim."

Charity saw Tasha and Eunique over near the grill flirting with two Bahamian islanders. Latoya was sitting under a shaded tree with another. Where was Beverly? She quickly scanned the area then shrugged. Beverly had probably found her own private entertainment with Bobby Barnett.

She slipped out of her sandals. "I've already browned a shade."

"And you'll brown even more if you aren't careful. The sun is dangerous. Why don't you lie down while I apply sunscreen to your back?"

Discarding her plate onto the sand, Charity rolled over onto her stomach and closed her eyes while Keelen took a seat beside her and spread generous amounts of lotion onto her back. Her body tingled from the contact and she couldn't resist the moan that escaped her lips. Thoughts of him kissing her from head to toe the night before danced in front of her lowered eyelids. She felt so relaxed that she was tempted to drift off to sleep.

Keelen wasn't sure how long he sat there spreading lotion across her body while his loins stirred from the contact with her warm, lush body. Suddenly he wanted her all to himself and was anxious to leave the loud music and chattering for the peace and quiet on the other side of the island. Keelen suggested that they take a walk around the island together. There wasn't much to see but it did allow them time alone.

Stepping out of their shoes, they laced their fingers together. They left the hot sand to walk along the shore, close enough for the cool salty ocean to rise to their ankles. The circumference of the island couldn't have been any more than a couple of miles of lush green plant life, palm trees and sand.

Charity inhaled the thick tropical air. It was at least eighty degrees, but with none of the humidity that Missouri had.

They walked without saying much, but they were thinking quite a bit. Keelen loved her and she was bursting inside at the discovery.

"This place is beautiful," she said in awe as she took in her surroundings. There was no one else around but the two of them. She felt as if what had happened earlier had been a bad dream.

"I really hope everyone else is having a good time."

"They're having a wonderful time. I guarantee we'll still be talking about this trip at our twentieth class reunion," she reassured.

"I hope so."

Despite the several mishaps, she was pretty confident they wouldn't be a reflection on the cruise line. If it had been anyone other than Olivia or Kimora maybe people would think otherwise. She hadn't said anything earlier, but she had a strong suspicion that Arika might somehow be responsible. What she had to figure out now was how she could have managed to steal her key card and sneak into her cabin. She had access to both Olivia and Kimora's room. How she had gotten into her cabin was another story altogether.

"What are you thinking about?" he asked, pulling her out of her thoughts.

She blinked then turned to him and smiled. "Nothing, just enjoying the afternoon." She was indeed having a wonderful time. The fact that she believed Arika was responsible was at least a burden lifted off her shoulders. She would just have to watch her back. When they got back to the ship, she would share her suspicions.

"I know. Let's come back during Christmas."

"What?" she asked as if she had misunderstood what he had said.

He stopped walking and turned to her. "Christmas, let's come back during the holidays."

Smiling, Charity lowered onto the sandy shore.

He also lowered but turned in the opposite direction so that they were facing one another. "Did you not believe me when I invited you and your family to come down?"

She shook her head. "Not at first, but I do now."

"I'm not letting you out of my life this time." Their gazes locked and Charity couldn't breath. There was no mistaking the gentleness in his voice, the solemnity of the tone.

He pulled her into his lap and met her parted lips with another kiss, devouring her mouth again and again.

"I just can't seem to get enough of you."

"I'm not complaining," she murmured against his lips.

She allowed him to lead her away, leaving the sounds of laughter and the blaring music behind. He led her into a secluded area surrounded by trees.

It was at that moment she realized that she had also fallen in love. How was it possible in such a short period of time? Maybe deep down she had always loved a part of him. But it was the part that satisfied her every desire that caused a knot to form in her stomach. Without realizing it, he had filled a deep need within her.

She had fallen in love with Keelen. Helplessly and desperately in love.

Keelen slid his arm around her waist and pulled her flush against him then leaned down to kiss her and push his tongue inside her mouth. He then deepened the kiss, losing himself inside her mouth. She felt the warm, relaxed firmness of his body with the curves of her own, desire surging though her again like new blood. She could feel the gradual tightening in her breasts and the hardening of her nipples, the aching in her womb and along her inner thighs. She enjoyed the pleasure of his mouth. Shivers of arousal coursed through her breasts then moved lower to throb between her thighs.

Before he knew it his hands were on her body, cupping her round breasts through her bikini top. He bit her jaw, nuzzled her neck and kissed her throat. She could feel him grow and harden against her abdomen. Somehow they sat down on the grass and she managed to get one thigh up and over his and he helped her, smoothing a hand over her bikini bottoms and cuddling her closer, letting his fingers probe and explore and entice.

She straddled his lap and he could feel her feminine heat from the juncture of her thighs against his abdomen and it made him nearly mad with need. He wanted her naked, in this same position, riding him gently. He reached up and tweeked each breast with his fingers.

Then they heard a shout.

Keelen opened his eyes trying to orient himself and then he heard it again.

Another scream interrupted the moment, a high-pitched scream so ear shattering that it couldn't have meant anything but misery.

Keelen and Charity raced back to join the crowd on the other side of the island. Once the group was in their line of vision they noticed that a body floating face down was being pulled out of the water.

Charity moved to get a closer look and gasped. "Oh, my God! That's Arika!"

Her heart was pounding. Two crewmembers dragged her onto the dry sand. Keelen stepped forward and rolled her onto her back. Arika's eyes were closed, her skin deathly pale. He wiped the water away from her face and lowered his ear to her mouth. "She isn't breathing!"

Donovan pushed through the crowd shouting, "Get out of my way!" He rushed to crouch down beside her and felt her pulse. Nothing. Applying light compression to her chest, together he and Keelen administered CPR.

Charity was wringing her hands nervously. How in the world had this happened? Looking out of the corner of her eyes, she found Beverly and Rhonda standing behind the crowd talking. Beverly's back was to her, however when Rhonda raised her eyes to find Charity watching her, she gave her a cynical grin.

Feeling uneasy, Charity dragged her eyes away. Keelen was sitting on his legs wearing a look of defeat. Donovan rose, eyes raw with pain. Her heart sank. She had seen that same bleak expression while he was still in medical school. He had come home one evening and told her a patient of his had died.

Arika was gone.

The next several hours were a big blur. All of the guests were buzzing about the drowning. Some said it was an accident, others gossiped that it had not been an accident.

Several passengers were questioned and it was confirmed that Arika was last seen swimming alone.

Charity was confused about a lot of things, but not Arika's death. An excellent swimmer, there was no way she could have drowned. However, there were no signs of a struggle and no bruise marks around her neck. Until an autopsy was performed, her death was being ruled an accident. However, Charity knew otherwise.

Someone had killed her.

You'll find out soon enough.

Shuddering, she found the words coming to life. Would she be next?

Their last dinner was gloomier than ever. The silence at the table closed in on her. Her appetite was gone so she spent most of the meal absently drawing invisible patterns on the tablecloth.

Beverly sighed loudly, cutting the silence. "You guys, we need to get out of this funk. This is our last night and I'm not about to let Arika ruin it, neither should any of you."

"She's right," Tasha nodded her head in agreement. "If it hadn't been Arika she wouldn't have batted an eyelash."

Charity licked her lips nervously, remembering the discussion she had had with Arika only yesterday. Tasha was right. Arika chose not to heed her warning. Nevertheless, she didn't deserve to die.

"Doesn't it scare you guys to know that someone in our class could be responsible for her death?" Charity asked. She rested her chin in her trembling hand.

Bev shook her head. "Not really 'cause I never did anything that I have to worry about."

"Well, I do," she began with a tremor in her voice. "You forget, but I was once a Cutie Pie and even though I wasn't anything like Arika, I did hang around them. I stood back and watched the things that she and the others did and I never did anything to help anyone." *Well . . . maybe once or twice.*

Eunique closed a comforting hand over hers. "Girl, any-one can see you have changed. So relax."

Latoya's smile carried across the table. "She's right. You need to relax."

How could she relax when she knew if she didn't hurry up and get off the ship, she might be next?

Turning in her seat, she glanced at Keelen sitting in a corner to her right. Close enough to keep an eye on her but far enough out of ear's way. Her heart went out to him. This type of publicity could not possibly be good for the cruise line. He reassured her that it was not that big of a deal but she begged to differ. Arika's father would not rest until justice was done.

After dinner, Keelen walked Charity backed to her cabin so she could pick up a few things. She no longer felt com-fortable being without Keelen. She was going to spend her last evening in his room.

Searching for her brush, she remembered that Beverly had used it earlier. Moving into the bathroom, she rum-maged through Beverly's toiletry bag. Her hand froze when something caught her eye.

My lost key card.

What was Beverly doing with her card, she asked her-self. It didn't make any sense. When she had asked Beverly earlier, she had claimed that she knew nothing about it, yet here it was in the bag she had been in several times since this morning.

What did this mean? Could Beverly somehow be re-sponsible for all of the incidents? Her thoughts horrified her. *No, not Beverly!* It had to be a mistake. She refused to believe it. Brushing the ill thoughts aside, Charity put the card back in the bag and exited the bathroom.

Keelen read her face. "Is something wrong?" he asked, rising from the bed.

"Nothing, nothing's wrong," she lied. "I'm just still shaken up about this afternoon."

Keelen didn't believe her but he went ahead and accepted her explanation for now. He reached for her suitcase and escorted her down the hall. Back in his room, he told her to make herself at home while he disappeared in the shower.

Staring out the window, Charity watched the ship as it headed back to Orlando. By nine o'clock tomorrow morning the nightmare would be over.

She hoped she had been wrong, that everything had been a coincidence, but it wasn't the case. Someone was out to get her. Unfortunately, Arika wasn't responsible, someone else was. And could that person be Beverly? What about Tasha? She had spent more time in the cabin that she had. Charity chewed on her lower lip. Yet, how else could she explain how her key card got in her tote bag? Could it have somehow fallen in there by accident? She remembered Rhonda's warning. Could Rhonda be responsible?

Hugging her arms around her knees, Charity just didn't know who or what to believe anymore.

When Keelen finally exited the bathroom, Charity was sitting up in bed shaking uncontrollably. Pulling the covers around her, he knew her chattering teeth had very little to do with the air-conditioning.

"Thanks." She managed a weak smile.

His heart went out to her. She was confused, scared, and had every right to be. She believed her life to be in danger and he agreed.

He sat down beside her and pulled her trembling body across his lap. "Baby, listen. Nothing is going to happen to you. I promise."

"Have any of the other passengers caught wind of what is going on?"

"No," he said, touched by her concern. "They think it

was just an accident. I've beefed up security. Anything suspicious between tonight and tomorrow morning are to be investigated and reported to me immediately." He paused, meeting the fear in her eyes. "I have to stay around until Arika's parents arrive tomorrow to claim her body. I want you to wait and catch a later flight with me."

She could think of several reasons why that was not a good idea but two immediately came to mind: she couldn't imagine being on this ship any longer than she had to, and she wasn't ready yet to face the Andersons.

Deciding to use her third reason, she shook her head. "I can't. Taylor is waiting for me."

"I don't want you flying alone," he persisted, eyes clinging to hers.

She raised her hand and cupped his cheek. "Everything is going to be okay once I get back home, you'll see," she reassured him.

Did she really believe that? Keelen cradled her in his arms.

Something was going on that was targeted directly at the Cutie Pies and until he could find out who was responsible he was going to do everything in his power to protect the woman he loved.

She gazed intently at her reflection in the mirror, taking note of the fatigue in her expression, the puffiness around her eyelids and the strain around her mouth. She was tired. She wasn't certain if she still wanted to go through with things but knew she had to. Already it had been a long trip and was almost over, however, she still had some unfinished business to attend to.

"Three down, one more to go," she murmured. "Charity, it's just you and me, baby."

Revenge is so sweet.

* * *

*Keelen bolted upright in bed. Something had awak-
ened him out of his sleep. Looking beside him he realized
that Charity was no longer lying next to him. He glanced
over at the bathroom. The door was open and the light
off.*

"Charity," he called. There was no answer.

*He tossed the covers aside and rose. Moving toward the
bathroom he realized the door to the stateroom was
slightly open.*

*From the moment he stepped out into the hallway, he
sensed danger. The light was dimmed, almost cloudy. He
slowly moved down the corridor. It was quiet. Too quiet.*

*Where was everyone? All the doors to the cabins were
open. A strong smell tainted the air. The floor was wet. As
he weaved down the hall he saw something crumpled at
the end of the hall. He quickened his pace. He crouched
down to remove a sheet and there laid Charity, unmoving.
Touching her wrist he couldn't find a pulse. A dark puddle
stained the floor beneath her head.*

"No!"

"Keelen, are you all right?"

He sprung up in bed, bringing himself out of the dream.
A dream. It had only been a dream. Lying beside him was
Charity, alive and well. "I'm fine, baby. Everything is just
fine." He pulled her close to him, planting a trail of kisses
across her forehead and cheeks.

Before they fell asleep they began touching, which led
to kissing which led to him burying himself inside her. He
moved rapidly between her legs bringing them quickly to
a climax; before dawn they made love a second, then a
third time. Long past the time Charity had fallen asleep,
drained and exhausted, Keelen found himself unable to
sleep. Instead he lay awake studying her lying beside him,

as her breathing deepened. He felt a fierce surge of possessiveness as he watched her.

Smart, funny, sexy, Charity was unlike anyone he had ever known before. Despite being a victim of peer pressure and marrying a crackpot like Donovan, she'd retained an innocence that touched something so deep inside him that his hand trembled as he caressed her cheek.

The devoted bachelor wanted nothing more than to spend the rest of his life holding her close to his heart. How quickly he had grown accustomed to having her in his bed each night. He tightened his hold around Charity and vowed somehow to find a way to protect her.

Fifteen

When Charity got off the plane she felt so relieved she smiled. She was almost home. She was looking forward to a couple of days of relaxation because for some reason she was exhausted.

When she had first left for her vacation she was under the assumption that she would have gotten plenty of rest during the reunion, but it had been the complete opposite. She had had a long and draining four days both mentally and physically.

With a tote bag draped over her shoulder she moved to the baggage claim area. Flashbacks of her last few minutes with Keelen came to mind. Even though he had tried to hide it, she knew he had been furious with her.

"I don't want you traveling alone!" he bellowed.

"I'll be fine," she repeated for the umpteenth time. He had been going on and on for over an hour about a dream that he had had. "I'm not going to change my mind so you might as well quick wasting your time."

He pulled her close to him. "Why do you have to be so stubborn? I don't want anything to happen to you."

Shaking her head, she removed the memory from her mind. She didn't want to think about the incidents that had occurred. Charity was confident that now that she was off the ship everything was going to be like it had been before she had left.

Making a right turn she halted, shocked to find Donovan standing in the rental car line. She considered ignoring him but was curious as to why he was in Missouri.

She tapped him lightly on the shoulder. "Don. What are you doing here?"

He swung around and didn't appear the least bit surprised to see her. "What do you think I'm doing? I'm on my way to Columbia to pick up my daughter."

She looked at him puzzled. "But I thought you weren't coming until next week?"

"I changed my mind," he stated without offering any further explanation. "Did you drive down?"

"Yes."

"Good, then there's no point in me wasting money on a rental car. Let's go." She was abruptly caught by the elbow and escorted to the baggage carousel.

He ignored her protest as he retrieved her bags and headed out to catch a shuttle to the long-term parking lot. Donovan then took the keys from her and insisted on driving the hour-and-a-half drive to Columbia. Before she could comment, he ripped out of the parking space leaving behind the scent of burnt rubber. Charity slumped down in the seat too tired to argue.

They had been driving for almost fifteen minutes before she broke the silence. "Are you staying for Arika's funeral?"

Donovan remained silent a moment longer. He hadn't planned on staying in the deadbeat college town any longer than it took to retrieve Taylor and catch another plane to his parents'. It was truly unfortunate that Arika had died from a tragic accident. However, all he could do was send his condolences, chalk it up as a loss, and move on.

"I don't think so. My parents are expecting us," he answered without a trace of emotion.

Charity had figured as much. Arika hadn't meant any more to him than she had. Even though she and Arika had fallen off months ago, she still felt obligated to attend and show her respect.

She chewed her upper lip a moment before blurting out, "Her death wasn't an accident."

His jaw flexed but he didn't look at her. "Why do you say that?"

"Because it's too much of a coincidence." She told him about what had happened to Olivia and Kimora and the television that had barely missed her.

Donovan laughed rudely. "I've never heard anything so absurd in my life. You're letting your imagination run away from you."

In a huff, Charity crossed her arms and pointedly looked away. "Oh, I should have known better than to try and have a serious conversation with you."

"We could if what you were saying made sense, but it doesn't."

"Whatever," she murmured.

She didn't know what to believe anymore. Maybe she was being paranoid. Maybe it had all been a coincidence. She just didn't think so. *At least Keelen believes me . . . so far.* She frowned. She hadn't told him yet about the key card or her suspicions about his cousin.

The conversation ended and they were content listening to the radio for almost a half hour before Charity glanced over at the speedometer. Donovan was going almost ninety miles an hour. Looking through the windshield she watched as he whipped carelessly between two cars. "Slow down," she ordered.

He grinned arrogantly. "You forgot who taught you how to drive. Just sit back and relax."

She made sure her seat belt was tightly secured. Donovan swerved around one car and barely missed another. "Would you slow down!" she cried.

"All right," he scowled. He put his foot on the brake while

mumbling something about women drivers. He pushed on the brake again and nothing happened. He frowned and tried pressing on it a third time.

Charity did not miss the puzzled look on his face. "What's wrong?"

"Nothing's wrong with me. What's wrong with your brakes?" he asked as he swerved around another car.

"Nothing is wrong with my brakes. Why?"

"Because they aren't working." Her emergency brake wasn't working either.

"Oh, my God! What are we going to do?" Fear knotted inside of her.

Donovan cast her a quick glance then brought his gaze back to the road. Now was not the time to panic. Using both hands, he turned the wheel sharply and successfully maneuvered around a Cutlass going sixty-five miles an hour, pulling into the far left lane.

"Watch out for that Jeep!" Charity cried.

"I see it!"

She was driving him crazy. He slammed his hand down on the horn and hit it several times. The driver ignored his warning, therefore Don had no choice but to swerve into another lane, throwing her sideways in her seat. "You've got to relax," he insisted.

She swallowed hard trying to calm her nerves. "How can I relax when someone is trying to kill me?"

His nostrils flared. "Would you stop saying that!" *This is the reason why people die,* he thought as he maneuvered in and out of traffic.

Her heart was in her throat. Staring out the windshield she saw cars ahead of them in both lanes, moving about ten miles slower than her car. If he didn't do something quick they were going to crash.

"Hold on," Don instructed.

Gripping tightly on to the door handle, Charity braced

herself as he pulled onto the shoulder and into a field. Taking his foot off the pedal the car coasted and at an incline it eventually came to a halt.

Getting out, Don slammed the door so hard it rattled the glass. After catching her breath, and thanking God for deliverance, Charity also climbed out the car. Donovan was looking under the hood of the car.

"What are you doing?" Charity asked.

"I'm going to prove once and for all that nobody sabotaged this car," he snapped.

His tone infuriated her. She rolled her eyes. Donovan always had to be right. Turning away, she gazed at the cars racing by them.

"Damn!"

She jumped. "What's wrong?"

"Nothing." He didn't look at her as he climbed back in the car.

"W—what do you mean, nothing?" Charity moved around the car and climbed into the passenger's side again.

Donovan was already on the phone with AAA. She waited impatiently for him to end his call before she asked him again, spacing out her words evenly. "Donovan, what is wrong with my brakes?"

Donovan was gripping the steering wheel saying nothing.

"Don, you're scaring me!"

"All right, all right!" He slowly turned his head to look at her, his expression both weary and serious. "Someone cut your brake line." A sudden chill hung on the edge of his words.

"Oh, my God! Oh, my God!" she gasped. Leaning her head back she closed her eyes as a feeling of total shock consumed her. When she opened her eyes again, she whispered, "Now do you believe me?"

Donovan ran his hand through his hair then met the fear

in her eyes. "Yes . . . I believe you. Someone is trying to kill you."

Charity had her car towed into a Phillip 66 gas station about a mile up the highway then called Tia to pick them up. Holding her daughter in her arms helped her push aside the fear that had overcome her for the past several hours. She had to hold on to her sanity for Taylor if not for anyone else.

Once at home she sighed with relief. She missed home and its familiar surroundings. Tia had not only taken care of watering her plants and bringing in the mail, but she had even tidied up a bit.

Charity leaned back on the couch and tried to relax.

Taylor raced into the room carrying a new doll. Charity held out her arms and she landed on her lap. "Mommy, are you going with Daddy and me to Grandma Gross's house?"

She looked down into her shiny walnut eyes. "No, baby."

"But I want you to come," she pouted.

Her heart broke. She was going to be away from her daughter again. "I know, sweetheart. But you'll have so much fun. Your daddy plans to take you to the beach."

A true daddy's girl, her eyes lit up. "Ooh! Can I wear my new pink swimsuit that Aunt Tia bought me?"

Charity looked at her sister and quirked a brow that read, "you've been spoiling her again."

She hugged Taylor close. "Sure, baby." She hated that her time with her daughter had been cut short. However, when she returned in two weeks, she would make it up to her. "Why don't you run along while your daddy and I talk."

"All right." She gave each adult a kiss on the cheek before she scrambled up to her room.

Donovan cleared his throat. "Charity, I think you need to come to my parents' with me until all this blows over."

"I'm not running away," she answered stubbornly.

"Don't be silly, someone is after you." Scowling, he shifted position on the chair.

"All I care about is that Taylor is safe."

Tia's eyes shifted from one to the next. Even though Donovan wasn't one of her favorite people, she had to agree with his suggestion. But knowing Charity would never agree she had no other choice but to support her sister's decision. "Don't worry, Don, I'll take care of my little sister. Besides, Keelen will be here tomorrow."

He shot her a penetrating stare at the mention of Keelen. In fact, the realization that his wife no longer needed him hurt in a strange way. All those months he'd sat back waiting for her to come crawling back, instead, she had built another life—a better life—that no longer included him.

He rose fluidly from the chair. "I guess it's settled. I'm going to go ahead and call a shuttle to take Taylor and me back to the airport. I think the sooner we get out of here the better." With that he moved into the kitchen to use the phone.

Tia slid across the couch. Searching her face, she tried to read her sister's thoughts. "Are you sure you don't want to go?"

Charity shook her head. "I'm positive. I'm not running. It took too many years for me to gain my independence for me to run like a scared child."

"This is not the same thing and you know it."

"I'll be fine. Trust me." With that she rose and went upstairs to spend a little more time with Taylor before she left.

Tia watched her climbed the stairs, eyes wide with concern.

* * *

Immediately after the shuttle pulled out of her driveway, Charity double-checked all the doors and windows and met her sister in the kitchen.

Tia leaned across the table. "Now that Don's gone, I want to know how you really feel."

"I'm fine. Really I am."

"Well, I don't believe you. I'm not letting you out of my sight until Keelen arrives. As a matter of fact, I'm going to give Will a call."

"Oh, no, I don't need a bodyguard!" Charity protested.

"Yes, you do, you just haven't realized it yet. Mom and Dad would have a fit if they found out what was going on."

"Don't you dare tell them!"

"I won't as long as you agree to at least listen to what Will has to say."

"All right," she grumbled. Tia dashed into the other room and returned with the cordless phone. Within seconds she reached William Gray, a local police officer and Tia's former boyfriend.

Tia handed Charity the phone. She explained to him what had happened on the cruise as well as on the way back from the airport. She assured him that Donovan had already filed a report on the car then promised him that she would be careful. After she agreed to allow him to periodically drive by her house, she hung up.

"There, satisfied?"

"Nope, but it will do for now. So ease my mind a little and tell me all about Keelen."

At the gas station, she had given her sister a quick summary of her weekend while Don was giving an officer a police report.

Despite her dilemma a smile crept on her lips. "He's still Keelen, only smarter and fine as wine." She went into detail about their last couple of days together.

"Ooh, I can't wait to see him tomorrow." Tia's eyes shone with excitement.

Charity rested her elbow on the table. "I can't wait until he gets here either. I feel so safe when he is around." She was certain he was going to be angry that she hadn't bothered to call him and tell him about what had transpired today. But she didn't want to worry him. Tomorrow was soon enough.

"What's on your mind?"

While sipping her coffee she explained her suspicions. "I almost made the mistake of telling Keelen that I thought his cousin was responsible for the incidents, but there was no way she could have sabotaged my car."

"You're going to have to be careful."

She nodded. "I know." There wasn't anything the police could do without some kind of proof.

If Beverly wasn't responsible, then who was?

Sixteen

What was going on?

She leaned against the wall for support while the room doubled then tripled. For almost four years she had awaited acceptance from the in crowd. Then when she finally got an invitation to the party of the year what does she do, she gets sick. The rest of the class was having a good time while she was holding on to the wall praying that she didn't lose her stomach all over the floor.

How much had she drunk? She remembered someone greeting her at the door with one drink and then stepping into the dining room and Charity handing her another. Two, no more. After one taste of the bitter liquid she knew the punch was spiked, but she never imagined it would affect her this way.

Feeling continuously light-headed, she headed toward the back of the house, hoping to find a quiet place to sit down long enough to catch her breath. She couldn't think straight. Something definitely wasn't right.

"What's wrong?"

Ignoring her aching temples she looked up to find Charity hovering over her with a look of concern.

Hundreds of dots clouded her vision. "I—I'm not sure."

"Follow me."

Latching on to her arm, Charity led her to the suite of bedrooms at the top of the stairs.

Arika stepped out into the hall. "What's going on?" she asked.

"She's not feeling well. I'm going to call her mother."

"And have her mother find out that we've been drinking? No way! My parents will kill me. Take her in there." She pointed to the first room on the left. "You can lie in there until you feel better," Arika suggested.

The girl collapsed on the bed, too tired to dwell on the fact that for once Arika was being nice.

Arika turned to Charity. "Why don't you go back downstairs? I'll make sure she is okay."

Anxious to return downstairs to Donovan, Charity nodded and left the room.

The girl lay across the bed with her eyelids half shut when she heard someone else walk into the room.

"Did y'all give her the drink?" asked a slurred male voice.

Arika chuckled softly. "I had Charity give it to her. She should have plenty of X in her system."

Ecstasy. The voice belonged to Arika. Charity gave her Ecstasy. She tried to sit up in the bed, but failed miserably. Think girl, think, *she told herself, trying not to panic.* What did your cousin teach you? You need to be strong, fight back. *She had to find a way to get out of there and call her mother. She tried to open her eyes.*

"You can leave us alone now," she heard the male voice order.

"Uh-uh, not until you pay up!" Arika commanded.

He swore softly then she heard him rattling change in his pockets.

"Wonderful doing business with you, Sis."

She tried again to get up from the bed, but found she was too weak to move. She tried to call out but found her throat dry. She tried to lift her head to identify the voice, but any sudden movement made her head swim. She felt immobilized and wasn't sure how much longer she could hold on.

She sensed him moving beside her on the bed and within seconds she could smell the stink of liquor. She tried to move away, to scream and couldn't. She had to do something quick or he was going to rape her.

"No," *she managed to whisper.*

"I love a woman who plays hard to get."

She smelled the stink of his sour breath on her face. Her dress was being pulled up her waist and her underwear being ripped from her body. She tried to free herself of his bruising grip, but he tightened his hold.

No! She tried to scream. Don't do this! He laid his heavy body on top of her and she found herself unable to breathe.

Help!

Gasping for air, she told herself that it was only a dream, there was no way this was happening to her. But it wasn't a dream. She should have known the invitation was too good to be true.

Even though Charity hung around Arika, she wouldn't do something like this. She had come to her defense several times before. But Charity had given her a drink laced with a drug powerful enough to kill her. She was no better than the rest. In fact, this stunt put her at the top of her hate list.

I'm going to get you, Charity.

As he parted her thighs and positioned himself between them, darkness swam up to claim her.

Charity heard the doorbell chime. She noticed the clock on the wall mantel read five in the morning. With a groan she reluctantly climbed out of bed. Slipping into her house shoes she padded down the hall past Taylor's room where Tia was sleeping soundly. She reached the bottom of the steps just as the doorbell rang again. "Hold your horses," she grumbled.

She swung open the door and her heart skipped a beat. "Keelen!" He lowered his bags on the floor just as she rushed into his arms. He touched his mouth to hers and she gasped, then made a sound of pleasure deep in her throat. Her hands, secured around his back, tightened just as he deepened the kiss, touching his tongue with hers.

When he finally came up for air Keelen spoke in a voice that combined affection with concern. "Are you okay?"

Staring into his eyes, she nodded. "I'm fine now that you are here. How did you know?"

"Don contacted me."

"Don?" she gaped.

With a smile he nodded. "Believe me, I was just as surprised. Somehow he tracked down my cell phone number. After he told me about your brakes being tampered with he told me if I truly loved you I'd get here as fast as I could." He hugged her closely again as if to assure her that now that he had arrived everything was going to be all right.

Unbelievable. It was hard to believe that Donovan had cared enough about her to put his pride aside. For once he was behaving like a man. She couldn't believe it.

For a long moment he rocked her gently in the circle of his arms. Never before had any man shown her such concern, never had she felt so safe and protected. She threw her head back and their eyes melted. She noticed the dark circles around his eyes. Just as she had expected, he had hopped on the first available plane.

Removing her arms she led him into the house and shut the door.

Keelen chuckled lightly. "Wow! This place definitely brings back memories." His eyes wandered around the living room. Besides the contemporary furnishings the house still looked the same as when they were kids. Gleaming hardwood floors with matching crown molding, and spacious rooms with nine-foot ceilings. Charity had added her own personality by adding a mauve area rug and floral couch with matching love seat.

Dropping his bags at the bottom of the stairs, Keelen bent and lifted her effortlessly in his arms and carried her up to the shower.

With the hot water beating on their bodies, Keelen backed her into a corner and parted her thighs with his knee. As he moved between her legs she could feel him hard and pulsating against her stomach. Her body was screaming, already addicted to his touch.

He reached up, capturing a nipple between his thumb and forefinger, tweaking it gently until it turned pebble-hard.

Charity was easily aroused and moaned with pleasure.

"What's the matter?" he whispered against her nose while capturing her other breast in his hand.

"N—nothing. That feels sooo good," she whimpered.

He smiled, pleased at the effect he had over her. "Let me make you feel better," he suggested, grabbing a foil packet.

She nodded as pleasure stirred through her body.

He slid one hand down and touched her; she was wet and ready for him. Placing his hands around her waist, he lifted her slightly for better access. Shifting his weight slightly, he entered her.

Burying her head in the hollow space between his neck and shoulder, she moaned.

"I can't get enough of you," he whispered, feeling her warmth surrounding him.

A wild jolt surged through him as he felt her tighten around his shaft. He cupped her bottom and brought her even closer, sliding even deeper inside of her. After brushing a kiss over her mouth, he arched his back and drove harder and harder.

For the next couple of days things began to feel like they were getting back to normal. They visited his parents who were both glad to see that the two of them had finally gotten together. Keelen even helped her bake cookies for the bookstore. Charity could tell that Tia was quite impressed with him.

Her days and nights were spent in the company of a man who made her laugh one minute and cry out in ecstasy the next. He taught her things in bed that made her feel like the most desirable woman on the face of the earth and when his tenderness extended beyond the boundaries of her bedroom she found herself thanking her Father from heaven above for returning him to her life.

Every day Keelen made a point of making her feel special. He made it a point to prepare her breakfast in bed and tried to duplicate the frozen drinks from the cruise. Each considerate gesture meant more to her than she could put into words.

When they weren't in bed making love, they spent time talking about their hopes and dreams and a future that included each other.

On Thursday, the two attended Arika's funeral.

As Charity had expected, Second Baptist Church was standing-room only. It came as no surprise. Arika had been a well-known person in the community. The service was moving and Charity felt an acute sense of loss, especially when her brother gave a eulogy that showed the good in his sister. Her vision clouded with faint memories as she rested her head on Keelen's shoulder while she listened.

After the service Charity decided against going to the cemetery. She couldn't take any more. Her fears were beginning to resurface and she was anxious to return to the safety of her home as quickly as possible.

Walking out to Keelen's rental car, she heard someone calling her name. She turned around to find Olivia and Kimora moving her way.

"Hi," Charity said.

To her surprise they each hugged her, showing their first true signs of affection for one another. There was then an awkward moment of silence as there always was when death was in the air.

Keelen threw a quick glance and smiled at both women then squeezed Charity's hand.

"I'm going to give the three of you a few minutes alone. I'll be waiting for you at the car." He said good-bye to the two then departed.

Pointing her cast toward the church, Olivia said with despair, "I never imagined it would come to this."

"I know," Charity answered in a troubled voice. "Someone cut my brake line and I almost had an accident."

"Oh, no!" Kimora exclaimed. "I was almost stung by a swarm of bees."

Charity's eyes grew large. Everyone knew Kimora was allergic to bee stings. She had always carried a kit in her purse.

She fingered her new short tapered cut nervously. "Someone put them in my car. I didn't realize it until I was driving through an intersection. Luckily, I got out in time."

"I think it is time we go to the police," Olivia suggested. No other attempts had been made on her life but she wasn't taking any chances. She had been sober for almost three days.

The other two agreed.

Keelen drove them downtown. After they gave their statements, the three embraced again, promising to stay in touch, and parted their separate ways.

Charity and Keelen returned to her house. Despair was thick, uncertainty had returned.

At his insistence, Charity agreed to relax while he prepared dinner. Keelen ran her a hot bubble bath and helped her undress. Once she was in the tub, he brought a CD player into the bathroom and stuck in her favorite nature sounds. After giving her strict instructions not to move for thirty minutes, he raced down to start the grill.

Keelen removed two steaks from the refrigerator that he

had allowed to marinate all night and moved out on the patio to light the grill.

He was chopping vegetables for a salad when Charity came down the stairs in a nightshirt. She looked much more relaxed. Although she was smiling, the sparkle still had not returned to her eyes. "How do you feel?" he asked.

"Wonderful. Thank you." She leaned over and kissed his cheek. "Need some help?"

"Why don't you try setting the table while I get the steaks off."

Dinner was quiet. Neither said much. Together they cleared off the table and washed the dishes. By eight, Charity was ready to call it a night and the two of them went off to bed.

Keelen took her hand and led her up the stairs. "Go ahead and lie down, sweetheart."

"Why, what are you about to do?"

He chuckled lightly. "Why don't you lie down and see?"

Curiously she obeyed and lay back with two pillows comfortably behind her head. Keelen took a seat beside her and reached for her left foot.

She flinched. "Hey, I'm ticklish."

"I'm not going to tickle you. So just relax."

He took her foot again and began kneading it softly. From the soles of her feet, he massaged his way along her ankles to her calves. The kind act brought tears to Charity's eyes. No one had ever done anything like that before.

Keelen continued to smooth away the stress, pausing to nibble whenever he felt the need. When he finally reached her thighs, Charity was moaning.

"Roll over onto your stomach and I will be right back."

She did as he instructed. She wasn't sure how long she had lain there before he returned. He moved to sit beside her again and raised her gown over her head.

Within minutes Charity felt him pour hot oil on her back.

He began kneading her neck and back and before long she was moaning again.

"You feel better?"

"I'd feel even better if you'd make love to me."

Her bold declaration caused heat to travel up his legs and settle in his loins. "Sweetheart, that's not why I gave you a massage. I wasn't trying to seduce you."

She rolled over and stared at him intensely. "Are you denying me? I thought you wanted to make me feel good?"

"You don't have to ask me twice." Her response told him all he needed to know. He smiled then removed his clothes and, after grabbing a condom, joined her on the bed.

Within mere seconds he slid into her, filling her with him. His hands grabbed her hips and he shoved harder, deeper into the core of her.

"Ah," she whimpered, her teeth clenched as turbulent pleasure filled her. She wrapped her long legs around his waist, hooking their bodies together. She was lost in the flames of erotic passion. She welcomed the power of his thrusts, meeting each one halfway. Unable to hold on any longer she screamed out release. Seconds later, her cry was quickly followed by his, and he collapsed beside her. Their heavy breathing filled the room.

"Hold me tight," she urged, fearing that if she closed her eyes, Keelen would disappear.

Keelen held her comfortably in his embrace and drifted off to sleep.

Around ten, the phone rang.

Sliding from under his arm, Charity reached over to the nightstand and removed the receiver. "Hello?"

"Charity, this is Tasha."

"Hey, girl," she said in a groggy voice.

"I didn't mean to wake you. I was calling to find out how the funeral went."

"Like all funerals, sad." Charity then told her about the

conversation she had had with Kimora and Olivia, and the close call with her brakes.

Tasha gasped. "Oh, my God! Are you okay?"

"I'm fine. Keelen is here with me," she reassured her.

She breathed a sigh of relief. "Good. Nevertheless, Beverly and I are coming down tomorrow to see you."

"Beverly?" She sat up in the bed suddenly wide awake. "What's she doing in Kansas City?"

"She's been here since Tuesday. She isn't teaching summer school so she decided to come and hang out. We're going to spend the weekend with her parents, but we're going to come and see you first. It sounds like you could use the support. Anyway, hang in there. We'll see you tomorrow."

Charity struggled to keep her hands from tightening around the phone. "I'll see you then."

She was silent long after they hung up. It couldn't be possible. Beverly couldn't be involved. Yet the signs were there again. Whenever there was an accident, Beverly was nearby. When Olivia fell, Beverly was out of the room. When Kimora's head was shaved, she was out of the room and when Arika drowned, Beverly was nowhere around. Was it a coincidence? She would have arrived in Kansas City on the exact day of Kimora's accident. Did that mean that she flew through St. Louis first, long enough to tamper with her car? She swallowed a large lump in her throat. Now she was coming to Columbia to see her. She wasn't quite convinced that was a good idea.

Maybe it's better to have your enemies where you can see them.

Charity was nervous and instead of sleeping, she pondered the questions long through the night and somehow managed to wait until breakfast to share her suspicions with Keelen. "Beverly's in Kansas City," she said while pouring a glass of orange juice.

He looked up from his pancakes, eyes sparkling. "That's great. Is she planning to come to Columbia?"

She nodded. "She'll be down today."

"Good, my parents will be glad to see her. Speaking of parents, they are having a barbecue tomorrow. Apparently my brother is flying down for a visit. He intended to surprise them, but at the last minute decided it would be better to tell them he was on his way. I guess I'll tell them Bev will be there too."

Charity lowered her fork and laced her fingers together. "Keelen, I want to talk to you about something that is bothering me."

The quiver in her voice drew his undivided attention. "Baby, you can talk to me about anything. What is it?"

She hesitated. "I think Beverly might be involved."

"Involved in what?"

There was a long pause. "The incidents during the cruise."

"What?" He stopped chewing.

She took a deep breath, pulling her thoughts together and explained to him her suspicions.

Keelen gave a throaty chuckle. "You've got to be kidding?"

His laughter infuriated her. "No, I'm not. Look at all the signs."

"Sweetheart, it's just a coincidence, nothing else. My cousin is not a killer."

"Then explain why she had my room key?"

He shrugged. "Maybe you dropped it in her bag."

"I can't believe you. I'm trying to talk to you and you think this is one big joke!" she exclaimed irritably as she rose to her feet.

"No, I think that this is a bunch of nonsense. Beverly is not a murderer. What reason would she have to hurt any of you?"

She carried her dishes over to the sink. "The same reason as half our graduating class—revenge."

Keelen pushed his plate away. "You can't be serious?"

Her brown eyes met his in an open challenge. "Maybe I'm wrong, but what if I'm right?"

"I don't believe it." His voice held a warning to let it drop.

"Then you couldn't possibly believe in us. Donovan didn't either."

Keelen gritted his teeth and drew in a deep breath before answering, "This doesn't have anything to do with him."

"No, but it has everything to do with us," she whispered brokenly. She couldn't believe that Keelen was not willing to see the possibility. If anybody was open-minded she thought it would at least have been him. "Why don't you go to your parents so I can have some time alone to think."

She saw the muscles around his jaw harden. "I'm not leaving you by yourself."

"Then I'll call Tia to come over."

He lifted his chin and held a calm level gaze with her. "When she arrives, I'll leave."

Charity was so mad that she left the kitchen, went up to her room and locked the door. Leaning against the door, she briefly closed her mind of all the events of the past week. She needed desperately to think, to gather all the information and put together some possibilities.

Maybe Keelen was right, maybe she was jumping to conclusions. Beverly didn't have any reason to want her dead. Maybe it was just as he said, a coincidence.

Charity took a seat on her bed and sighed. This entire situation had her so upset she couldn't think straight. Maybe she needed to think through all the possibilities again. After all, she couldn't remember if she had even told Beverly what kind of car she drove.

She lowered her face in her hands. Oh, she didn't want to think right now. She was thankful that Donovan had taken Taylor with him until she was certain.

Seventeen

Charity was just pulling out her last batch of cookies when she heard the doorbell ring. Wiping her hands on an old red apron before removing it, she laid it on the kitchen counter then went into the living room to answer it.

"Hey, girl," Tasha grinned.

"You made it." They embraced in a hug.

Beverly also moved to her. After a friendly embrace she frowned. "Tasha told me what happened. I'm so glad you're okay."

Seeing her again Charity thought to herself there was no way Bev could be responsible for something so terrible. She just wished she could be sure. Shrugging off the thought she decided to watch her just the same.

"Come in and make yourselves at home."

Tasha moved over to the fireplace where a dozen or more photos of Taylor were on the mantel. "Where is that darling little girl of yours?"

She couldn't resist a smile. "She's visiting her grand-parents."

"That's too bad. I was hoping to see her."

"What's that smell?" Beverly inquired.

"I just pulled the last batch of cookies out of the oven. Come on back." She signaled for the two to follow her into the kitchen.

Tasha sniffed. "Mmm, it sure smells good."

"Have a seat at the table." Charity reached for a spatula and brought a plate to the table.

"Wow!" Tasha said when she saw the gourmet-style cookies with big chunks of chocolate chips. "This looks wonderful."

Taking a seat at the table, Charity smiled proudly. "I'm entering them in a cook-off next month. Try one and tell me what you think."

Beverly took a bite. "Oh, my goodness! These are wonderful."

Tasha agreed. "Mmm, I have never tasted anything so good."

Beverly crossed her legs and laughed. "Girlfriend, you definitely have got talent."

Keelen slipped on his shoes and headed for the stairs.

Charity hadn't spoken to him once since their disagreement that morning. After finding out Tia was tied up at the store, she agreed to let him stay until Tasha arrived. However, she informed him that once the women arrived she no longer needed his protection.

He was willing to give her a couple of hours, nothing more. However, he had one thing to check out first before he could comply.

Keelen moved into the kitchen, walked over to his cousin and kissed her lightly on the cheek.

"Hey, Keelen," Tasha managed around a chocolate morsel.

He smiled at each. "I see you two have already found the cookies."

"They are wonderful!" Tasha exclaimed.

He nodded. "I've already eaten a couple dozen myself." He dropped a hand to Beverly's shoulder. "Can I speak to you privately for a minute?"

"Sure."

Frowning, Charity looked up at him searching for his thoughts, communicating with his eyes. She pressed her lips together grimly. She knew what they were going to talk about.

Beverly followed him into the living room and outside onto the covered porch.

"What's up, Kee?" she asked after taking a seat on the swing beside him and noticing the blank expression on his face.

"I'm still trying to piece together what happened last week."

Pushing her feet, she rocked them slightly back and forth. "I wish I could help you, but I don't know. I was snorkeling."

The look on his face was intense and thoughtful. "I was told you were seen not too far from where Arika's body was found," he commented quietly, not taking his eyes off his cousin's adorable face.

She looked at him for a long moment as if she was trying to make sense of his statement. A stunned look altered her expression. "What are you asking me?" Keelen could hear the defensive tone in her voice.

"Enchanted stands to lose a great deal behind this if . . ." He purposely allowed his voice to trail off. Keelen held her gaze with a questioning glint in his gray eyes.

Beverly's gaze didn't waver. "Like I'd said before, I was already out of the water flirting with some islander."

His eyes clung to her, analyzing her reaction before he finally sighed with relief and covered her hand with his. He had known all along she was telling the truth. "I know. I just needed to hear it again. I know how much you despised Arika."

"I didn't care that much for Charity either, but that hasn't stopped me from being her friend again."

Keelen simply nodded.

Beverly patted his hand. "Sorry, Cuz. I didn't kill her."

"I know you didn't," he smirked, clasping their fingers together.

"I didn't like her any more than the next person. I even wished her dead a couple of times, but I would never have killed her."

"Thanks. I needed to hear that."

There was a prolonged pause. "Does Charity think I did it?"

He looked over at her questioning expression and lied. "No, no, she doesn't."

He saw the look of relief on her face and was glad that he had lied. He didn't want to hurt her feelings.

"Well, if there isn't anything else, I'm going back in for another cookie."

She rose but he held on to her hand. "Can you do me a favor?" he asked.

Beverly nodded her head, smiling. "Sure, Cuz, anything."

"Keep a close eye on Charity."

She could see his gray eyes were filled with raw emotion. "You love her don't you?"

"With all my heart."

Keelen finally left Charity's house after the two assured him they would keep an eye on her. He arrived at his parents' house in time to find his mother putting the finishing touches on a potato salad.

"Hi, Mom."

Kathleen Brooks turned around at the sound of her son's voice. She hadn't heard him come through the front door.

"You're early," she commented as she smiled brilliantly at him.

He moved to her and planted a kiss to her wrinkle-free cheek.

"I thought I'd see if you needed anything."

Keelen looked down at his mother, dressed in khaki slacks and a white blouse protected by a large apron. She carried her age well and didn't look a day over fifty. She definitely didn't look like a woman with three grown children and two grandchildren.

"I think I have everything I need, but I'm sure your father could use some help with the grill."

He gave her a knowing smile before strolling toward the door. Opening French doors he moved out onto the deck where smoke was leaking around the edge of a barbecue grill. From several feet away, Keelen observed his father, Terrance Brooks, as he slipped an oven mitt over one hand then opened the lid and began attacking a couple of thick steaks with a pair of long-handled tongs.

"Daddy, why don't you let me do that for you," Keelen offered.

"Son, I don't need any help. It just takes me a little longer than usual." At that exact moment he removed two juicy steaks from the grill and onto a large platter. Setting it down on a round patio table he stabbed a slab of ribs and layered the grill. With a hand planted on his hip, he beamed triumphantly over at his son. "See, didn't I tell you? Your old man still has the touch."

Keelen smiled as he stared up at an older version of himself. He had inherited his father's pecan complexion and body type. Evidence of the handsome man that he had been as a young man was still quite evident. Traces of gray in Keelen's own sandy brown hair were a clear indication that his own head would someday resemble his father's silver top.

"What's on your mind?" his father asked, breaking into his thoughts.

Keelen dropped his eyes before his father's keenly observant gaze and reached up to adjust a sturdy green umbrella at the center of the table that shot out like a flower in full bloom. "Nothing is on my mind, Dad. Why do you ask?"

His father squinted against the sunlight and said pointedly, "I've known you long enough to know when something is bothering you, son."

As Keelen sat in a patio chair, he raised his eyes to find his father still watching him. He chuckled despite himself. He never had been able to get anything past his ole' man.

Laugh lines crinkled around Terrance's eyes as he added, "This by chance doesn't have anything to do with Charity does it?" Keelen didn't even have to answer—a revealing scowl gave him away.

He took a long deep breath of the scent of fresh-cut grass while Charity's beautiful face flashed through his mind. "Yeah, I'm having a little problem." He stared out at the grill trying to decide just how much he should tell his father. He didn't want to do anything to trigger another stroke. However, they had always been completely open in the past. Besides, the *where* and *how* of Arika's death were already public knowledge.

Leaning forward in his chair, he went into detail as he told his father about what had transpired during the reunion all the way to the close call Charity had had on the way back from the airport. "She doesn't want my help," he finally said.

His father, who had taken a seat across from him at the patio table, scratched his bearded chin. "It seems to me you need to show her who's boss."

Falling back against the chair Keelen roared with laughter. "You have forgotten who we are talking about."

"I know Charity can be a little feisty, but right now she doesn't have much of a choice. If you think her life is in any danger and the police can't do anything to protect her then you have no choice but to make her see reason."

His eyes traveled to his father's close-cropped gray hair to his broad nose then down to the wrinkles that were pronounced around his mouth. The frown on his face deepened. He remained silent while he thought about what his dad had said.

Terrance was speaking from experience. As far back as Keelen could remember his parents had always had a good relationship. But there had been times when he remembered hearing his father mumbling, "She's as stubborn as a mule."

"What do you suggest that I do?" Keelen asked as if desperate for his opinion.

Terrance smiled and deliberately watched his son's reaction when he suggested, "A kiss would be a good start. Then lock her in the room and show her how much you love her."

Keelen raised an eyebrow as he glanced over at his father with absolute surprise on his face. He wasn't sure if he was serious or joking.

"You still love her don't you?" he asked, smiling across at him.

Keelen narrowed his eyes at him. "How did you . . ." his voice trailed off with the words.

Now it was his father's turn to laugh with a deep rumble that caused his protruding tummy to jiggle. "A father always knows." His son might be trying to say one thing, but his heart was definitely saying something else. He had seen the wistful look in his eyes. Terrance shook his head, grinning, remembering the day the two first met. Back then Charity had made a permanent impact on his son and that was something that just didn't go away.

Terrance winked then rose and headed into the kitchen carrying the platter of meat.

After he left Keelen decided to take a stroll around the yard while he tried to figure out what he needed to do.

He followed the brick red path that led him in the direction of his mother's rose garden until he reached an iron archway. Lowering onto a bench, he released a heavy sigh. He should have known that love wouldn't come easy. He smirked. Charity was definitely something else. Nonetheless she had a stubborn streak that would be a force to reckon with.

Keelen took a deep mind-clearing breath. He had never been one to chase a woman. But that was not the way to think of it. Anything good was worth fighting for.

After Kathleen Brooks called to make sure that she was planning to attend the barbecue, Charity didn't have much choice but to show up. The three rode over in Tasha's BMW.

The Brooks had a stunning white Victorian-style house located south of town. When they arrived the driveway was already lined with cars.

Tasha pulled in front and turned off the engine of her cream-colored car. "We're here." She lowered her visor and took a quick moment to fix her makeup.

"I didn't know it was supposed to be such a large turnout," Charity mumbled as she climbed out of the car.

Beverly met her surprised expression and shrugged matter-of-factly. "Everything my aunt Kathleen does is a big deal. Girl, did Keelen tell you Tristian is home?"

Charity's gaze narrowed at the mention of Keelen's name. "Yes, he told me this morning." Swinging her purse over her shoulder, she retrieved the batch of cookies she had baked that morning from the backseat, while Beverly removed a case of orange soda.

Tasha climbed out of the car and moved beside her. "What does he look like?"

Charity slammed the door shut and strode up the driveway along with the others as she tried to recall the image of Tristian Brooks. "I haven't seen him in years but he was definitely a cutie when he was little."

Beverly clucked her tongue again her teeth. "My little cousin is just as fine as his brother."

Tasha's eyes shone with excitement. "If he looks anything like his brother, I am looking forward to an interesting afternoon."

Keelen's rental car was already in the driveway. Charity took a deep breath to calm her nerves. It was inevitable that they talk about what had happened. She just wasn't sure if she was ready to discuss it, especially not around his family and friends.

Together they climbed a charming wraparound porch then moved through a stately wooden door surrounded by leaded glass windows.

Kathleen greeted them in a grand entry hall that was reminiscent of days gone by.

After embracing each of them she turned back to Charity with her eyes crinkling in a friendly smile. She admired the woman she had become. She remembered when she'd first met her, she was a little tomboy and as feisty as they came.

She looked down at the brown bag in her hands. "What do we have here?"

"These are for you." Charity handed the bag to her hostess. "They're just some cookies I baked this morning."

Kathleen leaned in to sniff its contents. "I've heard the rave reviews. I can't wait to sink my teeth into them."

She directed the three through the house where there were a lot of familiar faces. The large deck was also flooded with friends and family. While Beverly and Tasha went in search of Tristian, Charity returned to the front of the house. She moved past a pair of gleaming oak pillars that graced the entrance to an impressive formal living room. Oak hardwood floors and ceilings over nine feet high graced the room. She found Kay sitting under a huge bay window on a cushioned window seat changing one of the twins' diaper.

"Hey, girl," she greeted.

Kay glanced over at her with a wide friendly smile that lit up her features.

She had inherited her father's sandy brown hair and gray eyes, while she was short and petite with a rich mahogany color like her mother. She had once worn her hair in a short blunt cut that she had since grown to shoulder length. She had pulled her hair back with a yellow ribbon to match her tunic outfit. Her face was rounder. She had gained several pounds during her pregnancy that she had yet to lose. However, the radiant smile proved she was happier than ever.

"Congratulations."

"Come on over and meet Italy. Asia is somewhere outside with her daddy." She didn't miss the look of surprise on Charity's face. She gave her a knowing smile. "Don't ask. My husband just retired from the army and those are the names of two of his favorite places."

Kay fastened the disposable diaper then placed Italy into her arms.

"She's beautiful." They were nearly six months old now and she smiled down at Italy when she smiled up at her. She loved the way babies smelled like baby powder. Taylor had been a lovely baby, however Kay's daughter was gorgeous. She had the same complexion as her uncle with big brown eyes. Would Keelen's child look like the twins? she found herself wondering as she stared down at her chubby face.

"She gets pretty heavy," Kay said, breaking into her thoughts.

Charity looked up to find her smiling down at her baby girl. "I don't mind."

While holding the baby she looked up to find Keelen staring across the room at her. She tried to ignore him, but found that she could not.

"I hear you and my brother are an item," Kay probed. She had always hoped something had finally transpired between the two. From as far back as she could remember Keelen had always had a thing for Charity. She was determined to get her brother married once and for all.

"We are seeing each other," she answered faintly. "However, he hadn't told me how beautiful his niece was. She's going to be a heartbreaker," she said, smoothly changing the direction of their conversation. Taking a deep breath she allowed herself to look across the room. Keelen stood near a large window where the sunlight beamed brilliantly against his smooth brown skin. Dressed in a pair of denim shorts and a Mizzou Tigers T-shirt he looked like a true Columbian. Keelen must have felt her intense gaze, for he turned and looked straight at her.

Charity felt the blood rush through her veins. The desire she felt for him was stronger than before. She missed him. Even though it had only been a couple of hours since he had left her house, she missed him still. Somehow she found the strength to break eye contact.

She gave the baby a kiss on her soft cheek then handed her back to her mother.

Charity went into the kitchen to get something cold from the cooler and had no idea Keelen had followed her. She didn't see him standing in the corner of the room.

As he had watched her stroll into the kitchen, his gray eyes darkened with emotion. She was ignoring him. He took in the khaki walking shorts and white blouse. Even though the outfit was simple, it caused emotions to stir.

"Are you going to try and ignore me all afternoon?"

At the sound of his voice she shuddered but didn't bother to look his way. Charity had hoped to escape his inquisitive questions. She still needed time to think. But Keelen obviously had other ideas.

Looking down at the counter she popped the cap on an

orange soda before responding. "I'm not ignoring you," she said at last, bringing her gaze to his. She found Keelen was standing in the doorway with his arms folded across his chest.

"Then what would you call it?"

Dropping his arms to his sides, he strode forward until their bodies were touching. The contact caused her to quiver while his masculine scent made her want to moan.

"I just need a little time to think."

He turned her around and backed her against the counter. He gazed down at her with a single brow raised in challenge. "To think about what?"

Her heart was beating much too fast. "What do you think? About what's going on. I have no idea who is trying to hurt me and right now more than anything I need the support of someone who believes in me."

Hurt registered in his eyes. "I believe in you. I just think you're wrong about my cousin."

Her spine stiffened. "Maybe you're right, but I need to be safe not sorry."

"I thought you felt safe with me."

"I—I do."

"Then what's the problem?"

She nibbled on her lip. It annoyed her that her breasts had tightened and her nipples hardened. She couldn't think when he was next to her. Since her divorce she'd tried her best not to rely on anyone. As far as she was concerned, she was not about to start now.

Keelen took in her upturned face. Her hair pulled away from her face, the shadows of worry beneath her eyes. It would be so easy to tell her everything was going to be all right but unless she wanted his help, his words had no meaning. "Charity, I love you. All I want to do is to protect you and make sure no harm comes to you. Why can't you just for once let me handle this for you?"

"Because the last time I put my trust in a man, he disappointed me," she answered truthfully.

"I'm not Donovan."

"True, but you are still a man."

Keelen tried to keep his anger at bay. "What's that supposed to mean?"

"It means I will never lose sight of who I am ever again," she retorted.

"What does that have to do with me protecting you?"

"I don't need protection. If someone is after me then they are going to have one hell of a fight on their hands."

"Are you really willing to take that chance?"

She did not respond right away. Keelen stared incredulously at her. He couldn't believe that she was willing to take such a chance with her own life. Studying the firm set of her mouth he knew she wasn't willing to listen to reason. The frustration of the last several days ruffled his patience. He didn't need this and neither did she. She was going to listen and accept his help whether she wanted it or not.

Keelen stepped closer, his arms braced on either side, trapping her against the counter. "I can't let you do that. I love you too much to take that chance."

"Then why can't you consider the possibility?" Her gaze locked with his, challenging him.

"If you tell me deep down in your heart that you truly believe she is responsible then I will explore the possibility further."

She stared up at him, shocked by his words. Would he really take her side over his own flesh and blood? His declaration touched her in more ways than he would ever know.

He was staring down at her with his beautiful eyes shining with love and it made her insides melt. All she needed was one kiss to satisfy her. Keelen must have read her mind for he dipped and she met him halfway. Thrusting his hands through her hair he pulled her closer to him and lost himself in her mouth. His lips were urgent, demanding as if he was trying to teach her a lesson that she was more than willing to learn.

A breathy shudder eased from her chest then the kiss ended just as quickly as it had begun. Before she could respond, the sliding glass door opened and she gasped at the man in front of her.

Tristian Brooks had grown more handsome with age. He had the same complexion as his brother, however he had large brown eyes and a firm mouth. He was sporting a standard military cut.

Boy, the Brooks brothers were handsome, she thought. Even though his brother's eyes were darker and his face squared, they both bore a resemblance.

Keelen released her and stepped toward his brother, wearing an affectionate grin. "I guess I can't call you little anymore." He reached for Tristian and patted him firmly on the back. "It's about time you got here," he said as they parted.

Tristian's eyes narrowed slightly. "My plane was delayed. I had no idea Mom was planning a big party for little ole' me."

"I asked her what the big fuss was but she wanted to do it anyway," Keelen joked.

"Who is this lovely woman I saw you kiss . . .?" His voice trailed off with recognition. "Charity, is that you?"

"Hi, Tristian." She moved forward and gave him a friendly hug. He kissed her noisily on the cheek.

"Well, I'll be damned." He whistled as soon as the two pulled apart. An intriguing smile curled his lips under his mustache. "Well you finally decided to give my ugly brother a chance. I don't know if I should thank you or take your temperature." He chuckled at his own joke while Keelen pretended to deck him in the shoulder.

Charity didn't know how to answer him so instead she giggled along with the two.

They had a wonderful afternoon with his parents. Keelen never got a chance to resume his conversation with Charity but he did make sure that she was always close by. When Tristian asked him to go out for a drink with the boys he was reluctant. He didn't want to leave Charity. They had spent the evening surrounded by others when all he really wanted was to have her for himself. He felt like he was being selfish and overly protective and when Beverly insisted that the two of them go out while she and Tasha took Charity to a club, he had no choice but to agree even though he had a strong suspicion that letting Charity out of his sight was not a good idea.

The three went back to the house to change into jeans then drove the short distance downtown to Lou's Lounge.

"I haven't been here in years," Tasha said as they climbed out of her car.

"Neither have I," Charity agreed.

Beverly looked around at the crowd hanging out in the parking lot. "When I last came here, Lou's was still located in the basement of Tony's Pizza."

Lou's Lounge was nothing more than a juke joint. It was a place where local black folks could go to catch up on gossip and be themselves. No frills.

They moved to the door where they paid their admission fee. After having being patted down by security they were finally allowed to enter where they were met by a cloud of smoke.

Charity coughed. "I see much hasn't changed."

Beverly laughed in agreement.

Moving into the room, she saw people that hadn't been around for years. Lou was behind the counter fixing drinks. Ballers were in the back playing pool and three fat girls were on the dance floor moving to the tunes of Nelly blaring from the speakers. Although ghetto, Lou's was definitely mixing the old with the new.

They took a seat at a table close to the dance floor.

Tasha smiled. "Girl, I feel right at home."

Charity raised her elbows to the table. "How else can you feel around your own people?"

She looked around and waved at several people. Columbia was so small that unless you were a college student, the entire black community knew one another.

"Anybody want a drink?" Beverly asked.

"Sure, get me a margarita," Tasha said.

Charity smiled, feeling some of the tension that had gripped her for the past week starting to ease. "I'll take a rum and Coke."

"Coming right up." Beverly moved to the crowded bar where she was met by several familiar faces.

"I can't believe I haven't been here," Charity said. "It's funny. I've been in this town almost six months and half of these faces I haven't even seen."

Tasha clicked her tongue. "Girl, you know in the summertime black folks only come out at night."

The two were still cracking up when Charity felt someone tap her on the shoulder. She turned to see Craig Crawford. He used to tutor her in English and had saved her from failing. She rose and hugged him. "How have you been?" she asked.

"Good, and yourself?" he said.

"Fine. How come you weren't at the reunion?"

"I just got a new job at the University and couldn't take off. I've got two kids now so I got to make that paper."

She nodded with understanding.

"Care to dance?"

"Sure." She allowed him to lead her onto the floor.

They danced two sets before she declined a third. When Charity finally returned to her seat she found Beverly talking with Rhonda. *She still lives here, too?*

"Hey, Rhonda," she greeted politely.

"Hello, Charity," she mumbled although her expression clearly registered her dislike. She mumbled something to Beverly then turned to leave.

Charity frowned as she lowered in her chair. "She didn't have to leave on my account."

Beverly shrugged, sipping on her drink. "She's here with someone."

"Hmm." Charity didn't buy it but left it alone. She reached for the drink in front of her and took a sip then choked. "Good God!"

Beverly chuckled. "Girl, you know Lou makes hellafide drinks."

She coughed again then smiled. "Some things never change."

While rap music blasted from the DJ stand Charity found herself wondering if maybe she really had been wrong about Beverly and perhaps Rhonda could be involved in Arika's death.

By the time Tasha had returned to the table, Charity excused herself and went to the pay phone at the back of the club to give Keelen a call.

Keelen was being pulled down the sidewalk by his long-time pet, Champion. Turning the corner the golden Labrador barked at a man crossing the street.

"Be quiet, boy." Obedience school had done him a world of good, but the dog still liked to control the neighborhood.

He, Tristian, and a couple of the fellas had dropped by Tropical Liquors for a round of frozen Silver Bullets and a few quick games of pool. On the way back they rode past

Lou's where he found Tasha's car in the parking lot. He was tempted to go in but he didn't want Charity to think he was following her so he had declined. He felt pretty comfortable that nothing would happen to her in a public place. As soon as they returned he was going back to her house even if it meant sleeping on the couch.

It felt good being home, he thought as he passed through campus. Summer-school students were still on the court playing a game of basketball. The rest were running around the quarter-mile track. Keelen moved to a light jog with Champion trotting beside him.

He couldn't blame Charity for being paranoid. Hell, he felt paranoid as well. Someone indeed wanted to get back at her. He had to admit she had a point when she had mentioned that Beverly was always missing when something was happening. But a killer? Not his cousin—she didn't have an evil bone in her body. So if Beverly wasn't responsible then who was?

Charity began to feel like the entire room was spinning. She thanked her partner for the dance and staggered in the direction of the table in a drunken haze. Could there have been that much rum in her drink? She knew Lou's drinks were strong but this was ridiculous. Bracing her weight against a chair she took a moment and waited for the room to stop moving. Only it got worse. Blinking her eyes, she watched the room and everyone in it become blurry. Shaking her head she struggled to make heads or tails of which direction her table was. Seeing a clear path of light in front of her, she swayed in that direction. She reached what she believed to be about where she had been sitting and stuck out a hand in front of her.

"Charity, what's wrong with you?" she heard Tasha ask.

"I—I'm not sure," she slurred as the room spun nause-atingly. "Can you help me to my seat?"

Tasha rose and clasped on to her elbow and helped her into her chair.

"Girl, what's wrong?" Beverly asked from her right. "Was that drink a little too much for you?"

"I believe so," Charity slurred. She could see either of them clearly. All she saw were dark shadows where their faces should have been. The world began to spin faster and faster until finally she had no choice but to lower her head to the table and groan.

"I think we need to take you home," Tasha suggested.

Beverly nodded. "I agree."

Charity tried to focus on the crowd as they led her to the door but was unable to make out anything.

Then everything went black.

"Charity, wake up."

Charity looked up to find a blurred woman standing over her.

She blinked her eyes and realized there were two women standing over her. Beverly and Tasha.

"Come on, girl," Tasha took one arm while Beverly took the other and together they helped her up the stairs and into the house.

She had been drugged. She was certain of it. Rum had never had this type of effect over her. While sitting in her living room chair, Charity tried to remember what had happened. How many drinks had she had? One . . . two . . . three? She shook her head. She just couldn't remember. She remembered Rhonda standing over her drink. Was there any way she could have been responsible? She groaned—her head felt like someone had hit her with a sledgehammer as her world moved around and around in circles.

"Charity, do you have any ibuprofen?" she heard Tasha ask.

"Umm . . ." She tried to focus. Where did she keep her medications?

"I tried the bathroom and couldn't find any," Beverly said.

The two sounded like they were on the other side of the room. Charity tried to raise her head and locate them, but she couldn't get past the pain burning behind her eyes.

"Why don't I go to the store and pick up a bottle? I could use a couple myself," Beverly said.

Tasha nodded then tossed her the keys to her car. "Are you sure you're sober enough to drive?"

"I'll be fine," she murmured as she headed for the door.

Beverly wheeled Tasha's car down the driveway and up the street to a nearby Walgreens. As she drove through an intersection a car swerved in front of her. She slammed down on the brakes and cursed silently. She hadn't seen the stop sign hidden behind the bushes. Maybe she was drunk after all.

After catching her breath she vowed to drive slower. She had just pushed down on the accelerator when she felt something slide down near her feet. Glancing down she found a small red book. Beverly waited until she reached the Walgreens parking lot before she reached down to pick it up. She thumbed through the pages before she began reading the last page.

"Oh, my God!" she gasped.

Quickly, she put the car back into gear and raced in the direction of the Brooks' house.

Eighteen

Dear Cousin,

If you are reading this then that means I have gone on to a better place.

Please don't be angry with me. I've tried for years to be accepted by my peers and just never could quite fit in. I tried so hard to be like you, Tasha, but I was just never as strong as you. Sometimes I felt like you were my only friend, but you're my cousin, so that doesn't count.

My life has been one big disappointment after another and I just can't take it anymore. The Cutie Pies have shown me that my life doesn't mean a thing. It has been hard and I tried to hang on just a little bit longer, but after Arika's brother raped me, I have decided it's time to let go.

I had hoped that college life would be different, but I have a strong suspicion that it would only get worse. I can't bear it. I am weak. I've always been weak. I can't go through all the ridicule again, no matter how much my acceptance to Harvard meant to my parents. I'll never forget the smiles on their faces and yours.

Take care. I love you.

Your cousin, Tabitha

* * *

Keelen looked up from the book and stared across the table at Beverly with utter astonishment.

"Tabitha and Tasha were cousins?"

Wringing her hands, Beverly was still too stunned to cry. "I—I had no idea. I saw a picture of the two of them together in her apartment but I . . . I just thought they had been good friends. I—I never put the connection together."

A quick and disturbing thought came to Keelen's mind. "Where's Charity?"

"She's at her house with Tasha. She wasn't feeling good so . . ." She gasped as realization flashed before her eyes. "You don't think she'll . . ."

Keelen had raced out the door before she could finish.

Once in his rental car, Keelen reached down for his cell phone and dialed Charity's number.

It's all my fault. I shouldn't have left her alone. He should have kept her by his side all night. He shouldn't have left her alone. If anything happened to her, he'd never forgive himself.

"Pick up, pick up," he chanted impatiently.

He frowned at the third ring. Why weren't either of them answering? By the sixth ring fear was rioting within him. He pushed down on the accelerator, praying he got there in time.

Tasha went downstairs and into the kitchen. After looking through several cabinets she finally found the tea bags in a ceramic canister over the stove.

She filled a mug with hot water and a single bag then put it in the microwave for two minutes. She tapped her foot impatiently. She didn't have much time. Beverly would be back at any moment.

The timer went off and she opened the microwave and removed the mug. Moving over to the counter, she spooned in two teaspoons of sugar. She then reached into her back pocket and removed three white tablets, dropped them in the water and stirred.

Humming, she went back upstairs.

Feeling someone tap her on the shoulder, Charity opened her heavy eyelids and the room began to spin.

"Easy, girl," Tasha warned. Taking a seat beside her on the bed she put several pillows behind Charity's head, elevating her so she could drink the tea.

"Here, drink this. It'll make you feel better." She brought the mug to her mouth.

Charity blinked several times, trying to bring her into focus. All she could see was a blurred image in front of her. "I don't feel so good," she slurred.

"I know, but everything will be clear real soon. You'll see." She tilted the mug and Charity took several sips.

"Where is . . . Beverly?"

"She'll be back soon." Tasha urged her to continue drinking.

Charity took another sip then pushed the mug away. Clutching Tasha's arm, she tried to pull herself upright, but fell back weakly against the pillow. "I—I need to talk to you before . . . before she returns."

Tasha compressed her lips and looked down at her distraught face. "What do you want to talk about?"

Charity sighed. "I think . . . someone . . . put . . . something . . . in my drink," she said slowly, sluggishly.

Tasha chuckled. "Girl, don't be silly, you drank too much."

She raised the tea back to her lips, but Charity shook her head. "No. Please listen."

"I'll listen to you after you get some rest. Now drink." Tasha raised the mug again, but Charity was too tired to drink and barely drank enough to satisfy her. She sat the mug on the nightstand and stared down at her.

Taking a deep breath, Charity fell back on the pillow and closed her eyes. She felt terrible. She just needed to sleep and then everything would be better. "This can't be happening," she mumbled.

"Now you know how Tabitha felt," Tasha murmured.

"What?" she asked hoarsely.

Tasha was appalled. "Don't tell me you've already forgotten who my cousin Tabitha White was?"

"No, I know who she is . . . was . . ." *Cousin! Did she say she was her cousin?*

"Of course you do. You're the reason why she's dead."

Renewed panic overtook her as she picked up on the lack of warmth in Tasha's voice. "I—I didn't kill her." *What is going on?*

"Don't lie to me," she snapped. "I know the truth."

Her head was spinning. *What was she talking about?*

"I guess you didn't have anything to do with her rape either?"

Rape! Oh, my God! Tabitha had been raped. She had had a sinking feeling for years that something had happened and now she knew. Alexander Anderson had raped Tabitha at the Senior Party. Even in her state, that night came back in a rush.

Arika handed Charity a glass. "Give this to Tabitha."

She took a sniff. "What's in this punch?"

"Alcohol. Maybe it'll loosen her up a bit."

With a shrug, Charity moved through the crowd of seniors and found Tabitha standing against the wall. She handed her the drink.

"Thanks, Charity," she smirked.

"You're welcome."

Tabitha took a sip and made a choking sound.

Charity slapped her across the back. "You okay, girl?"

She nodded while coughing and laughing at the same time. "I'm just not used to drinking."

"Neither am I. You can either fake it or drink it down fast."

Tabitha chose the latter and tilted the glass.

Charity barked. "I didn't mean that fast."

She returned to the kitchen where Arika was waiting.

"Did you give her the drink?" Arika asked.

Charity nodded.

"Did you make sure she drank it?"

"What does it matter?"

"I told you I want her to loosen up. I got an exciting evening ahead of us."

Charity was uncomfortable with the wicked smile Arika gave her, but brushed it off.

She should have followed her senses and asked questions. Even later when she helped Tabitha up to a room, she should have known then that something was wrong.

She was talking to Kimora when she saw Tabitha coming down the stairs. Something was wrong. She was supposed to have been taking a nap. Charity headed toward her when Donovan swung her around in his arms.

"Where you going, sweetheart?" he crooned.

"I need to check on someone."

"How about checking on me?" He rained a trail of kisses down her cheek.

Charity pulled free. "I'll be right back." She moved out of his reach before he could grab her again and went into the living room.

Tabitha was gone.

* * *

"My cousin never spoke to me about what happened at that party. If it weren't for her diary, I would never have known. She named you as being responsible."

"Ididnotknow," Charity slurred hoarsely. It was becoming hard to think.

"You gave her the Ecstasy."

Ecstasy? There had been Ecstasy in that glass? She had no idea. A lot of the kids took it, but she didn't think Arika had put any in Tabitha's glass.

"Arika . . ." she whispered. *She did it, not me.*

"Oh, Ms. Arika," she repeated, shaking her head. "On the beach I slipped enough in her drink to . . . well . . . you know the rest." She laughed.

Tasha had killed Arika! Which meant Olivia's fall wasn't an accident either. And Kimora's drink had been drugged.

Oh, my God! Tasha drugged me tonight!

Charity struggled to sit up, but her body felt like a ton of rocks.

Tasha removed a vial from her pocket that contained a liquid form of the drug. She then removed a needle and lifted Charity's arm.

"W—what are you doing?"

"I'm going to try to make this as painless and quick as possible," she said in a calm yet gentle voice.

"No!" Charity shrieked as she tried again to find the strength to get away. Instead she was helpless to do anything but allow Tasha to push the liquid through her vein.

Keelen knocked on the door a second time then pressed his face against the glass. The light was on in the living room, but there were no signs of any movement. He was preparing to walk around to the back when the door opened and Tasha appeared.

"Keelen, what are you doing over so late?" she asked with a courteous smile.

"I came to speak to Charity," he answered, managing to sound as calm as he possibly could.

"She's in the shower. Come on in and join me for a cup of tea." She stepped aside so that he could follow her into the room.

Hearing the water running in the bathroom upstairs, confirming her words, he felt a fraction of relief. She was okay. He considered climbing the stairs and joining Charity in the shower, but after giving it some thought, decided to wait and followed Tasha into the kitchen. When Charity got done with her shower they would confront her together.

Keelen!

He was here to rescue her. All she had to do was make some kind of noise, do something so he would come upstairs. Charity willed her arm to move, but it was weightless. She tried to scream through her parched throat, but it was hopeless.

Please, God! I haven't even had a chance to tell him I love him.

Lying on her back, she prayed until darkness took over again.

While Tasha reached for two tea bags, Keelen took a seat. Seeing the batch of homemade peanut butter cookies on a plate on the table, he helped himself to two.

"Charity was acting very unusual this evening," Tasha offered.

"How so?" he asked absently. He was looking off to his

right, watching, waiting for the water to stop and Charity to surface.

She shrugged as she removed his mug from the microwave. "I don't know. Sluggish maybe. Do you think she could be on drugs?"

Her back was to him, so Keelen was unable to see the expression on her face.

He snorted. "Not likely."

She carried his mug to the table and sat it in front of him.

"Thanks." He reached for the sugar bowl.

Tasha took a seat across from him. "Well . . . maybe it was something else."

He raised his eyes to meet her gaze. "Something like what?"

She heard something in his voice that told her he didn't believe it. *Drink the damn tea!* When he wasn't looking, she had slipped several tablets into his mug. "I don't know. Probably just the stress of everything that has been happening."

Keelen considered telling her right then that Beverly had found the diary. Instead he raised the mug to his lips and took a sip.

Tasha smiled and pushed the plate of cookies closer to him. If he would hurry she could finish before Beverly returned.

Keelen raised the mug to his lips again and was about to take another sip when he heard a loud crash upstairs. He jumped out of the seat and raced up the stairs two at a time, heading straight for the bathroom. Barging through the door, he pulled the shower curtain back and found it empty with the water running. He rushed across the hallway to Charity's room and found her face down on the floor next to a broken lamp.

"Oh, no!" The blood drained from his face. He dropped

down beside her and reached for her pulse then sighed with relief. She was alive. Pulling her into his lap, he cradled her.

"Charity, Charity, can you hear me?"

"Keeeeelen . . ." she slurred then sagged against him.

"Yes, Baby. I'm here. I'm going to get some help. Hang on, hang on," he repeated over and over. He lifted her in his arms and carried her over to the bed where he laid her head gently on the pillow.

Reaching for the phone, he dialed 911 and waited impatiently for someone to pick up. There was a mug on the nightstand. He lifted it to his nose and smelled it. Nothing unusual. What had Tasha given her?

It took several seconds before her heard a dispatcher on the other end. "Nine-one-one emergency, can I help you?"

Before he had a chance to speak, Keelen heard movement to his right. He turned his head and was met with something hard across his face. Then blackness engulfed him.

Nineteen

Tasha looked down at Keelen's crumpled body and cursed. Why did he have to come to Charity's rescue? She didn't want to hurt him, but he had left her little choice.

The phone rang, startling her. She dropped the umbrella onto the floor and moved to pick up the receiver.

"Hello?"

"This is the nine-one-one dispatcher. We just received a call from this number."

"Uh . . . yeah, I'm sorry, my son was playing with the phone."

"Please stress to him that this number is not for playing games."

"Yes, I will. I'm sorry for bothering you."

She hung up the phone. That was a close one. Now what was she going to do? Not only did she have to get rid of Charity, but she also had to get rid of Keelen. Damn! *And I really liked him.* Charity stirred slightly. She would have to act fast. Seeing a red lighter sitting on the end of the dresser, her lips curled into a cynical smile. She reached for it and raced down the stairs.

Keelen opened his eyes and tried to raise his head, but the pain was overwhelming. What had Tasha hit him with? Whatever it had been he was going to have a lump the size of a golf ball. He tried again to rise and this time was successful. The pain had him slightly off balance. He found Charity still lying across the bed, unconscious. He moved over to the bed and took a seat and reached for the phone. This time he had his back to the wall. He picked up the receiver. The phone was dead. Damn! He wasn't sure if he had the strength to carry Charity down the stairs by himself. Where was Tasha?

Then he smelled smoke.

He pushed himself off the bed and moved to the door and sure enough smoke was coming down the hall. The house was on fire!

Beverly turned into the subdivision nibbling nervously on the inside of her lip. She watched another fire truck race pass her. There must be a fire, she thought, then her thoughts trailed back to what she had found as she had continued to read the diary. Tabitha had been drugged. Now she understood who had drugged Kimora and Charity. Tabitha said it had been Ecstasy. She didn't even know they had Ecstasy back then.

Beverly knew that Keelen was capable of handling things, but she just didn't feel comfortable letting him do it by himself. She and Tasha had been friends for too many years for her to let him handle it. She needed to talk to Tasha herself. Her friend owed her an explanation. She wouldn't condemn her, instead she would listen. She would, however, insist that she go to the police, then she would aid her in finding help. They had been through too much for her to abandon her now.

She turned the corner onto Charity's road and found the collection of fire trucks blocking the corner. *Oh, no, it can't be!* She pulled into the nearest parking spot and climbed out of the car. Noticing the commotion in front of

Charity's house, she began to panic. It was then she noticed the black smoke coming from the roof and the flames roaring from the front of the house. *Oh, no! Please, don't let them still be in there.* She moved quickly to the house and noticed that Keelen and Charity's cars were still in the driveway. She sprinted up the sidewalk where a police officer stopped her.

"My cousin's in there!"

"I'm sorry, ma'am, I can't let you in."

She stood by helplessly. She looked around frantically to see if she saw Keelen and Charity somewhere in the crowd. Tasha too, for that matter. Just as she finished scanning the area two firemen came out the front door carrying a stretcher. She rushed over to the stretcher to find Keelen covered in soot.

"Keelen, Keelen. Are you all right?"

"Charity, where's Charity?" he gasped.

"I—I don't know. What happened?"

He began coughing uncontrollably. Beverly moved alongside the stretcher to the back of the ambulance. "I'll call your parents and I will be at the hospital as fast as I can get there."

She then returned to the front of the crowd to find them bringing out another body, this one being zipped into a body bag. She pushed through the crowd and stopped the lady just before she closed the bag. Looking down at the face, she cried, "Oh, no, no!"

Then something exploded and the firemen came racing out of the house just as a second explosion was heard.

Beverly dropped to her knees. It was all her fault. She should have known.

Tears streaming down her face, she reached for her cell phone on her hip and dialed the first number.

Twenty

After blinking several times, Charity forced open her eyes to find sunlight flooding the room. She looked around confused before realizing she was in a hospital.

She turned her head to the left and found Keelen sleeping uncomfortably in a hard chair next to her bed.

"Kee," she called, her throat dry.

His eyelids flew open. "Sweetheart." Finding her awake, he stood, leaned over and kissed her forehead. His eyes were sparkling with relief as he looked down at her lying in the hospital bed with a look of joy. He had been so afraid that he had lost her. "Thank God you're okay." He had been by her side all night, refusing to leave. He watched her lie there lifeless with an IV in place thinking how close he had come to losing her forever.

He stroked her hair away from her pale face. "How are you feeling?"

"Thirsty," she whispered.

He reached for a cup on her bedside table and helped her sit up so she could drink.

Charity took several small sips then refused any more. "Thanks." Her eyes drifted over his face where she found a large bandage on his forehead. Raising her hand, she touched his face. "What happened?"

His eyes drifted half closed. It felt so good having her

touch him. "Tasha hit me with that large umbrella you kept in the hall."

She lowered her hand and laced her fingers with his. "I was so afraid. I heard you when you came into the house and I tried to get you to come upstairs, but I was so drugged that I couldn't move. What happened?"

"Bev found Tabitha's diary. Unfortunately, I only read the last page. Tasha drugged you and was probably trying to do the same to me when I heard you fall. Not realizing how dangerous she was I made the mistake of turning my back. Thank goodness the dispatcher sent out a car to respond to my nine-one-one call or it could have been far worse." He told her about Tasha setting the house on fire.

"Tasha died in the fire."

The curtain moved and Charity looked to see Tia and Beverly peeking around the corner.

"She's awake!" Beverly shrieked.

Tia shed tears of relief. "Thank God! You had me worried. How're you feeling?"

She forced a smile. "Tired, but glad to be alive."

"I need to go call Mom and Dad and Donovan. They're all planning to arrive this evening." She quickly scrambled out of the room.

Beverly moved to the other side of the bed and held her hand. Her face was bleak with sorrow. "I'm so sorry. I feel kind of responsible."

"Why? It wasn't your fault."

"I know, but Tasha was my friend."

Keelen draped an arm about her shoulders. "Quit beating yourself up. You had no idea what she was capable of."

She slowly nodded. "Well, I'm going to leave the two of you alone."

Charity squeezed her hand. "Thanks for being my friend."

Beverly shook away the tears and exited.

Keelen pulled his chair closer and took her hand in his. "You get your rest and when you wake up I'll be sitting right here."

"I love you," she said. "I want you to know that. I was so scared I wouldn't get a chance to tell you. I didn't think I could ever love again after Don and then my feelings for you scared me. I still have a lot of self-confidence issues that I need to conquer, but nothing is going to change the way I feel about you."

Tipping up her chin, he joined their mouths in a tender kiss.

"We'll get through them together. I spent a decade getting you back in my life and there is no way I'm going to lose you again." With that, he reached into his pocket, pulled out something black and slid it over her finger.

"What is that?" She raised her hand trying to get a closer look at the black object.

His entire face spread into a smile. "It's the spider ring you gave me for Halloween one year. I used to wear it on a shoestring around my neck. I want you to wear it until we have a chance to pick out a real engagement ring."

Her eyes clouded with tears. She was so touched she didn't know what to say.

"I love you, Charity Rose, and I plan to spend the rest of my life proving to you how much."

Charity was laughing and crying at the same time. Tears blinded her eyes and choked her voice. "You got your work cut out because I plan to be around a long time."

Epilogue

Christmas had always been her favorite holiday and the suggestion of taking a private cruise on the Caribbean was nothing short of memorable. However, as Charity looked around at her friends and family scattering around the stateroom, she realized this was one Christmas she would never forget.

Tia glanced away from the mirror with a sympathetic grin and cooed. "Oh, no, she's crying again."

Mrs. Rose reached for another Kleenex and moved to take a seat on the bed next to the bride-to-be. "Charity, you can't keep ruining your makeup," she lightly scolded as she dabbed lightly under her eyes.

Sitting comfortably on the bed in a white slip, Charity sniffled. "I'm sorry. I just can't believe this is happening."

Tia snorted. "Neither can I. I thought I was going to beat you down the aisle." She still hadn't gotten her fiancé to commit to a date.

Her mother smiled at her firstborn. "Sweetheart, you're next." Turning back to Charity she said, "I have something for you." She reached over into a purse and removed a string of pearls.

Charity fingered them. "Mom, these are beautiful."

"They used to belong to your grandmother. Now you have something old." She took the necklace and clasped it around her neck.

"Oh, it's my turn." Tia dug into her bag and removed a small box. "This is for you."

Charity looked down at the box with surprise then took it from Tia's hand and opened it. Inside was a blue garter.

"Aw, sookie, sookie," Beverly said as she came through the door to the cabin followed by Kimora and Olivia. They were all wearing sleeveless floor-length dresses with satin bodices and an empire waist. In sync with the holiday spirit, their dresses were red while Tia's was green.

"We have something for you. We put our heads together and came up with something new." Beverly handed her a large box.

"Oh, you guys, you didn't have to do this."

"Yes, we did."

She rose and Beverly was the first to hug her. "Thank you so much for being my friend. My cousin couldn't have picked a better bride."

"Thank you."

She moved to Kimora. Her hair had grown in enough for her to wear a short flip. She draped her arms around Kimora's waist and whispered, "Thanks for being a good friend." When she pulled away tears were spilling from each of their eyes. The last several months had been a time for strengthening friendships.

"Thank you for showing me what friendship really is."

"Let me in on this." Olivia came over and encircled both of them. "Thank you both for your strength and support these past several weeks."

"What are friends for." Together they had gotten Olivia into rehab. She had since left her fiancé and was living at home with her mother and her son.

A knock was heard at the door, then Taylor came charging through the room with the ribbon in her hair already coming undone.

"Taylor, where have you been?" her grandmother scolded.

"I was upstairs with Grandpa."

Her grandmother shook her head. Her husband sometimes forgot that Taylor was not a little boy.

"Come here, sweetheart, so I can fix your hair." Mrs. Rose quickly retied the sash and used a brush to smooth down her side. She then slipped the sundress over her head.

Taylor moved to Charity. "Mom, why are you crying?"

She kissed her nose. "Because Mommy's happy."

She fingered the spiral curls in front back into place. "All right, let's get you dressed."

Her mother reached for the green A-line dress that lay across the bed. "Why don't I help Taylor while the rest of you help Charity into her dress."

With growing excitement the four helped Charity into her gown. The bride was wearing a sleeveless ivory satin gown with a round neckline, empire waist, and bodice adorned with pearls and sequins. It also featured a chapel-length train covered with pearls. She slipped the garter over her silk hose then slipped into a pair of satin-covered pumps.

Tia pin-curled her hair, leaving tendrils around her face, then Kimora positioned her headpiece that was covered with sequins and pearls with a long veil.

Olivia and Kimora spoke at the same time. "Oh, you look beautiful!"

"Thanks."

A knock was heard at the door then her father appeared. "They're ready for you," he said, staring proudly at his baby girl.

"We'll see you on the deck. . . ." Olivia squeezed her hand. They each reached for their bouquets and left. Tia took Taylor's hand and escorted her out with her flower basket in hand.

To the sounds of Jagged Edge's "Let's Get Married" she watched as her bridesmaids moved slowly down the aisle.

Kimora and Olivia were both escorted by Keelen's first
cousins. Holding six roses cuffed with green tulle and fastened with pearl-tipped pins, Charity stepped out onto the
deck on her father's arm. She gasped. Keelen had forbid-
den her to appear on deck all morning, now she knew why.
He had transformed it into a dream. A floral archway was
created with clusters of chrysanthemums and ivy. A dramatic arrangement of white and red roses in urns were
strategically positioned around the deck. Rows of white
folding chairs were graced with tulle garlands of ivory
roses and rioting red and green ribbons. A white runner
where Taylor had dropped petals leading to an archway
was covered with red roses.

It was a beautiful day. The sun was shining brightly. The
ocean was bluer than she had ever seen.

For five months they had maintained a long-distance re-
lationship, with Keelen traveling back and forth to see her.
After the wedding, she and Taylor were joining him in
Florida.

Keelen was standing beside his brother who had flown
back from Spain for the occasion. Olivia and Kimora were
smiling brightly.

She couldn't stop the tears when her daughter took her
time dropping petals along the way. She was so proud. She
sniffled.

"Sweetheart, are you okay?"

She turned and looked at her father and nodded. "I
couldn't be happier."

He kissed her cheek and lowered her veil and, once the
crowd rose, they made their way down the aisle where her
mother was blubbering uncontrollably at the front. Charity held a cascading bouquet of red and white roses tied
with ivy and green ribbons.

Keelen stood at the altar waiting for his bride. There
were only several dozen people present, just the people

most important in both their lives, who'd come to see the two exchange their vows.

His parents and his future mother-in-law were sitting in the front row as well as his sister, her husband and the twins. Several of the crew that had the day off also attended. He saw several sitting in the back rows.

And Tristian was standing by his side as his best man. He watched as Olivia, Kimora and Tia came down the aisle. His smile broadened when Taylor strolled by; taking pride in her job as the flower girl, she dropped petals strategically as she moved. Tears came to the corners of his eyes. In a few short months, he had grown to love Taylor as though she were his own.

All eyes were toward the staircase and when the top of Charity's veil came into view, everyone stood. Mr. Rose came into view moving proudly with his youngest daughter on his arm. There were *oohs* and *aahs* heard in the aisle. Keelen didn't hear anything but the banging of his heart. His bride took his breath away. She was beautiful. The dress as well as the gold tones of her hair shimmered under the sun. His wife. His life.

She moved down the aisle smiling at her friends and family at her left and right. He watched her coming his way. Even with the veil covering her face her chestnut eyes were fixed steadily on him. When she smiled, happiness shone from her eyes. He realized that he too was smiling. When Mr. Rose put her hand in his and moved to take a seat, Keelen smiled at his future wife and suddenly the two started laughing uncontrollably as they turned to face the minister. The guests looked at one another with curious grins.

The two were looking forward to a lifetime of endless enchantment.

ABOUT THE AUTHOR

Angie Daniels is a chronic daydreamer who loves a page-turner. Already an avid reader by age seven, she knew early on that someday she wanted to create stories of love and adventure. During the fifth grade, she began her journey writing comical short stories. As her talent evolved, she found herself writing full-length novels that offered her readers a full dose of romantic suspense. "I enjoy writing whodunits because they allow me to use my imagination to the fullest extent. When I combine it with a love story, it's like spreading icing on a cake."

Angie was born in Chicago, but after spending fifteen years in Missouri she considered it her home. Currently she resides in Delaware with her family. She holds a bachelor's degree in business. Occasionally she works on contract and enjoys the option of either working a nine-to-five or just staying at home to write full-time. You can contact her via e-mail at daniels_angie@yahoo.com or visit her Web site at www.angiedaniels.com.